Season of Forgiveness

LAUREL RIDGE SERIES, BOOK #16

TARA BAISDEN

STERLING RIDGE PRESS LLC

Dedication

To everyone who believes in second chances—

To the firefighters who run toward the flames when others run away, especially those who understand that the heart is sometimes the most dangerous fire of all to fight.

To the small-town restaurant owners who feed both bodies and souls, creating gathering places where community happens one shared meal at a time.

To the divorced parents who choose grace over grudges and love over pride, showing their children that families can be beautiful in all kinds of ways.

And to my own community of faith—

Thank you for showing me that forgiveness isn't just a Sunday school lesson; it's a daily choice that changes everything.

Most of all, to the God of second chances, who writes the most beautiful love stories and never gives up on any of us—even when we've given up on ourselves.

This one's for everyone who's ever stood in the ruins of their dreams and wondered if it's possible to build something even more beautiful from the pieces.

Spoiler alert: It always is.

With love and hope,

Tara

Contents

Chapter 1

"Sue, table six needs extra napkins, and the Martins just walked in with their grandson!" Carla Henderson called across the dining room, her voice carrying over the cheerful din of laughter and conversation that filled every corner of Sue's Pizza.

Sue Smith caught the pack of napkins Carla tossed her way and pivoted toward the front entrance, with a smile on her face. The familiar chaos of a Saturday afternoon rush hummed around her—forks scraping against plates, the oven door clanging shut in the kitchen, and a toddler's delighted squeal from the booth by the window. This was her world, the life she'd built from determination, and most days it felt like enough.

"Mr. and Mrs. Martin!" Sue wove between tables with ease. "Hello, Jason, you've grown so much since the last time I saw you. Your grandparents have been telling everyone about your visit from Florida."

The boy, maybe nine or ten, ducked his head with a shy grin. Mrs. Martin beamed and patted her grandson's shoulder. "He's been asking about your pizza since we picked him up from the airport yesterday. I told him, Nowhere makes it better than Sue's."

"Well, we'd better live up to that reputation." Sue led them to a booth near the front windows where afternoon sunlight streamed through lace curtains. "Your server will be right over to take your order. Jason, if you've got room after pizza, our cinnamon dessert knots are pretty popular."

"They are the best," Mr. Martin added with a wink. "I'll probably order a few extra to take home."

Sue laughed, the sound genuine and warm. She loved this—the banter, the familiarity, the way her restaurant had become woven into the fabric of Laurel Ridge life. As she turned back toward the counter, her gaze swept across the dining room in the automatic assessment she'd perfected over the years. The Sullivan family occupied their usual corner booth, their three kids coloring on the paper placemats Sue kept stocked for exactly this purpose. The Tuesday night book club ladies had commandeered two tables near the back, their weekly pizza tradition apparently moving to Saturday this week based on the stack of novels she saw. Near the window, Pastor Andrew Whitman and his wife, Lily, sat close together, their heads bent in conversation over half-eaten slices of pepperoni and mushroom.

The cash register dinged as Carla rang up another order. Sue caught her friend's eye and received a thumbs-up that meant everything was running smoothly. Carla had been with her since the beginning, working her way from server to manager, and Sue trusted her completely. More than that—she needed her. Running a restaurant alone would be manageable. Running it while raising Lindsey and maintaining the community involvement that made Sue's Pizza more than just a business required someone like Carla.

"Sue!" A hand waved from table twelve, and Sue recognized Eleanor Parker from the church quilting guild. "We've got a situation."

Sue navigated past a server carrying a steaming pizza and arrived at Eleanor's table to find the elderly woman pointing at her water glass with an expression of mock horror. "This water is far too cold. I'm going to need you to warm it up by at least ten degrees, or I simply cannot enjoy my meal."

The twinkle in Eleanor's eyes gave away the joke, and Sue played along without missing a beat. "I'll have Carla fetch the thermometer immediately. Though I should warn you, our water temperature adjustment services do come with a surcharge."

Eleanor's tablemates—three other women from church—erupted in laughter. "Don't you dare encourage her," Margaret Collins said. "She's been impossible since she won the chili cook-off last month."

"That's because my chili was exceptional," Eleanor retorted. "Unlike some people's dry cornbread."

"Ladies, please." Sue held up both hands in a gesture of peace, fighting back a grin. "This is a respectable establishment. Save your feuding for the church potluck like civilized people."

More laughter rippled around the table, and Sue felt the familiar warmth that came from being part of this community as she walked back to the checkout counter. She'd grown up in Laurel Ridge and had gone to school with some of those women's children.

Across the dining room, Lily Whitman rose from her table and made her way toward her.

"How are you feeling?" Sue asked as Lily approached.

"Nauseated and grateful." Lily's smile was radiant despite the slight shadows under her eyes. "The morning sickness is supposed to get better soon, according to all the books. Andrew thinks I should try ginger tea, but honestly, nothing sounds good except your garlic knots."

"The baby has excellent taste already." Sue grabbed a paper bag from beneath the counter and began filling it with the pillowy, butter-brushed rolls from the nearby warmer. "Take these home. On the house."

"Sue, you can't keep giving away food—"

"I can, and I will." Sue pressed the warm bag into Lily's hands. "Consider it an investment in the next generation of Sue's Pizza customers. Besides, you and Andrew do enough for this community. Let me do this small thing."

Lily's eyes grew suspiciously bright. "Pregnancy hormones," she said quickly, dabbing at her eyes with a napkin. "Everything makes me cry lately. Andrew recited our wedding vows yesterday morning, and I sobbed into my oatmeal."

"That man adores you," Sue said, and she meant it. Watching the young pastor with his wife always stirred something in her chest—part joy, part ache. They had what she'd once believed she and Steve possessed. What she'd thought would last forever.

She pushed the thought aside as Lily headed back to join Andrew. No sense dwelling on ancient history on a perfectly good Saturday.

"Sue?" Carla appeared at her elbow. "We've got a problem with the Miller's catering order. They just called—they've moved their party up to tomorrow afternoon instead of next weekend."

Sue's mind immediately shifted into problem-solving mode. Tomorrow was Sunday, which meant she wouldn't be here. She never worked on Sundays, a boundary she'd maintained since opening the restaurant. Sundays were for church, for family, and for rest. "How big is the order?"

"Ten large pizzas, four full orders of garlic knots, and a sheet of brownies. They want it delivered to the church fellowship hall by two o'clock."

"We can do it." Sue reached for the tablet Carla held, scanning the schedule. "Mark it down for Sunday delivery. I'll have one of the cooks prep everything—get the dough ready, toppings measured, and brownies baked. Or I'll go prep everything myself if we stay busy. That way, all the crew has to do tomorrow will be assemble and bake. You'll be here to oversee, right?"

"Wouldn't miss it."

"Good. Text me tomorrow if you get slammed with customers; I can deliver the order myself if you need me to." Sue handed back the tablet. "And remember, they get free delivery and a twenty percent discount; it's for the youth group's mission fundraiser. We're supporting a good cause."

"You support every good cause that walks through that door," Carla said, but her tone was affectionate rather than critical. "It's one of the reasons everyone loves this place. And you."

Sue waved off the compliment, suddenly uncomfortable with the praise. She didn't run Sue's Pizza for recognition. She ran it because it was hers, because she was good at it, and because it meant something to serve the people she'd known her whole life.

A crash from the kitchen sent both women spinning toward the sound.

"I'm okay!" One of the line cooks—Jeremy, a college kid from two towns over—appeared in the doorway looking sheepish. "Dropped a pan. Nothing broke except my dignity."

"Your dignity was already questionable," Carla called back, earning a good-natured laugh from Jeremy.

The afternoon continued in its predictable rhythm. Sue refilled drinks, boxed up leftovers for customers, answered questions about gluten-free options, and admired photos of someone's new puppy. She recommended her Margherita pizza to first-time tourists looking for something simple and personally delivered a small pepperoni pizza to Mr. Abbott, who sat alone at his regular table reading the newspaper like he did every Saturday afternoon.

By two o'clock, the rush had mellowed into a gentle lull. Sue stood behind the counter, reviewing the day's receipts so far, while Carla coordinated the early dinner prep with the kitchen staff. The numbers looked good—better than good, actually. November wasn't typically their busiest month, but business remained steady.

She should feel proud. The restaurant was successful, her daughter was thriving, and she had the respect and affection of her entire community. Everything she'd worked for had come to fruition.

So why did today leave her feeling hollowed out?

Sue's gaze drifted to the front windows, where the Leonard family was preparing to leave, Corrine animatedly telling her parents something while her hands gestured wildly. At the next table, a young couple leaned close over their shared pizza, laughing at some private joke. Near the back, Don and Marla Anderson were gathering coats and scarves, the couple working in that synchronized way long-married couples developed, anticipating each other's movements without conscious thought.

She looked away, busying herself with straightening the menus stacked beside the register.

"You're doing it again," Carla said quietly, appearing beside her with two glasses of sweet tea.

"Doing what?"

"That thing where you get that look on your face." Carla set a glass in front of her. "The wistful one."

"I don't know what you're talking about." Sue took a long drink of tea, avoiding her friend's eyes.

"Sure you don't." Carla leaned against the counter, lowering her voice so the few remaining customers wouldn't overhear. "Sue, you've built something incredible here. Everyone in Laurel Ridge knows they can count on you; your business is thriving, and you're raising a wonderful daughter. But—"

"No buts." Sue cut her off gently but firmly. "I'm exactly where I need to be. Where I choose to be."

Carla studied her for a long moment, then sighed. "Okay. But for what it's worth, it's okay to take some time off and enjoy life a bit... to want more than just working and going home. In fact, you know I've got everything covered here. Why don't you take off a little early and go walk around town and get some fresh air? Go on a quick hike. Go do something just for yourself."

"What I want," Sue said carefully, "is to pick up my daughter in a little while, make a gigantic batch of buttered popcorn, and watch a movie this evening with her. That's enough."

"If you say so." Carla squeezed her shoulder and moved away, calling something to Jeremy about tomorrow's dough preparation.

Sue glanced at the clock above the doorway. Two-thirty. In an hour and a half she'd leave, drive to her parents' house, pick up Lindsey, and they'd go home and curl up on the couch together with popcorn and whatever animated movie Lindsey picked out. It was their Saturday tradition, the highlight of Sue's week, at least when Lindsey was with her and not at her dad's apartment.

The little bell above the door jingled as the last of the lunch crowd filtered out, calling goodbyes and see-you-Sundays. Sue waved, returned their well-wishes, and tried to ignore the question that had been whispering in the back of her mind for months now.

When had "enough" started feeling like "almost enough"?

She pulled the next day's schedule up on the tablet again, scanning the names to confirm everything was covered for tomorrow. The restaurant would run smoothly without her—it always did. Carla managed the staff efficiently, the kitchen ran like clockwork, and Sue's careful systems ensured consistency even in her absence.

Everything was under control.

Everything was exactly as it should be.

She pressed her palm flat against the cool countertop, grounding herself. This restaurant, this community, this independence—she'd fought for all of it.

"Lord, help me be grateful for what I have instead of longing for more," she whispered.

Chapter 2

"*A mazing grace, how sweet the sound...*"

Sue's voice rose clear and true above the congregation, her soprano carrying through the sanctuary of Laurel Ridge Community Church like a prayer made tangible as she sang with the choir. Sunlight streamed through the stained-glass windows, painting the wooden pews in shades of amber and blue, and Sue felt the familiar peace that came from worship and from being surrounded by voices lifted together in faith.

"*That saved a wretch like me...*"

Lindsey stood in the pew between her mother, Anna, and her father, Earl, hymnal open but unnecessary—she knew every word by heart.

"*I once was lost, but now am found...*"

This was Sue's favorite part of Sunday mornings. The unity of voices, the shared faith, and the sense of being part of something larger than herself. Her grandmother had led this choir before her, and standing here in the same sanctuary where she'd been baptized and married felt like walking in footsteps worn smooth by generations of faithful women.

"*Was blind, but now I see.*"

The final note hung in the air as Pastor Andrew rose from his seat behind the pulpit. He was young for a pastor—only thirty-four—but he carried himself with a quiet authority that had won over even the most skeptical members. His wife, Lily, sat in the front pew.

"Let us pray," Andrew said, and the congregation bowed their heads.

Sue closed her eyes as the familiar words of the benediction washed over her, and she added her own silent prayer. *Thank You for this community, Lord. For these people who love and support me. For the stability of this church and for the comfort of knowing where I belong.*

"Amen."

The word echoed through the sanctuary, followed by the soft rustle of movement as people reached for purses, Bibles, and coats. Stepping down from the platform where she'd been standing with the choir, Sue retrieved her purse from the pew, automatically checking that Lindsey had her things before joining the steady flow of congregants moving down the center aisle.

"That was beautiful, Sue," Eleanor Parker said as she shuffled past, leaning on her cane.

"Thank you, Mrs. Parker."

"Lindsey, dear, you're getting so tall." Eleanor patted Lindsey's cheek with a papery hand. "Pretty soon you'll be leading the choir yourself."

"Maybe. Mom says I need to work on my breathing technique first."

"Your mother knows what she's talking about."

They moved slowly down the aisle, stopping every few feet for brief conversations. Martha Kincaid caught Sue's arm to discuss Tuesday's church council meeting. The Sullivan family wanted to schedule a birthday party at Sue's Pizza for their youngest.

Pastor Andrew stood at the double doors near the back of the church, shaking hands and exchanging words with each departing worshipper. When Sue reached him, Lily materialized at his side, her face glowing despite the faint circles under her eyes that betrayed her ongoing battle with morning sickness.

"Sue, I wanted to catch you before you left." Lily's enthusiasm bubbled over despite her fatigue. "Can we finalize the Christmas pageant schedule? I know choir rehearsals start the first Monday in December, but I wanted to make sure we're coordinating with the children's program."

"Of course." Sue shifted her purse to her other shoulder. "Why don't you come by the restaurant tomorrow afternoon? We can go over everything with some coffee and a snack."

"You're an angel." Lily squeezed her hand. "How you manage the restaurant and the choir and everything else, I'll never know."

"Lots of coffee and stubbornness," Sue said, then softened it with a smile. "And God's grace. Mostly that."

She and Lindsey moved through the doors and out onto the church steps. The November air was crisp and clean, carrying the scent of pine from the surrounding mountains. The church sat on a gentle rise at the edge of town, offering a view of Laurel Ridge's main street and the valley beyond. From here, Sue could see the white gazebo in the town square in the distance and the glint of sunlight off the New River across the road.

The congregation spread across the front lawn and gravel parking lot in the comfortable chaos of a Sunday morning. Children darted between adults, their Sunday shoes crunching on fallen leaves. Earl and Anna stood near the large oak tree that shaded one corner of the churchyard, already surrounded by friends. Graham, her youngest brother, was talking to the youth pastor near the edge of the parking lot, while her other brother, Matt, leaned against his truck with his arms crossed, waiting patiently for his girlfriend.

Sue descended the steps with Lindsey, nodding to familiar faces, her mind already shifting to the afternoon ahead. She and Lindsey would spend it with her mom, dad, and siblings, enjoying Sunday dinner and family time.

When she was halfway across the front church lawn, a scent caught her attention.

Smoke.

Sue paused mid-step, her nose lifting automatically to catch the breeze. It was faint but distinct—the sharp tang of something burning that didn't quite match the cozy smell of a fireplace. Probably someone burning leaves despite the county regulations.

A patrol car pulled into the parking lot. Deputy Reed Dunbar's cruiser stopped abruptly near the entrance, and Reed emerged with the kind of purposeful urgency that made Sue's stomach clench.

Their eyes met as Reed walked toward her.

Lindsey must have sensed something. "Mom?"

"It's okay, baby." Sue's hand found her daughter's shoulder, holding on tighter than necessary. Around them, conversations had begun to falter as other congregation members noticed the deputy's hurried approach toward Sue.

Reed reached them, his face grim. The apology in his eyes made her want to turn around and walk away, to refuse to hear whatever came next.

"Sue." He glanced at Lindsey, then back to Sue. "I need to speak with you."

"What's wrong?"

"There's a fire." The words came quickly, like ripping off a bandage. "At your restaurant. The department's on scene now, but—"

The world tilted.

Sue heard the words, understood them individually, but her brain refused to assemble them into meaning. Fire. Restaurant. Her restaurant. Sue's Pizza.

"How bad?" The question came from somewhere outside herself.

"I don't know all the details yet. Fire Chief Johnson sent me to find you."

Steve. Of course it would be Steve responding, Steve fighting the fire, Steve trying to save what they'd once built together. The bitter irony wasn't lost on her.

"Mom?" Lindsey's voice had gone small and scared.

Sue looked down at her daughter's upturned face and felt the familiar maternal override click into place. Whatever was happening downtown, Lindsey didn't need to see it. She didn't need to stand in the parking lot of their church and watch her mother fall apart.

"Lindsey, baby, I need you to stay with Grandma and Grandpa." Sue kept her voice steady through sheer force of will. "Can you do that for me?"

"But—"

"Please, sweetheart. I need to know you're safe while I go figure out what's happening."

Earl and Anna had already started across the lawn, drawn by the patrol car and the deputy's presence. Sue's father's face was set in the hard lines of a man preparing for the worst, while her mother's expression held the kind of practical worry that came from raising three children and managing a lifetime of small crises.

"What's going on?" Earl asked.

"Fire at the restaurant," Sue said, the words tasting like ash in her mouth. "I need to get there. Can you—"

"We'll take Lindsey home with us," Anna said immediately, already reaching for her granddaughter. "Don't you worry about a thing, honey. You go."

Lindsey clung to Sue for a moment, and Sue pressed a kiss to the top of her daughter's head, breathing in the familiar scent of her strawberry shampoo. "I love you. I'll call as soon as I know anything."

"I love you too, Mom."

Graham and Matt had materialized at her elbows, both of them wearing identical expressions of barely contained alarm. "We're coming with you," Graham said.

Sue wanted to argue—wanted to handle this alone like she handled everything—but the thought of driving toward the smoke with no one beside her made something in her chest constrict painfully.

"Okay."

The walk to her car felt surreal, her feet moving while her mind raced in circles. The restaurant. Her restaurant. The place she'd poured her heart into, her identity.

She could see more smoke now, a gray smudge against the blue November sky.

Sue's hands shook as she fumbled with her keys. Matt took them gently from her fingers and unlocked the back passenger door of her SUV, holding it open while she slid in. Matt climbed into the driver's seat. Graham climbed in the passenger side, his jaw tight.

"It's going to be okay," Graham said, but his voice lacked conviction.

Matt started the engine and pulled out of the parking lot. Down the hill from the church, left onto Main Street, following the patrol car that led the way with lights flashing but no siren. Behind them, other cars from the church parking lot had begun to follow, drawn by curiosity or concern or the simple magnetic pull of disaster.

The smoke grew thicker as they drove, no longer just a distant smudge but a real, tangible presence. Sue leaned forward in her seat, her fingers gripping the door handle.

Please, God. The prayer formed wordlessly, desperate and formless. Please, please, please.

The restaurant came into view as they turned onto Cedar Avenue, and Sue's breath caught in her throat.

Smoke poured from the kitchen windows. The dining-room windows were dark with smoke. Two fire engines blocked the street, their lights painting everything in alternating shades of red and white. Firefighters moved with controlled urgency, wrestling hoses and shouting instructions.

Matt pulled to a stop behind a barricade. Through the windshield, she watched her life surrounded by a smoky cloud.

A figure in turnout gear emerged from the smoke, and even at this distance, even with his face partially obscured by his helmet, Sue recognized Steve's height, his shoulders, and the way he moved. He was shouting orders to his crew, directing them, and for one irrational moment Sue wanted to run toward him.

Instead, she sat frozen in her car in the back seat, watching smoke pour from the building where she'd served thousands of meals, where she'd celebrated birthdays and anniversaries and graduations.

Graham turned in his seat to face her and reached back for her hand. "Sue—"

"I can't lose this." The words came out broken, barely above a whisper. "I can't."

Chapter 3

"Miller, I want water on that southeast corner—now!"

Steve Johnson's voice cut through the chaos of shouts and rushing water, his eyes tracking the smoke pouring from Sue's Pizza kitchen windows. The fire was contained but stubborn, and every second mattered when it came to saving what could be saved.

"On it, Chief!" Lieutenant Ray Miller adjusted his grip on the hose.

Steve moved closer to the building, his turnout gear heavy, boots crunching over debris and broken glass. The radio on his shoulder crackled with updates from the crew inside, their voices calm despite the heat and smoke.

"Chief, we've got it knocked down in here," Mark Talley's voice came through the radio. "Checking for extension into the walls."

"Copy that. Stay alert." Steve's gaze swept the building's exterior with the practiced assessment of someone who'd fought hundreds of fires. Smoke poured out of the kitchen's broken windows. The dining-room windows were intact but clouded with soot. The roof showed no signs of involvement—a small mercy.

He knew this building intimately. Not from pre-fire inspections or community safety checks, but from the years when it was as familiar as his own home. He'd helped Sue paint the dining room walls a soft cream color. He'd been there the day the wood-fired ovens were installed, watching her face light up with excitement. He'd fixed that back door three times because the frame always swelled in humid weather.

The memory felt like smoke itself—insubstantial and choking.

"Luke, check the breaker box again," Steve called to the young firefighter emerging from the building. "I want to confirm we've got a full electrical shutdown."

"Yes, sir." Luke Benton jogged toward the side of the building where the main electrical panel was located, his movements quick and efficient.

Steve had taught Luke most of what the kid knew about firefighting. Had mentored him through his rookie year, pushed him to get his EMT certification, and watched him grow into a solid member of the department. Teaching came naturally to Steve—sharing knowledge, building competence, and creating a team he could trust with his life.

If only he'd been half as good at building a marriage.

The radio crackled again. "Chief, the origin point looks like the electrical system near the prep station. Wiring's melted pretty bad."

Steve pressed the transmit button. "Understood. Keep documenting. I'll need photos for the fire marshal's report."

Fire marshal. The words sat heavy in his chest. The state fire marshal's office had been courting him for months, offering a position that would mean better pay, regular hours, and a chance to work arson investigations across West Virginia. A promotion that would take him two hours away from Laurel Ridge.

Away from Lindsey.

Away from Sue.

Not that Sue's proximity should have mattered. They'd been divorced for six years, and in all that time, they'd maintained a cordial distance punctuated by necessary exchanges about Lindsey's schedule. Sue was polite when he picked up their daughter, civil when circumstances required conversation, and careful never to let him see anything beyond the capable, independent woman she'd become.

The woman she'd had to become because he'd been too focused on his career to notice his marriage dying.

"Chief?" Ray appeared at his elbow, his weathered face streaked with soot. "We're about done here. Fire's out, just doing overhaul now."

"Good work. Start ventilation procedures. I want this smoke cleared so we can do a more thorough assessment."

"You got it."

Steve pulled off his helmet, running a gloved hand through sweat-dampened hair. The November air felt cool against his overheated face. Around him, his crew worked with the synchronized efficiency that came from training and trust. They knew their jobs, knew each other, and knew he'd never ask them to do anything he wouldn't do himself.

He'd built that. Through years of late nights and weekend trainings and leading by example, he'd created a department Laurel Ridge could be proud of.

He just wished it didn't feel like every professional achievement was built on the ruins of his personal life.

Movement at the barricade caught his attention—Matt Smith climbed out of the driver's side of Sue's vehicle.

Steve forced himself to scan the scene with professional detachment. Civilians secured behind the barricade, check. All crew members accounted for, check. No active flames visible, check. Everything was under control.

Except his suddenly racing pulse.

Through the SUV's back window, he could make out Sue's silhouette. She hadn't gotten out yet—probably still processing the sight of her restaurant wreathed in smoke and surrounded by emergency vehicles. Graham had exited the passenger side and stood beside his brother, both of them wearing matching expressions of grim concern.

Steve looked away again, focusing on the thermal imaging camera readings one of his crew was showing him. He would not stare. Would not let his attention drift toward Sue like a compass finding north. Would not allow personal feelings to interfere with the job that still needed doing.

"Chief, you want me to start talking to witnesses?" Luke asked, gesturing toward the small crowd of onlookers gathering at a safe distance. "Deputy Dunbar said the manager and a few employees were here when it started."

"Yeah, find Carla Henderson." Steve scanned the crowd and spotted her sitting in the back of an ambulance, an oxygen mask held loosely in her lap. Tim Henderson stood beside her, one hand on his wife's shoulder. "She'll need to give a statement about what she saw."

"On it."

Steve returned his attention to the building, but his awareness of Sue's presence pulled at him like gravity. He could feel her watching, could imagine the devastation on her face, and something in his chest twisted painfully.

This restaurant was everything to her.

"Steve!" Mark emerged from the building, pulling off his breathing apparatus. "You need to see this."

Steve crossed to his second-in-command, grateful for something concrete to focus on. "What've we got?"

"The electrical fire started in the wall behind the prep station and spread through the wiring. Breaker box never tripped—looks like it might've been overloaded for a while." Mark wiped soot from his face with the back of his glove. "The dining room's got heavy smoke damage but looks structurally sound. Steve, the kitchen's bad. The ovens in the kitchen are a total loss, the refrigeration system is damaged... everything..."

"Everything will need to be replaced," Steve finished.

"Yeah." Mark's expression was sympathetic. He'd been Steve's closest friend since high school, had been best man at Steve and Sue's wedding, and had watched their marriage fall apart. "This will be expensive."

"I know."

"She's here, isn't she?"

"Yeah."

"You going to talk to her?"

"I'll give her the preliminary report once we're done here. It's protocol."

Mark studied him for a long moment, then nodded slowly. "Right. Protocol."

Steve ignored the skepticism in his friend's voice and turned back toward the building. "Get me a complete damage assessment. I need to know if the structure's safe to enter without gear, and I want that electrical system traced from the breaker box to every outlet."

"You got it, Chief."

The next twenty minutes passed in a blur of procedure and documentation. Steve moved through the familiar rhythm of post-fire operations—photographing evidence, noting observations, and coordinating with his crew to ensure nothing was missed. This was what he was good at. This was where he excelled. In a crisis, with lives and property at stake, Steve Johnson knew exactly who he was and what needed to be done.

It was only in the quiet moments—in Sue's carefully neutral expression during custody exchanges or in his empty apartment at the end of long shifts—that certainty dissolved into regret.

"Chief, we're clear," Ray reported, approaching with a clipboard full of notes. "Fire's out, scene's secure. The main structure's solid."

"Good. Get the trucks ready to roll back to the station. I'll finish up here and meet you there."

As his crew began breaking down equipment and preparing to leave, Steve allowed himself to look toward Sue's SUV. She'd gotten out now and stood between her brothers at the barricade, her arms wrapped around herself despite the relatively mild November day. Even from this distance, he could see the rigid set of her shoulders and the way she held herself together through sheer force of will.

He'd seen that posture before. He'd seen it the day she filed for divorce and when she'd been sitting across from him in the lawyer's office. He had seen it at Lindsey's school events when she smiled at their daughter while carefully avoiding his eyes. Had seen it in a thousand small moments over six years, each one a reminder of what his choices had cost them both.

Steve pulled off his gloves and tucked them into his coat pocket, then ducked under the caution tape and made his way toward her. Each step felt weighted with history and things left unsaid, but this was his job. She deserved answers, and he could provide them.

Sue's gaze tracked his approach, her hazel eyes unreadable behind her determined expression. Matt and Graham shifted slightly, a subtle movement that reminded Steve they were her brothers first and his friends second. The Smith men had always been protective of their sister—more so since the divorce.

"Sue." He stopped at a professional distance, close enough to speak without shouting but far enough to respect boundaries. "I'm sorry."

"How bad is it?" Her voice was steady, but Steve heard the tremor underneath—the same tremor that used to appear when she was fighting tears.

"Kitchen's a total loss. The fire originated in the electrical system behind your prep station. Looks like the wiring couldn't handle the load and overheated." He kept his tone factual and clinical. "The dining room has smoke damage, but the structure is sound."

"Can I go inside?"

"Not yet. Maybe tomorrow, once everything's been cleared."

Sue's jaw tightened, and she nodded once. "Okay."

Graham cleared his throat. "Tell me more about the electrical damage."

"It'll need to be completely replaced and brought up to current code. The wiring's old—probably original to the building." Steve addressed Graham but remained aware of Sue's reaction in his peripheral vision. "You're looking at significant renovation work."

"How long?" Sue asked.

The question he'd been dreading. "Hard to say, but if I had to estimate—six to eight weeks minimum. Could be longer depending on contractor availability and code requirements."

"Six to eight weeks." Sue repeated the words as if she were testing their weight.

"I'm sorry." The inadequacy of the apology settled between them, paper-thin and useless.

"I'm having a hard time dealing with this right now. What caused this? Was it—" She stopped, swallowed hard. "Was it something we did wrong?"

"No." Steve's response came quickly, firmly. "This was an electrical failure, not negligence. This was—" He paused, choosing words carefully. "Sometimes things just fail. It's nobody's fault."

Sue's eyes met his directly for the first time, and he saw the devastation in them as she fought back tears.

He wanted to promise her it would be okay. He wanted to tell her he'd help however she needed, that she wouldn't face this alone, and that somehow they'd figure it out together.

Instead, he said, "The fire marshal will be out early tomorrow morning to complete the official investigation. You'll need that report for your insurance claim."

"Right. Insurance." Sue seemed to pull herself together, straightening her shoulders. "Thank you for—for getting here so fast. For saving what you could."

"Just doing my job."

The words came out more curtly than he'd intended, and Steve watched Sue's expression shutter closed. That wall she'd built between them—the one made of polite distance and careful neutrality—slid back into place.

"Of course." She glanced at the building behind him, then back to her brothers. "We should go. There's nothing we can do here."

Matt's hand found his sister's elbow, a gesture of support that Steve used to provide. "Come on. Mom and Dad are probably wearing a hole in the floor waiting for news."

"Sue," Steve said as they turned to leave.

She paused, looking back over her shoulder.

"If you need anything—" He stopped, recognizing the presumption. "The department has resources. For business owners dealing with fire damage. I can get you that information."

"Thank you." Her tone was polite, distant. "I appreciate it."

Then, she and her brothers were climbing back into her SUV. Steve watched them drive away and thought about how he'd become someone she thanked like a stranger for doing his job.

The radio crackled. "Chief, rolling out now."

Steve pressed the transmit button. "Copy that. I'll be there in five."

He turned back to look at the building—the restaurant where he'd shared countless meals with Sue and Lindsey, where he'd been happy before he'd forgotten happiness required attention and care.

The building stood wounded but standing, smoke-stained and damaged but not destroyed.

The irony wasn't lost on him.

Chapter 4

Sue's hand trembled as she reached for the back door. Carla stood beside her, silent and steady, her presence the only thing keeping Sue's knees from buckling.

"We don't have to do this today," Carla said quietly.

"I need to see it," she said as she jerked the warp door open. "Waiting won't make it any better."

The smell hit her like a physical blow—acrid smoke mixed with melted plastic and something she couldn't name but would never forget. Sue pressed her hand to her mouth, fighting the nausea rising in her throat.

"Oh, Sue." Carla's voice cracked.

The kitchen was a blackened shell. The walls were charred and blistered. Electrical wiring hung from the ceiling like dead vines, their copper cores exposed and twisted. The prep station where she'd rolled out thousands of pizza crusts was nothing but a warped metal frame; the stainless-steel surface bubbled and discolored beyond recognition.

Her feet crunched on debris as she moved deeper into the space. The industrial refrigerator stood slightly ajar, its white exterior now streaked with soot. Inside, she could see ruined containers of sauce, cheese turned to liquid, and vegetables wilted and spoiled. The smell intensified, and Sue had to turn away.

"Let's go look at the dining area," Carla offered, though her tone held little hope.

Sue pushed through the swinging door that separated the kitchen from the dining area, and her heart broke a little more.

Every surface told the story of devastation. The cream-colored walls were now gray with soot. The photos she'd hung with such care—images of Lindsey's birthday parties, the grand opening day, and various community fundraisers—were warped behind smoke-damaged glass. The antique cash register her grandmother had given her sat on the counter, its brass fittings tarnished black.

Sue walked to the nearest table and ran her finger across its surface. It came away dark with ash. The cheerful checkered tablecloths looked gray and lifeless.

"Sue, maybe we should—"

The front door opened, and Steve stepped inside.

He wore jeans and a department polo. His blue eyes swept the dining room before settling on her, and Sue saw something flicker in his expression—concern, possibly, or pity. She didn't want either.

"I wasn't sure if you'd come today." His voice was careful, neutral.

"I needed to see it." Sue crossed her arms, suddenly aware of how she must look—in her comfortable leggings and oversized sweatshirt, hair disheveled, mascara probably smudged beneath her eyes. She lifted her chin anyway. "You said the structure was sound."

"It is." Steve pulled a small notebook from his pocket; the gesture was so familiar it made Sue's chest ache. He'd always kept one of those notebooks, jotting down observations, thoughts, and reminders to himself. "I can walk you through what needs to happen, if you'd like."

Sue wanted to say no, wanted to send him away and figure this out herself, the way she'd figured out everything else in the six years since their divorce. But she also needed answers, and Steve could provide them.

"Okay."

They started in the kitchen. Steve moved through the space with efficiency, pointing out damage Sue had missed in her initial shock. The breaker box would need complete replacement. The ventilation system had melted in places. The gas lines required inspection before the building could even be considered safe for contractors.

Steve crouched beside one of the wood-fired units she'd saved for months to buy. His hand—still large and capable, she noticed before forcing her gaze elsewhere—traced the brick exterior. "I'm deeply sorry, Sue. You don't deserve this."

She hugged herself tighter.

"I came back last night and looked over the entire kitchen again. Nothing in here is salvageable." Steve straightened, and Sue had to tilt her head back slightly to meet his eyes. When had he gotten taller? Or had she just forgotten? "The electrical, as I said before, will need to be completely replaced. Everything has to be brought up to current code."

Carla appeared in the doorway, notebook in hand. "What about the dining room?"

"Cosmetic damage—I went through the entire dining room again yesterday evening when I came back." Steve led them back through the swinging door. "New paint, new tablecloths, professional cleaning for the furniture and fixtures. A few windows will need to be replaced—smoke damage to the seals."

He walked to the wall where Sue's favorite family photos hung and carefully lifted one frame down. Behind it, the wall showed a perfect rectangle of clean cream paint, untouched by smoke.

"See? The structure's fine. It's just surface damage out here." He set the frame back in place with surprising gentleness. "Still expensive, but not catastrophic."

Sue watched his hands as he adjusted the frame, ensuring it hung straight despite the warped backing. Those hands had once held hers during wedding vows. Had cradled Lindsey minutes after her birth. Had fixed the leaky sink in their first apartment and built the bookshelf that still stood in Lindsey's bedroom.

Those same hands now cataloged the destruction of her dream with clinical precision.

"How long?" Sue asked, though Steve had already told her at the scene yesterday. She needed to hear it again, needed the reality of it to sink past the numbness coating her thoughts.

"Six to eight weeks if everything goes smoothly. It could stretch to ten or twelve if there are complications with permits or inspections." Steve pulled out his phone, scrolling through something. "I can send you contact information for contractors who specialize in fire restoration. The insurance company will have its own list, but these guys are good. Fair prices, quality work."

"That's helpful." Carla was taking notes, her pen moving quickly across the page. "What else do we need to know?"

Steve launched into an explanation of building codes, inspection requirements, and the process for obtaining the necessary permits to reopen. Sue tried to focus on his words, but her attention kept fragmenting. The way he stood with his weight slightly on his right leg—a habit from an old high school football injury. The furrow between his brows. The careful distance he maintained between them, never getting close to her.

"Sue?" Carla's voice pulled her back. "Did you hear that?"

"Sorry, what?"

"Steve said you'll need to contact the insurance company soon." Carla's expression was sympathetic. "Start the claim process."

"Right." Sue pressed her fingers to her temples. Her head had started to ache, a dull throb behind her eyes that matched the heaviness in her chest.

"You should go home," Steve said, and there it was—that gentle concern she remembered from years ago, when he'd notice she was pushing herself too hard and insist she rest. "There's nothing you can do here today."

Sue's spine stiffened. "I'm fine."

"Sue—"

"I said I'm fine." The words came out sharply, and she saw Steve's jaw tighten in response. Good. She didn't need his concern and didn't want his careful consideration. She needed—

What did she need?

The question hovered unanswered as silence stretched between them. Carla glanced away, clearly sensing the undercurrent but wisely staying quiet.

"I'll leave you to it, then." Steve's tone had gone flat, professional. "Call if you need anything. For the insurance or contractors or—" He stopped, seeming to reconsider whatever he'd been about to say. "Just call if you need anything."

He left without waiting for a response, the front door closing behind him with a soft click that somehow felt louder than a slam.

"You didn't have to bite his head off," Carla said mildly.

"I didn't bite his head off."

"Sue." Carla set down her notebook and crossed to where Sue stood frozen in the middle of her ruined restaurant. "He's trying to help."

"I know." Sue's voice cracked. "I know he is, and that's... that's the problem, Carla. I can't—" She gestured helplessly at the smoke-damaged walls, the soot-covered tables, and the evidence of everything she'd lost.

"Hush... you need help," Carla said gently. "And Steve happens to be the most qualified person to give it."

"It's not that simple."

"Isn't it?"

Sue wanted to argue, wanted to explain all the complicated history that made accepting his help feel like losing ground she'd fought too hard to gain. But the words wouldn't come. Instead, she turned away, walked to a window, and rubbed off some soot to look out at Cedar Avenue, where life continued normally. A couple walked past with a stroller, their dog pulling on its leash, eager to explore. The world kept spinning while hers had ground to a halt.

"I should inventory what's salvageable," Sue said finally. "For the insurance claim."

Carla didn't argue. For the next hour, they moved through the restaurant with methodical determination, making lists of damaged equipment, ruined supplies, and items that might be saved. The work gave Sue something to focus on besides the ache in her chest.

By four o'clock, Carla had to leave—something about picking up her daughter from a friend's house. Sue assured her she'd be fine, that she just needed a few more minutes, and watched her friend leave.

The restaurant felt cavernous in the quiet. Sue stood at the counter where she'd rung up thousands of orders, where she'd chatted with customers and tallied receipts. Her fingers traced the soot-covered surface, and she thought about all the hours she'd spent here. All the early mornings and late nights. All the holidays she'd worked because employees had called off. All the choices she'd made in the name of independence.

For what?

The question whispered through her mind, unwelcome and persistent. She'd built this place because it had been her dream. She'd proven to herself after the divorce that she could stand on her own, provide for herself and her daughter, and continue something lasting and meaningful.

Sue closed her eyes, and for just a moment—just one brief, dangerous moment—she let herself imagine what it would feel like to lean into someone. To admit she was scared and overwhelmed and didn't know how she'd rebuild. To let Steve's calm competence shoulder some of this crushing weight.

The thought terrified her.

Sue opened her eyes and looked around again. She'd survived worse than this. She'd survived divorce and single motherhood and the thousand small humiliations of starting over in life. She would survive this too.

Chapter 5

The drive home from the restaurant had passed in a blur of mountain curves and darkening sky, her body moving through familiar motions while her mind remained trapped in that smoke-damaged shell of what used to be her restaurant.

Sue's hand trembled as she fitted the key into her front door, the simple motion requiring concentration she didn't have left to give. The door swung open to silence.

Not the peaceful quiet she usually cherished after long days at the restaurant, but something heavier. Emptier. The kind of silence that pressed against her eardrums and made her aware of her own breathing. Her parents had insisted on keeping Lindsey for the night, giving Sue "time to process," though what she was supposed to process remained unclear.

The fire.

The destruction.

The next six to eight weeks.

Steve's careful distance. The way he'd looked at her with something that might have been concern or might have been pity before walking away.

Sue dropped her purse on the entry table and moved through the familiar space of her log cabin home. The vaulted ceilings that usually made her feel embraced by warmth now seemed cavernous. Her footsteps echoed on the hardwood floors as she walked to the kitchen, each sound magnified by Lindsey's absence.

The coffeemaker sat ready on the counter. Sue pressed the brew button and listened to the machine gurgle and hiss, filling the kitchen with the rich aroma of dark roast. Her go-to comfort.

While the pot filled, Sue wandered to the living room and selected a novel from the built-in bookshelf—one of those clean romances Carla had recommended, something about second chances and small-town love. The irony wasn't lost on her. She carried it back to the kitchen and set it on the table, then poured coffee into her favorite mug, the one Lindsey had painted in art class three years ago with wobbly letters spelling "World's Best Mom."

Sue sat at the kitchen table, opened the book to page one, and read the same paragraph four times without absorbing a single word.

The coffee grew cold.

She looked outside through the large kitchen window; twilight had deepened to full dark. The motion-sensor light on the back of the garage clicked on as a deer wandered past, then off again when the animal disappeared into the woods. Sue watched the light cycle through its automated routine and thought about electrical systems, about wiring that couldn't handle the load, and about things that failed unexpectedly and destroyed everything around them.

Her phone buzzed against the table, Lindsey's name lighting up the screen.

Sue answered before the second ring. "Hey, sweetheart."

"Mom!" Lindsey's voice burst through the speaker, bright and untroubled. "Guess what Grandma and I made?"

"What did you make?" Sue kept her voice light, injecting enthusiasm she didn't feel.

"Snickerdoodles! Like, tons of them. Grandpa said we're trying to make him fat." Lindsey's laugh rang clear and pure, untouched by the weight crushing Sue's chest. "We saved you some."

"That sounds good, baby. I can't wait to try them."

"How's the restaurant? Did you and Carla go inside today?"

Sue closed her eyes, organizing words that would be true without being terrifying. "We did. It needs some work. We'll get it fixed back up."

"When can I see it?"

"Not yet, sweetheart. But I promise you can see it once everything's cleaned up a little."

"Dad said maybe you can have it opened by Christmas. Is that true?"

Of course, Steve had talked to Lindsey. Of course, he'd offered her reassurance and hope.

"That's the hope. I'll do my best."

"You can do it, Mom. You can do anything." The absolute faith in Lindsey's voice made Sue want to cry and laugh simultaneously. "Hey, Grandma wants to know what time you're picking me up tomorrow."

"After school. You're taking the bus to their house. Maybe we can grab dinner somewhere if you want."

"Can we get pizza?" Lindsey asked, then immediately gasped. "Oh no, Mom, I'm sorry, I didn't mean—"

"It's okay, baby. We can absolutely get pizza." Sue managed a smile, though Lindsey couldn't see it. "How about The Pizza Shop over in Fayetteville? We haven't been there in forever."

"Yes! The one with the arcade games?" Lindsey's enthusiasm rebuilt itself quickly, the way only eleven-year-olds could bounce back from awkwardness. "Grandma says I need to let you go so you can rest. Love you, Mom."

"Love you too, sweetheart. See you tomorrow."

The call ended, and silence rushed back in like water filling a bathtub.

She set her phone down and stared at the cold coffee in her mug, at the unread book, and at the empty chair across from her where Lindsey usually sat. The kitchen that normally hummed with activity and conversation felt like a museum exhibit—*Kitchen, circa present day, showing signs of habitation but lacking actual life.*

She should eat something. The thought drifted through her mind without any accompanying motivation to act on it. When had she last eaten? Breakfast, maybe.

She pushed back from the table and walked to the refrigerator, opening it to survey the contents without really seeing them. Leftover casserole. Greek yogurt. String cheese. Apples. Multiple ingredients for a dozen different meals, but nothing that looked remotely appealing.

She closed the refrigerator and leaned her forehead against the cool stainless-steel door.

Lord, I'm trying to understand Your timing here.

The prayer formed quietly, tentatively, like testing ice that might not hold her weight.

Why now? Why right before Christmas, when the restaurant's busiest? Why after I've worked so hard? I thought—

She stopped, the words tangling in her throat. What had she thought? That if she worked hard enough, served faithfully enough, and built carefully enough, she'd somehow earn protection from disaster? That God owed her smooth sailing because she'd already survived the wreck of her marriage?

Sue opened her eyes and straightened, wrapping her arms around herself. The home she loved suddenly felt like the walls surrounding her were closing in, pressing the quiet against her until it became something physical and suffocating.

She needed air.

Sue grabbed a jacket from the hook by the door and stepped out onto the wraparound porch. The November night bit at her cheeks, cold enough to make her breath visible in small puffs of white. She walked to the porch swing and sat, setting it in motion with one foot while pulling her jacket tighter.

The valley spread below her property, dotted with lights from houses and the distant glow of Laurel Ridge proper. From here, she could make out the church steeple, backlit against the night sky. Somewhere down there in the dark, her restaurant sat wounded and waiting.

Steve's words echoed in her memory: Six to eight weeks if everything goes smoothly.

If.

That single syllable contained multitudes—insurance delays, contractor availability, inspection complications, permit red tape, and weather delays. A thousand ways for "if" to become "longer."

Sue pushed harder with her foot, making the swing move faster. The chains creaked in rhythm, a sound she'd heard a thousand times but tonight felt almost plaintive.

She thought about the insurance claim she'd need to file soon. The paperwork. The photographs she'd have to submit, documenting every ruined piece of equipment and every smoke-stained surface. The investigators would want statements, timelines, and proof that she'd maintained the building properly and hadn't somehow caused this through negligence.

As if she would ever be negligent about something she loved.

The thought caught her sharply and unexpectedly. Loved. Not past tense. Present. Despite the destruction, despite the overwhelming prospect of rebuilding, she still loved that restaurant. It represented more than just her livelihood or her independence—it was the physical manifestation of every choice she'd ever made.

A memory surfaced unbidden: Sue at twenty years old, standing in the empty building that would become Sue's Pizza, Steve's arm around her shoulders as they surveyed the bare walls and concrete floors.

"You sure about this?" he'd asked, his voice warm with the uncomplicated support of their early marriage. *"It's a big risk."*

"I'm sure," she'd said, leaning into his solid presence. *"This is ours. Something we will build together."*

But it hadn't been together, had it? Well, some of it had been. By the time Lindsey turned two, Steve had already started picking up extra shifts. By the time she was three, he was working toward his lieutenant certification. By four, Sue had learned to manage the restaurant's daily operations alone, care for Lindsey, and take care of the household's maintenance without expecting Steve's presence or input.

She'd told herself he was providing for them. His dedication to his career meant he cared about their family's security. That temporary sacrifice would lead to future stability.

She'd been lying to herself.

Steve hadn't been working those hours for the family. He'd been working for himself—for the satisfaction of advancement, for the identity he found in being the best, and for the simple fact that work was easier than marriage and fatherhood. You could measure success in a job. You could earn promotions and recognition and the respect of your peers.

Marriage didn't come with performance reviews or clear metrics for success. You couldn't get certified in being a good husband. There was no rank structure in fatherhood.

So Steve had chosen the fire department, where he knew how to excel, and Sue had learned to stop expecting anything from him.

Sue stopped the swing's motion, planting both feet flat on the porch boards. The memory left a familiar bitter taste, like stale coffee.

She'd filed for divorce because staying meant accepting a partnership where she carried everything alone. Better to be actually alone than to live with the illusion of togetherness. Better to build something entirely hers than to keep pretending "ours" meant anything.

And she'd succeeded. Sue's Pizza was hers—her vision, her work, her heart. She'd proven she could stand on her own, provide for her daughter, and create something lasting and meaningful.

Now the restaurant was damaged, and accepting Steve's help felt like erasing everything she'd proven. It felt like admitting she couldn't actually manage alone. And it felt like sliding backward into dependence on someone who'd taught her the cost of depending on anyone.

But the practical reality remained: she needed help. Needed contractors and electricians and painters and cleaners. Needed people who knew how to navigate building codes and insurance claims and fire marshal reports. She needed expertise she didn't possess.

And Steve—frustratingly, inconveniently—possessed exactly the expertise she needed.

Sue stood and walked to the porch railing, gripping the smooth wood with both hands. In the distance, a car's headlights swept along the road toward town. Normal life continuing for people whose worlds hadn't nearly burned down.

How do I do this, Lord?

The question felt raw.

How do I accept help without losing myself again? How do I let Steve get close enough to help me without letting him get close enough to hurt me? How do I trust anyone when I've learned that people leave, people fail, and the only person I can count on is myself?

The wind picked up, rustling through the trees surrounding her property. Sue shivered and turned back toward the house, the warm glow of lights inside suddenly looking less like comfort and more like a lonely outpost against the surrounding dark.

Inside, she locked the door and reset the coffeemaker for the morning. Rinsed her coffee mug and left it in the sink. Turned off the lights in the living room and kitchen, leaving only the small lamp on the entry table burning.

The stairs to her bedroom seemed impossibly steep. Sue made it halfway up before her legs felt like jelly, her body finally registering what her mind had been trying to ignore all day—she was exhausted. Completely and utterly depleted in ways that went deeper than physical tiredness.

She sank onto the step, her back against the wall, and let her head fall into her hands.

The tears came hot and fierce and soundless. They burned tracks down her cheeks and dripped off her chin, soaking into the knees of her leggings. Sue pressed her palms against her eyes, trying to stem the flow, but it was useless. Everything she'd held back since yesterday, everything she'd pushed down while touring the damage and maintaining composure—it all came pouring out in gasping, shaking sobs that left her ribs aching.

She cried for the restaurant. For the time and money and heart she'd poured into those walls. For the community gathering place that now sat dark and empty. And for the income she'd lose over the coming weeks and the uncertainty of whether insurance would cover everything.

She cried for Lindsey, who deserved better than a mother who fell apart on staircases and couldn't even make it to her bedroom before breaking down.

She cried for the girl she'd been at twenty, full of dreams and certainty that love would be enough. For the woman she'd become at twenty-eight, signing divorce papers and taking back her maiden name and rebuilding a life from pieces.

She cried for reasons she couldn't name, grief that went deeper than the fire and wider than the restaurant, pooling in spaces she'd thought she'd sealed closed years ago.

Eventually the tears slowed, then stopped. Sue sat on her stairs in the dim light, empty and hollowed out, too tired to move but knowing she couldn't stay here.

She pulled herself upright using the banister and climbed the remaining steps to her bedroom. She didn't bother changing clothes or washing her face or doing any of the nightly routines she normally maintained. She just kicked off her shoes, pulled back the handmade quilt her mother had made, and collapsed onto the bed.

Sleep should have come quickly, but instead Sue lay staring at the ceiling, following the familiar patterns of exposed beams with her eyes while her mind spun in circles.

Insurance adjusters.

Contractor estimates.

Lost revenue.

Permit applications.

Employee uncertainty.

Customer loyalty.

Steve's offer: *Call if you need anything.*

Sue rolled onto her side, pulling the quilt up to her chin. Through her bedroom window, she could just make out the lights of Laurel Ridge twinkling in the valley below. Somewhere down there, Steve was probably still awake too at the firehouse, maybe reviewing his report from yesterday or checking on equipment at the station. Or doing whatever fire chiefs did when they weren't fighting fires or offering help to ex-wives who didn't want to need it.

Her eyes drifted closed finally, exhaustion winning over anxiety.

Chapter 6

Steve's pen hovered over the incident report, the blank signature line waiting for his approval. He'd read through the document three times now, checking equipment response times, noting the electrical system failure, and confirming Ray's observations about the structural integrity of the dining room. Everything was thorough, accurate, and professional.

Everything except his ability to focus on any of it.

He set the pen down and rubbed his eyes with the heels of his hands. Through the glass-paneled door of his office, he could see the quiet bustle of the evening shift—Luke wiping down Engine Two with methodical precision, voices drifting from the kitchen where someone was making a late evening dinner. The familiar sounds should have grounded him. Usually did. Tonight they felt like static, background noise to the conversation playing on repeat in his head.

"I'm fine." Sue had said when he'd offered contact information for contractors. The sharp edge in her words had sliced through him.

The tone that said, I don't need you, even when the reality shouted otherwise.

Steve picked up his pen again, then set it down. Stood. Walked to the window overlooking the apparatus bay, stood there for a while, and then sat back down.

He knew what she was doing. Had watched her do it for years—the self-reliance that bordered on martyrdom, the refusal to accept help even when drowning, and the careful construction of walls that kept everyone at arm's length. Especially him.

Not that he could blame her.

He leaned back in his chair, the leather creaking in the quiet office. The framed photo of Sue and Lindsey on his desk caught the lamplight—taken at Lindsey's eighth birthday party. Sue's smile looked genuine in the photo, though Steve remembered the tension in her shoulders when he'd arrived late, still in his turnout gear from a call.

He'd made it to the party. That's what mattered, right?

Except it didn't matter. Not when "making it" meant showing up physically while being absent everywhere that counted. Not when Sue had planned the entire party, baked the cake, wrapped the presents, entertained fifteen children, and tried to control the chaos while Steve fielded work calls in the corner of the room.

His phone buzzed, vibrating against the desk. Lindsey's name appeared on the screen, and Steve's chest tightened the way it always did when she called unexpectedly.

"Hey, princess, everything okay?"

"Dad?" Lindsey's voice came through small and worried. "Are you at the station?"

"Yeah, I'm here. What's wrong?" Steve straightened in his chair immediately, cataloging potential emergencies. "Are you okay? Is Grandma—"

"Everyone's fine. I just—" She paused, and Steve heard the shuffle of movement, a door closing. When she spoke again, her voice was lower. "How bad was the fire at Mom's restaurant?"

Steve's throat constricted. He should have expected this.

"It was serious," he said carefully. "But we got there in time."

"Mom said it needs work, but she said it the way she says things when she doesn't want me to worry. Like when Grandpa had his surgery, and she kept saying everything was under control." Lindsey's observation skills were too sharp for her own good sometimes. "So how bad is it, really?"

Steve closed his eyes. He could lie. Could offer the same sanitized version Sue was probably maintaining. Or he could trust his daughter with a truth that wouldn't terrify her but wouldn't insult her intelligence either.

"The kitchen took the worst of it. The dining room has mostly smoke damage—that can be cleaned and repainted." He paused, then added, "It's going to take several weeks to fix, sweetheart. Maybe months."

"Months?" The dismay in Lindsey's voice cut deep. "But that's... that's past Christmas."

"We're going to do everything possible to get it open before then. Your mom's restaurant is important to many people. Including me."

"Are you going to help her?"

Steve stared at the incident report on his desk, at his list of contractor recommendations he'd been compiling, and at the building code requirements he'd pulled up on his computer "just to review."

"I offered," he said finally. "But it's up to your mom whether she wants my help."

"Why wouldn't she want your help? You're the fire chief. You know all about this stuff." Lindsey's logic was eleven-year-old simple, uncluttered by adult complications like divorce and hurt and the careful dance of post-marriage boundaries.

"It's complicated, princess."

"That's what grown-ups always say." Lindsey's frustration bled through the phone. "Mom needs help. You want to help. What's so hard about that? She needs you."

Everything, Steve thought. Years of everything.

"Your mom is very independent," Steve said instead. "She's built that restaurant into something amazing, and she did most of it on her own. She might want to keep handling things herself."

"That's dumb." Lindsey's bluntness would have made Steve smile under different circumstances. "Grandma says pride makes people do dumb things. Is Mom being prideful?"

"Lindsey—"

"Because if she is, maybe you should just help anyway. Like, show up and fix things whether she asks or not. That's what heroes do in movies."

"Real life doesn't work like movies, sweetheart." Steve pinched the bridge of his nose. "I can't just show up and take over your mom's business without her permission. That would be disrespectful."

"But you want to help?"

"Of course I do."

"Then tell her that." Lindsey made it sound so easy. "Just call her and say, 'Sue, I want to help you rebuild the restaurant because I care about you and I'm really good at this stuff.'"

Steve's breath caught on an unexpected laugh. "You think I should say it exactly like that?"

"Well, maybe use fewer words. Mom says you always use too many words when you're nervous." Lindsey paused, then added with the careful hopefulness only children of divorce could master, "You still care about Mom, right?"

The question sucker-punched him. Steve stared at the photo on his desk—Sue's genuine smile, Lindsey's joy, the life they'd built before he'd systematically dismantled it through a thousand absences and misplaced priorities.

"I do," he said quietly. "I never stopped."

"Then help her. Please, Dad. She's going to try to do everything herself and work herself like crazy and not ask anybody for anything because that's what she does. And then she'll be stressed and tired and—" Lindsey's voice wavered slightly.

"I'll do what I can, princess. I promise."

"Okay." Lindsey exhaled, satisfied in the way kids get when adults finally agree with them. "Love you, Dad."

"Love you too, sweetheart. Talk soon."

The call ended, and Steve set his phone down on the desk. His daughter's words echoed in the sudden quiet of his office: She needs you.

He wanted to believe that. Gosh, he wanted to believe that Sue might need him for something beyond fire code expertise and contractor recommendations.

But wanting and reality rarely aligned.

Steve opened the bottom drawer of his desk and pulled out a folder he hadn't looked at in months. Inside were photos from the early days—Sue and him at the restaurant's grand opening, both of them impossibly young and hopeful. Sue was standing in front of the brick facade with an "Opening Soon" sign, her smile so wide it looked like it might split her face. The two of them were covered in paint after spending a weekend painting the entire building, exhausted but happy.

He'd been there for that. Had helped her sand tables, had held the ladder while she hung the first set of photos on the wall, and had tested every menu item and offered honest feedback. Even when it meant telling her the garlic knots needed more butter.

When had that stopped? When had "helping Sue pursue her dreams," become "making an appearance when work allowed?"

Steve knew the answer. Lindsey was two when he'd started working toward his lieutenant certification. The extra studying, the additional shifts to prove his reliability, and the networking with other departments to build his reputation. All of it necessary, he'd told himself. All of it a temporary sacrifice for long-term gain.

Except it hadn't been temporary. Lieutenant became captain. Captain became deputy chief. Deputy chief became his current position. Each promotion came with more responsibility, longer hours, and greater demands. And each time, Sue had smiled and said she was proud of him while the distance between them grew wider.

By the time Lindsey turned six, Sue had stopped asking him to help with restaurant decisions. Had stopped expecting him at school events. Had stopped including him in her daily life in any meaningful way.

Steve closed the folder and shoved it back in the drawer. The past couldn't be changed, but maybe the present could be navigated differently. If Sue would let him.

His computer screen had gone dark. Steve tapped the keyboard, bringing up the document he'd been working on earlier—a comprehensive list of local contractors specializing in fire restoration, their contact information, average timelines, and price ranges. Below that, notes on current building codes for commercial kitchens, electrical requirements, and ventilation system standards.

He'd told himself he was just being thorough. Making sure he had all the information ready in case Sue asked for recommendations.

Who was he kidding?

Steve opened a new document and began typing. A step-by-step guide for navigating insurance claims after fire damage. Common pitfalls to avoid. Questions to ask adjusters. Documentation requirements. The kind of information someone would need if they were tackling this process for the first time.

The kind of information Sue would need.

His fingers moved across the keyboard with purpose now, organizing everything he knew from years of fire safety work into practical, actionable guidance. He couldn't force Sue to accept his help. Couldn't show up at her restaurant tomorrow and start issuing orders. He couldn't fix this the way he wanted to with his own two hands.

But he could give her tools. Information. Support from a distance that respected her independence while acknowledging she shouldn't have to figure this out alone.

Steve was three pages into the document when a knock on his door made him look up. Mark Talley stood in the doorway, still in his uniform but with the slightly rumpled look that came at the end of a long shift.

"What are you working on so late?" Mark asked, leaning against the doorframe.

"Just finishing up some paperwork."

Mark's eyes narrowed slightly. "Want to tell me what's really going on?"

"Nope."

"Steve." Mark's tone carried the weight of years of friendship. "You look like you're wrestling a bear while being a million miles away. What's going on?"

Steve hesitated, then sighed. There was no point in hiding it. Mark knew him too well, and the whole department had responded to Sue's Pizza yesterday. Everyone knew the personal complications involved.

"I'm trying to figure out how to help Sue without making things worse," Steve admitted.

"Worse than her restaurant burning down?" Mark moved into the office and dropped into the chair across from Steve's desk. "Pretty sure it can't get much worse."

"Worse between us." Steve gestured vaguely. "She barely tolerates me on good days. Now that her business is damaged, she's going to need help with the restoration process, and I'm—" He stopped, struggling to articulate the tangle of thoughts that had been cycling through his head all day.

"You're the most qualified person to help her," Mark finished. "And also the last person she probably wants help from."

"You got that right."

Mark leaned back in the chair, studying Steve with the kind of frank assessment that made him an excellent fire captain. "So what are you going to do?"

"What can I do? She made it pretty clear today that she doesn't need me hovering around offering assistance." Steve clicked his mouse, closing the document on his screen. "If she wants more, she knows where to find me."

"That's it? You're just going to wait?"

"What else am I supposed to do, Mark? Show up at her house uninvited and beg to help? Start calling contractors on her behalf?"

"There's a difference between respecting her independence and using it as an excuse to keep your distance."

He looked at his friend sharply. "What's that supposed to mean?"

"It means you've spent six years dancing around Sue. Maybe what she needs isn't a grand gesture or you taking over. Maybe she just needs to know you're available. Actually available, not theoretically available if she jumps through the right hoops to ask for help."

Steve thought about Sue's expression earlier today in her restaurant—the exhaustion, the devastation, the rigid control that kept her spine straight when everything else was crumbling. He thought about Lindsey's voice on the phone: She needs you.

"I don't know how to do that," Steve said quietly. "How to be available without being invasive. How to offer support without taking over. How to—" He stopped, the words catching. "How to show her I've changed when every instinct I have says to fix this for her?"

Mark's expression softened. "Start small. Show up. Be present. Offer specific help, not general 'call if you need anything' stuff. And for goodness sake, stop treating her like a stranger you're trying not to offend... be a man."

"She is a stranger in a lot of ways. I don't know the woman she's become since the divorce."

"Then get to know her again." Mark stood, stretching. "Look, I'm not saying it'll be easy. Or that Sue's going to welcome you with open arms. But you've spent six years regretting how you lost her. This fire—awful as it is—might be the chance to prove you've actually learned something in that time."

After Mark left, Steve sat in his office staring at his computer.

He could close the document and forget he had ever started it. Go home to his empty apartment and a frozen dinner.

Or he could email it to her with a brief note. Nothing pushy. Nothing that demanded a response. Just information she might need.

Steve pulled up his email, attached the document, and stared at the empty message field. What did you say to your ex-wife when her business had just burned down and you desperately wanted to help but had no idea if that help would be welcome?

His fingers hovered over the keyboard.

Then he closed the email without sending it, the cursor blinking in accusation against the white screen.

Tomorrow. He'd figure out what to say tomorrow.

Steve signed the incident report with quick, practiced strokes, filed it in the appropriate folder, and shut down his computer. The office fell into shadow as he turned off the desk lamp, leaving only the glow from the apparatus bay to light his way out.

He paused at the door. When had helping the woman he loved become so complicated that he couldn't even send an email?

The question followed him out of the office and all the way home.

Chapter 7

Steve's truck idled at the red light on Main Street, two to-go coffees secured in the cup holders and a manila folder thick with documentation riding shotgun. He told himself he was just being helpful, being professional.

He was lying to himself.

When Sue's silver SUV came into view parked in front of the restaurant, Steve's grip tightened on the steering wheel. He'd known she'd be here—some instinct that had nothing to do with logic and everything to do with years of knowing her. Of course she'd show up first thing this morning, alone, trying to tackle the overwhelming mess.

Steve pulled into the space behind her vehicle and cut the engine.

He grabbed both coffees—hers with two creams and one sugar the way she preferred it, though he had no business remembering that—and the folder he'd spent the morning expanding. He'd been unable to sleep last night. He'd left his apartment before dawn and then poured everything he knew into making the information for Sue as comprehensive as possible. Contact numbers for specialty suppliers she might not know existed. Timeline templates for coordinating multiple contractors. Even a sample insurance claim letter formatted specifically for fire damage.

The folder felt inadequate in his hands.

As Steve opened the front door, he noticed the bell that used to jingle when customers entered lying on the floor near the threshold.

"Sue?"

She turned at his voice, and Steve watched the sequence of emotions cross her face—surprise, wariness, irritation, then that careful neutrality she'd perfected over six years.

"Steve." His name came out flat. "What are you doing here?"

"Saw your car. Thought you might need this." He held up the folder, keeping his tone professional. Clinical. "Information packet for fire restoration. Incident report copies, contractor recommendations, building code requirements, and permit procedures... among other things."

Sue's gaze dropped to the folder, then back to his face. Her chin lifted slightly—that stubborn pride he knew so well making its appearance. "I can handle this myself. I don't need—"

"I know you can handle it." Steve cut her off gently, stepping further into the dining room. The acrid smell of smoke hung heavy despite ventilation efforts. "But there's a difference between handling something and having to reinvent the wheel when someone's already done the research."

"I'm not asking for charity."

"Good. Because I'm not offering any." Steve set one coffee cup on the least soot-covered table surface he could find nearest her, keeping the other in his hand. "This is standard protocol. Any business owner dealing with fire damage gets access to these resources. It's part of the fire marshal's public safety mandate."

The words tasted like the bureaucratic nonsense they were, but they gave Sue an out—a way to accept help without it being personal. Without it being them.

Sue crossed her arms, and Steve recognized the defensive posture. "Fine. Leave it. I'll look through it later."

"You should look at it now." Steve opened the folder, pulling out the top sheet. "Emergency demolition permit. You'll need to file this right away if you want to start removing damaged materials this week."

Sue moved closer despite herself, squinting at the form.

Steve flipped to the next section. "Electrical inspection requirements. Before any contractor can touch your wiring, the county inspector needs to do a preliminary assessment. That's a three-week wait unless you file an expedited request. Here's the form already filled out with your restaurant information. You just need to sign and submit."

Sue took the paper from his hand, her fingers careful not to touch his. She scanned the form, and Steve watched her expression shift from defensive to overwhelmed as the reality of the bureaucratic maze ahead became clear.

"Three weeks just for an inspection?"

"Unless you expedite. Then it's just a couple of business days." Steve pulled out another document. "Building code compliance checklist. Everything needs to be brought up to current standards, not just replaced. That means your entire electrical system, ventilation, fire suppression, and plumbing if they encounter any issues while the walls are open."

"Plumbing?" Sue's voice had lost its edge, replaced by something that sounded dangerously close to panic. "What's wrong with the plumbing?"

"Probably nothing. But once walls are opened for electrical work, inspectors are required to verify all systems. It's standard procedure." Steve gestured to the next section. "Here's a contractor list. Your brother Graham's company is at the top—they're licensed for commercial fire restoration and have the fastest turnaround in the county. I've also included three other options in case Graham's crew is too booked."

Sue stared at the papers in her hands, then at the thick folder still in Steve's grip. "How much information is in there?"

"Everything you need to get you through this." Steve set the folder on the table beside her. "Contact information for every supplier you might need—electrical, plumbing, HVAC, commercial kitchen equipment, flooring, paint. I've noted which one's offer business accounts with net-thirty payment terms in case insurance reimbursement is delayed."

"Insurance reimbursement." Sue repeated the words as if they were in a foreign language. "Right. I need to call them today."

"You need documentation first. Photos of everything, itemized lists of damaged equipment, and original purchase receipts if you have them." Steve pulled out yet another checklist from the folder. "This walks you through exactly what insurance adjusters require. Common mistakes business owners make. Questions to ask about your coverage."

Sue took the papers, and this time her hands trembled slightly. She was reading through the insurance documentation checklist, and Steve watched her face as the scope of work ahead registered fully.

"The ovens," she said quietly. "The ones I saved six months to buy. Are you sure they're—"

"Complete loss." Steve kept his voice gentle. "I've included contact information for several companies that specialize in commercial kitchen equipment and have in-stock items that aren't on back order."

Sue looked up at him then, really looked at him, and Steve saw past the defensive walls to the exhaustion and fear beneath. "Why are you doing this?"

The question hung between them, loaded with everything they'd been carefully not saying. Steve could have deflected. Could have repeated his line about public safety protocols or fire chief responsibilities.

Instead, he told her the truth.

"Because you shouldn't have to figure this out alone. And because I know you will try anyway. You built something beautiful here, Sue. Something that matters to this community. You deserve support while you rebuild it."

"I divorced you."

The words were quiet, almost wondering, like she couldn't quite reconcile his help with the history between them.

"You did." Steve met her gaze steadily. "And you had good reason. That doesn't change the fact that your restaurant caught fire and you need information to navigate the restoration process."

Sue's jaw worked, emotions warring across her face. Pride. Gratitude. Resentment. Relief. Fear. "I don't want to owe you anything."

"You don't. This isn't—" Steve stopped, choosing his words carefully. "This is me doing my job. Nothing more."

The lie tasted bitter. This was everything more—every regret he carried, every wish that he could undo the past, every desperate hope that maybe helping her now could somehow balance the scales for all the times he'd failed to help her before.

"Okay." Sue's voice was small, uncertain in a way that made Steve's chest ache. "Thank you. For the information."

"You're welcome." Steve gestured to the folder. "Everything's organized by timeline. Things you need to do this week are flagged in red. Things that can wait until next week are yellow. Green flags are longer-term items."

Sue opened the folder, flipping through the color-coded sections with something like wonder. "This is... incredibly detailed."

"I had some time this morning."

"Steve." Sue closed the folder, her hands resting on the cover. "This must have taken hours."

He shrugged uncomfortably. "It's my job to know this stuff. Just took some time to compile it in one place."

"Still." Sue bit her lip, and Steve recognized the gesture—she was fighting tears. "I appreciate it. Even if I—" She stopped, swallowed hard. "Even if I should probably be able to figure all this out on my own."

"Nobody can figure this out on their own. That's not weakness, Sue. It's just reality." Steve picked up the papers she'd set down and began organizing them. "Fire restoration is complicated. There are regulations and requirements that most business owners have never heard of. No one expects you to just know all these things."

"But you do."

"Because I've seen dozens of these cases. You've seen one. Your own." Steve handed her back the organized stack of papers. "Use the information. Call those contractors. File the permits. Let people who know what they're doing help you through this."

Sue took the papers, and for a moment her fingers brushed his—accidental contact that sent sparks up Steve's arm. They both froze, then

Sue pulled back quickly, clutching the documents to her chest like a shield.

"I should get started on these calls," she said, her voice overly bright. "The sooner I file permits, the sooner work can begin."

"Right." Steve backed toward the door, giving her space. "If you have questions about any of the forms, just call me."

"I'll figure it out."

"I know you will." Steve paused at the threshold. "But the offer stands anyway."

Sue nodded without meeting his eyes, already turning back to survey the dining room with its smoke-stained walls and furniture. Steve watched her straighten and pull on that armor of competence and determination that had carried her through years of single parenthood and business ownership.

He wanted to tell her she didn't have to be strong every minute. That it was okay to lean on people who cared about her. And that he would gladly carry some of this burden if she'd let him.

Instead, he said, "Take care of yourself, Sue."

Then he walked out before he could say anything else. Anything true. Anything that would reveal just how much watching her struggle hurt and how desperately he wanted to fix it all for her.

His truck felt cold as he climbed inside. Steve started the engine and sat for a moment, staring at the building.

She was going to handle this. Of course, she was. Sue handled everything that got thrown at her with grace and determination and an independence that refused to break.

Steve just wished that she'd let him stand beside her while she did it.

He watched her step outside the front door, her phone pressed to her ear, already moving forward without him.

Just like she always did.

Just like he'd taught her to.

Chapter 8

Sue pressed the phone against her ear with one shoulder while highlighting another completed task on Steve's checklist. She sat outside at the patio table where she'd set up her temporary command center. The November sun felt warm against her face despite the crisp air, and the manila folder had transformed from an unwanted gift into her strategic roadmap forward.

"Yes, I can be here at eight-thirty tomorrow morning," she said to the building inspector's assistant. "I have all the preliminary documentation ready—incident report, property deed, insurance policy number. I'll bring originals and copies."

"That's perfect, Ms. Smith. Mr. Harrison will meet you at the property address. The assessment should take about an hour."

Sue drew a neat checkmark beside *Schedule Building Inspector Meeting* and felt a small surge of satisfaction. *One down. Seventeen to go.*

After she hung up, Sue opened Steve's folder to the section marked WEEK ONE—CRITICAL. His handwriting filled the margins with notes and clarifications, and a yellow Post-it stuck to one page made her pause: *Don't let them rush you through the inspection. Ask about the plumbing while they're checking the electrical—saves a second visit. - S*

She traced the letters with one finger, imagining Steve at his desk, thinking through every detail she might encounter. The care embedded in these preparations felt both touching and frustrating—proof that he understood her needs better than she wanted to admit.

Sue shook off the thought and made the next call to the county electrical inspector's office, where Sue navigated the automated menu system with Steve's notes guiding her to the right extension. She explained her situation with confidence, using terminology from his documentation—*commercial kitchen electrical failure, expedited inspection request, and fire marshal incident report number 2024-1114.*

"We can have someone out Friday morning if you file the online request by the end of business today," the scheduler told her.

"Friday works perfectly. I'll submit the paperwork within the hour." Sue made another checkmark. She was doing this. Actually doing this.

By ten, Sue had scheduled three inspections, contacted her insurance company to initiate the claims process, and left detailed messages for two electrical contractors from Steve's vetted list. Her notebook was filled with appointment times, reference numbers, and follow-up tasks in neat columns that would have made her business school professors proud.

When her phone rang with an unfamiliar number, Sue answered with professional efficiency. "This is Sue Smith."

"Ms. Smith, this is David Carter from Mountain Valley Electric. Returning your call about fire damage assessment."

Sue flipped to Steve's contractor section, finding Carter's name at the top with three stars drawn beside it and a note: *Fast, thorough, fair prices. Used him in the fire station renovation.*

"Mr. Carter, thank you for calling back so quickly. I need a complete electrical system evaluation and replacement estimate for a commercial kitchen." She rattled off the restaurant's address, square footage, and basic specifications, pulling information from various documents spread across the patio table.

"I can be there Thursday at two o'clock for the assessment. It will take about ninety minutes."

Sue penciled the appointment on her rapidly filling schedule. "That works. I'll have the building inspector's report by then, and the power will be disconnected per safety protocols."

"Sounds like you've done your homework."

"I had a good teacher." The words slipped out before Sue could stop them, and she felt heat creep up her neck. "I mean, I had a little help from my local fire chief."

They confirmed the details and ended the call, leaving Sue staring at another completed checkmark with mixed feelings churning in her stomach.

She was succeeding. Making real progress. Proving she could handle this crisis with competence and organization. So why did every accomplishment feel slightly hollow, like reading someone else's instruction manual rather than charting her own course?

Sue pushed the thought aside and reached for the next red-flagged item: *Contact Insurance Adjuster—DO NOT accept first settlement offer without contractor estimates in hand.*

Another Post-it note, this one attached to a sample letter: *Insurance companies lowball initial offers. Be polite but firm. You're entitled to full restoration, not just minimal repairs. Don't let them bully you. - S*

The protectiveness in those words made something twist in Sue's chest. This was the Steve she'd fallen in love with years ago—the man who'd stayed up all night helping her write the business plan for Sue's Pizza, who'd researched supplier contracts and negotiated with the building's previous owner on her behalf, and who'd celebrated every small victory like it was his own triumph.

Before ambition had consumed him. Before she'd become an afterthought.

Sue shook her head sharply and dialed her insurance company, forcing her focus back to the immediate task. The claims representative walked her through the preliminary documentation requirements, and Sue took meticulous notes while cross-referencing Steve's checklist.

"The adjuster will need to visit the property before we can provide settlement figures," the representative explained. "We're scheduling assessments for next week—"

"Next week?" Sue sat up straighter, her business instincts kicking in. "I have three contractor inspections scheduled this week. I'll need the adjuster's assessment before I can accept any bids or begin demolition."

"I understand your urgency, Ms. Smith, but our adjusters are quite busy—"

"I'm sure they are." Sue kept her voice pleasant but unyielding, channeling every difficult customer negotiation she'd ever navigated. "However, every day of delay costs me revenue. I have an inspection report from the responding fire chief, detailed photographs, and a complete equipment inventory. If your adjuster can coordinate with my Thursday electrical assessment, you'll have everything needed for accurate evaluation in one visit."

A pause. "Let me check the schedule."

Sue held her breath, surprised by her own assertiveness. When had she become someone who pushed back against bureaucratic timelines and demanded accommodation?

Since she'd started running a business alone. Since she'd learned that waiting for help meant falling behind.

"We can do Thursday at four o'clock. That's the best I can offer."

"Thursday at four is perfect. Thank you." Sue added it to her schedule with a small flourish of victory.

By eleven, Sue's stomach was growling with the reminder that she'd skipped breakfast. She'd also scheduled the insurance assessment, left messages for two more electrical contractors as backup options, and confirmed Graham's construction company could do the structural evaluation on Friday afternoon.

Sue surveyed her notes with genuine satisfaction. Earlier this morning she'd been standing in her ruined restaurant feeling utterly lost. Now she had a plan. Appointments. Progress. Control over a situation that had felt completely uncontrollable.

Her phone buzzed with a text from Carla: *How's it going? Need anything?*

Sue typed back: *Making progress. Can you come? Need to discuss staff scheduling.*

Within thirty minutes, Carla's sedan pulled into the parking lot. She emerged carrying two paper bags that released the unmistakable aroma of Martha's meatloaf sub-sandwiches and fresh fries.

"You need to eat," Carla said, setting the bags on the patio table. "Martha sent this on the house. She said—and I quote—That girl needs to keep her strength up, and I won't have her wasting away on my watch."

Sue's throat tightened at the gesture.

"Now catch me up. What's all this?" Carla settled into the chair across from Sue and started unpacking sandwiches.

Between bites of the best food she'd tasted in two days, Sue walked Carla through her morning's accomplishments. Her manager listened with growing amazement, occasionally stopping to ask questions or provide suggestions.

"You did all this since this morning?" Carla shook her head. "Sue, this is impressive. Really impressive."

"I had help." Sue gestured to Steve's folder, trying to keep her voice neutral. "The fire chief provided comprehensive guidance."

"Steve."

"Fire Chief Johnson," Sue corrected, suddenly defensive. "In his official capacity of providing public safety resources."

"Well, however you got the information, you're handling this like a boss. What do you need from me?"

Sue flipped to a fresh notebook page, grateful for the shift to safer topics. "Staff scheduling. The restaurant will be closed for at least six weeks, maybe longer. I need to keep everyone employed if possible."

They spent the next hour brainstorming solutions. Sue had already researched temporary catering licenses and identified several church and community events coming up that could use food service. If she could arrange access to another kitchen—maybe the church's commercial setup—she could maintain some revenue and keep her employees working.

"The Christmas bazaar is the first weekend in December," Carla noted. "Usually has at least two hundred people. And the town's doing an expanded tree-lighting ceremony this year. Entertainment, activities, the whole deal."

"Both perfect opportunities." Sue made notes, her mind already calculating staffing needs and menu options. "If they can get licensed for temporary food service by next week, they won't miss out on as much income as I feared."

"You're really thinking this entire process through."

"I don't have a choice." Sue set down her pen and looked at her ruined restaurant. "My employees need to keep earning a living. This restaurant—it's everything to me. I can't just sit around waiting for the contractors to fix it. I need to be doing something."

"I know." Carla reached across the table and squeezed her hand. "And you're doing an outstanding job. But don't forget to breathe occasionally, okay? And honestly, why don't you just take this time to focus on the restaurant itself? I'll handle making sure our employees have a temporary income. I'll make a few phone calls and see what I can do."

After Carla left, Sue returned to her checklist with renewed energy.

By two o'clock, her hand was cramping from writing and her head buzzed with information, but she'd accomplished more in one day than she'd thought possible this morning. Sue stood and stretched, then walked into the restaurant to survey the damage with fresh eyes.

The smoke-stained walls looked less terrifying now that she had a plan for addressing them. The ruined kitchen equipment felt manageable. Even the overwhelming bureaucracy of permits and inspections seemed navigable with Steve's detailed guidance.

Sue paused at that thought, her gaze falling on the forgotten coffee cup still sitting on the table where Steve had left it. She picked it up and removed the lid, noticing how cream had been added. She took a sip of the day-old coffee. Two creams and one sugar.

He'd remembered. After six years, Steve Johnson still remembered how she took her coffee.

Sue walked into the bathroom and dumped the cold liquid into the soot-filled sink and tossed the cup in the garbage. She didn't want to think about what those small details of him remembering how she liked her coffee meant. Didn't want to acknowledge the care embedded in every Post-it note, every margin comment, and every thoughtfully organized section of his documentation.

She especially didn't want to admit how much easier today had been because of the folder full of information that he had prepared for her.

Chapter 9

Sue spread the contents of the folder across the chrome-edged table at Martha's Diner as Martha herself appeared with a coffee pot, her weathered face creasing into a warm smile. "Honey, you look like you've been wrestling mountains all day."

"Just bureaucracy." Sue managed a tired smile. "Same thing, really."

"Mm-hmm." Martha poured coffee into the thick ceramic mug in front of Sue. "And before you even ask, that meat loaf sandwich I sent over with Carla today was on the house. Don't you dare argue with me about it."

"Martha, I can't—"

"Can't?" Martha's eyebrows rose. "Sue Smith, I've known you since you were in pigtails ordering grilled cheese with your daddy. If I want to send over a sandwich when your restaurant just nearly burned down to the ground, I'll do exactly that. Now, what can I get you?"

Sue felt her throat tighten at the simple kindness. "Cherry pie. With ice cream. And I'll pay for this."

"We'll see. Be right back, sugar."

Sue watched Martha disappear into the kitchen, then turned her attention back to Steve's meticulously organized documents. Post-it notes marked key sections, margin notes clarified complex terminology, and his handwriting filled the spaces between official documents with guidance she hadn't known she needed.

It was overwhelming. Not just the scope of work ahead, but the care embedded in every detail. This wasn't a fire chief fulfilling professional obligations. This was Steve—the man who'd once stayed up all night helping her practice for her business license exam, who'd painted the restaurant's dining room alongside her, and who'd believed in her dreams before she'd fully believed in them herself.

Before he'd stopped believing in anything except the next promotion and himself.

Martha returned with a generous slice of cherry pie, vanilla ice cream already melting into the lattice crust. She slid into the booth across from Sue without asking, settling in with the comfortable authority of someone who'd been feeding this town's troubles for forty years.

"Talk," Martha said simply.

"There's nothing to—"

"Sue. The building inspector's office called my nephew this morning asking if he could fit in an emergency commercial inspection this week. Small town, honey. Word travels. And you sitting here looking like you're trying to solve a puzzle with half the pieces missing tells me you need more than just pie."

Sue set down her fork, the first bite of cherry sweetness still coating her tongue. "It's not the restaurant. I mean, it is the restaurant, but I'm handling that. I've scheduled inspections, contacted contractors, and talked to the insurance company. I'm getting things done."

"With Steve's help."

The statement landed between them like a stone in still water. Sue looked up sharply, but Martha's expression held no judgment—only understanding.

"How did you—"

"Honey, Steve was in here at six this morning. Ordered coffee, opened his laptop, spread out half a forest's worth of paperwork, and spent two hours writing notes and googling stuff before heading to the station." Martha sipped her own coffee. "When I asked what had him up before the roosters, he said he was preparing information for a business owner affected by a fire. It wasn't difficult to figure out which business owner."

Sue's chest constricted. "He didn't have to do that."

"No, he didn't." Martha cut a piece from Sue's pie and ate it without bothering to ask. "But he did anyway. And now you're sitting here looking confused about whether to be grateful or angry."

"I'm grateful." The word came out defensive. "This information is incredibly helpful. I couldn't have scheduled half of today's appointments without it."

"But?"

Sue traced the rim of her coffee mug with one finger. "But I don't understand why. We've been divorced for six years, Martha. We coordinate custody exchanges through text messages. We maintain a polite distance whenever possible. We don't—we're not—"

"You don't get to care about each other anymore?" Martha's tone was knowing, almost amused.

"That's not what I meant."

"Isn't it?" Martha leaned forward, her expression softening. "Sue, I've watched you two dance around each other for years now. Both of you are pretending you don't still feel whatever it was that got you married in the first place. Maybe the marriage ended for good reasons—Lord knows I'm not one to judge that—but feelings don't just evaporate because you sign papers."

"They should. It'd be easier if they did."

"Easier isn't always better." Martha reached across the table and patted Sue's hand. "And speaking of easier—you've got enough on your plate without trying to rebuild that restaurant completely alone. What's your plan for your employees?"

Sue latched onto the safer topic gratefully. "That's actually one of my concerns. They need an income."

"Well." Martha sat back, her eyes brightening with the look she got when solving problems. "I could use a couple of extra hands around here. Thanksgiving and the Christmas rush are coming, which means additional tourists and extended families will be in town, and I'm not getting any younger. If any of your staff want to pick up some shifts waiting tables or helping in my kitchen, send them my way. It won't be full time, but it'll be something."

"Martha, that would be—you're sure?"

"Wouldn't offer if I wasn't. And here's another thought—you're going to need that restaurant cleaned up, right? Smoke damage, ash, broken glass, all that mess?"

"Yes, but I was going to hire—"

"Hire your own people. Pay them to do the cleanup work. They know your restaurant better than anyone; they'll treat it with care, and you keep them earning while speeding up the whole process. Two birds, one stone."

Sue stared at Martha as the elegance of the solution settled over her. "That's brilliant."

"I have my moments." Martha's smile was satisfied. "Now eat your pie before it gets soggy."

Sue pulled out her phone and quickly typed a message to Carla: *Can you coordinate with staff? Need to schedule paid cleanup work ASAP. Also, let them know Martha has shifts available at the diner if they're interested.*

Carla's response came within seconds: *On it. This is perfect. I'll make calls right away.*

Sue felt something loosen in her chest—the tight knot of worry about her employees finally starting to ease. She took another bite of pie, and this time it tasted like more than just cherries and sugar. It tasted like community and support and the reminder that she wasn't as alone as she sometimes felt.

The diner's bell chimed, announcing a new customer. Sue glanced up reflexively and felt her stomach drop.

Steve walked to the counter and spoke to the waitress there.

He hadn't seen her yet. She could duck her head, hide behind the folder, and hope he'd leave without noticing—

"Steve!" Martha called out cheerfully.

Steve turned, and his gaze found Sue immediately. Something flickered across his face—surprise, maybe, or pleasure, or that complicated mix of emotions that always seemed to surface when they occupied the same space.

"Martha." He approached with the careful courtesy of someone navigating uncertain territory. "Sue."

"Steve." Sue kept her voice neutral, professional.

"Why don't you sit while you wait?" Martha said as she slid over in the booth. "Hank's still working on your order. Might as well rest your feet."

"I don't want to interrupt—"

"You're not." Martha's tone brooked no argument as she gestured to the space beside her.

Steve hesitated, then slid into the booth, putting him at an angle to Sue across the small table. The booth that had felt comfortably private moments ago suddenly shrank.

"How's the planning going?" Steve directed the question to Sue, his posture careful, hands folded on the table.

Sue gestured to the open folder and documents between them on the table. "I scheduled the building inspector for tomorrow morning at eight-thirty. County electrical inspector Friday morning. Your electrician contact—David Carter—is coming Thursday afternoon for a preliminary assessment."

"That was fast." Steve's expression showed genuine approval.

"I had good documentation." Sue met his eyes, acknowledging the help without making it more than it was. "Graham's construction company is doing the structural evaluation Friday afternoon too. The insurance adjuster is coming Thursday."

"You've been busy."

"I told you I could handle it."

"I never doubted you." Steve's response was quiet, almost gentle, and somehow that felt more dangerous than if he'd challenged her.

Martha watched this exchange with poorly disguised interest, her head swiveling between them like a spectator at a tennis match.

"I can be there Friday," Steve said almost casually. "When Graham's crew does the structural assessment."

Sue felt her spine stiffen. "I don't need a chaperone."

"Not a chaperone. A fire safety consultant." Steve leaned forward slightly. "Sue, I know you can handle this yourself. I respect that. But there are technical aspects of fire damage assessment that require specialized knowledge. Load-bearing capacity after heat exposure, hidden structural compromises, smoke penetration in materials—"

"Graham and his crew know construction."

"He knows building, and yes, he is fire restoration certified. I know fire." Steve's tone remained patient, reasonable, which somehow made Sue's defensive walls rise higher. "There's a difference. And if Graham's crew misses something because they're not trained to look for specific fire-related damage, you could end up with serious problems down the line."

Sue opened her mouth to argue, then caught Martha's expression—a subtle, knowing look that said, "He has a point, honey."

"I don't want you taking over my project," Sue said firmly.

"I don't want to take over anything." Steve held her gaze steadily. "I want to make sure the assessment is thorough and accurate. That's it. Graham's crew makes the construction recommendations. You make all the decisions. I just provide fire safety expertise where it's needed."

"In a consulting capacity." Sue heard herself negotiating as if this were a business contract rather than a conversation with her ex-husband.

"Exactly."

"No decision-making authority."

"None. That's all yours."

"And you leave when the safety assessment is complete. You don't hover around offering opinions on paint colors or cabinet configurations."

A ghost of a smile crossed Steve's face. "Wouldn't dream of it. You have much better taste than I do, anyway."

The comment hung in the air—innocent on the surface but carrying echoes of their early marriage when Steve had deferred to her judgment on every design decision for the restaurant.

Sue picked up her coffee mug, needing something to do with her hands. "Fine. Friday afternoon. But I'm serious about the boundaries, Steve."

"I know you are. I'll stick to structural safety issues. Nothing else."

"Good."

Hank appeared from the kitchen carrying two large bags loaded with containers. "Order's ready, Chief. It should still be hot when you get it back to the station."

Steve slid out of the booth, then paused. "Thanks for letting me help, Sue. Even with the parameters."

"You're helping Graham, not me." Sue kept her tone businesslike.

"Right." That almost-smile again. "See you Friday then."

He collected the bags and headed for the door, throwing a wave to Martha. The bell chimed his exit, and the diner felt suddenly larger, the air less charged.

Martha waited exactly three seconds before speaking. "Well."

"Don't start." Sue stabbed her fork into the remaining pie.

"I wasn't going to say anything." Martha's innocent expression was utterly unconvincing. "Just noting that for two people who maintain a polite distance and enjoy waltzing around one another, that was a remarkably detailed negotiation."

"It's my restaurant. Of course, I'm going to set clear boundaries about who has what authority."

"Mm-hmm. And it has nothing to do with the fact that Steve compiled all this information for you or that he just offered to spend his Friday afternoon making sure your building gets properly evaluated."

"He's doing his job." But even as she said it, she knew it was a lie. Fire chiefs didn't spend personal time preparing comprehensive documentation folders. They didn't offer to attend assessments of buildings. And they certainly didn't remember coffee preferences after six years of divorce.

"If you say so, honey." Martha stood and collected Sue's empty pie plate. "But for what it's worth, I've known that boy since he moved to this town with his family. I've watched him pine over you, get married, get divorced, and spend the last six years looking like he lost something precious and doesn't know how to get it back. Whatever he's doing with all this help—it's not just his job."

Sue stared at the papers still spread across the table, at Steve's handwriting filling margins and Post-it notes, and at the hours of care invested in making her rebuilding process easier.

"I don't know what to do with that," she admitted quietly.

"You don't have to do anything with it." Martha's hand landed gently on Sue's shoulder. "Just don't slam the door completely closed, okay? Sometimes grace means letting people prove they've changed. Even when we're scared, they haven't."

After Martha left, Sue gathered the papers back into their folder with mechanical precision. She'd accomplished what she came for—had something sweet to calm her nerves and had even arranged for staff income during the closure. She'd set firm boundaries with Steve about Friday's inspection. She was maintaining control, independence, and self-sufficiency.

So why did Martha's words echo in her mind with uncomfortable persistence? *Sometimes grace means letting people prove they've changed.*

Sue paid for her pie despite Martha's protests and walked out into the November afternoon. Her SUV sat in the parking lot, a familiar pickup truck next to it.

Steve stood near his truck, phone to his ear, gesturing as he talked. When he saw Sue as she crossed the street, he held up one finger in a "just a minute" gesture.

She should have gotten into her vehicle and driven away.

Instead, she waited.

Steve finished his call, his expression uncertain. "You okay?"

"Fine. I just—" Sue stopped, surprised by her own hesitation. "Thank you. For the information packet. And for offering to help Friday. Even with my terms and conditions."

"You don't need to thank me, Sue."

"I do, though." Sue looked down at the folder in her hands. "This must have taken hours. And you didn't have to do any of it."

Steve was quiet for a moment. When he spoke, his voice was soft, almost vulnerable. "Yes, I did."

She nodded, not trusting herself to speak, and turned toward her SUV.

"Sue?"

She paused, hand on the door handle.

"I meant what I said earlier. About respecting your boundaries. I know—" Steve stopped, seemingly searching for words. "I know when we were married I wasn't the best husband. I'm trying to be a better person."

Sue's throat tightened. She wanted to dismiss the statement, to armor herself, to maintain the safe distance that kept her heart protected.

But Martha's voice echoed: *Sometimes grace means letting people prove they've changed.*

"I'll see you Friday," Sue said finally. "Two o'clock at the restaurant."

"I'll be there."

Sue drove away, and when she looked in her rearview mirror, she caught a glimpse of Steve still standing beside his truck, watching her leave.

And for the first time in six years, she wondered what might happen if she stopped holding him at a distance.

Chapter 10

Steve set the bags from Martha's Diner on the firehouse kitchen counter and caught Mark's raised eyebrow from across the room. The whole crew had gathered for their delayed lunch—nine hungry firefighters who'd spent the morning running medical calls and conducting equipment checks. The smell of Martha's meatloaf sub-sandwiches and mac and cheese filled the space, but Steve's mind was still back in that red vinyl booth, watching Sue's carefully constructed walls show their first hairline cracks.

"Everything okay, Chief?" Ray Miller asked, already reaching for plates from the cabinet. "You look like you haven't slept a wink in days."

Steve pulled containers out of the bags, lining them up on the counter. "Sue. The fire."

"Right." Luke grabbed utensils from the drawer beside him. "How's she handling everything?"

"She's—" Steve paused, searching for accurate words. "She's handling it the way Sue handles everything. With fierce independence and determination."

"Sounds familiar." Mark's tone was dry, knowing. He'd been Steve's best friend long enough to recognize the complicated history there.

Steve distributed containers while his crew settled around the long table where they'd shared countless meals over the years. This space had always felt like home—more than his apartment ever had, if he was being honest. The easy camaraderie, the shared purpose, the brotherhood that came from trusting people with your life daily.

"I gave her all the documentation she'd need this morning," Steve continued, taking his usual seat at the head of the table. "Contractors, permits, building codes, the whole works. And she's already scheduled half a dozen appointments based on it."

"That's good, right?" Luke looked confused.

"It's great. But it's also—" Steve set down his fork without taking a bite. "The restaurant's going to be closed for at least six weeks. Maybe longer. That's Sue's entire income gone right before Christmas. Insurance will eventually cover repairs, but it won't cover lost revenue."

Ray whistled low. "That's a tough spot."

"She'll figure it out," Mark said. "Sue's smart and resourceful. But yeah, that's a lot to handle."

Steve looked around the table at faces he'd worked alongside for years. Some of these men had been at his wedding. Had celebrated Lindsey's birth. Had quietly supported him through the divorce without judgment. They were more than colleagues—they were family.

"What if we did something?" The words came out before Steve had fully formed the thought. "For Sue. For the restaurant. A fundraiser."

The table went quiet, forks pausing mid-bite.

"What kind of fundraiser?" Ray leaned forward, interested.

"Fill the Boot." Steve's mind was already racing through logistics. "Classic firefighter community outreach. We stand at intersections, collecting donations in our turnout boots."

"I'm in." Luke spoke immediately. "When and where?"

"Hold on." Mark held up a hand, but his expression showed interest rather than skepticism. "Let's think this through. If we're doing this, we do it right. Professional. Organized."

"Agreed." Steve grabbed a napkin and pulled out his pen. "So let's plan it. What do we need?"

The next thirty minutes transformed their lunch into a strategic planning session. Food grew cold as they mapped out details with the same precision they'd use for any emergency response.

"Two locations at least," Ray said. "Main Street and Cedar Avenue intersection—that's a high-traffic area. And the Route 19 junction by the grocery store catches both commuters and weekend shoppers."

"We'll need city permits for each location." Mark was already making notes on his phone. "Can't just show up and start collecting money. Has to be official."

"I'll handle the permits." Steve added it to his mental checklist. "Mom works at City Hall. She can expedite the paperwork."

"Safety protocols." Ray's lieutenant training kicked in. "Reflective vests over turnout gear. No standing in active traffic lanes. Two-person teams minimum at each location. Proper cash handling procedures with sealed collection containers."

Luke raised his hand as if he were back in school. "I'll coordinate with local businesses. See if any of them want to match donations or contribute directly. Earl's Hardware would go for it for sure—after all, it's her dad's store."

"Smart thinking." Steve felt something loosening in his chest—the tight knot of helplessness that had been there since Sunday. This was something concrete. Something that helped without overstepping. "What about timing?"

"This weekend," Mark said decisively. "Friday and Saturday. Friday catches the before and after-work crowd and tourist traffic heading to the gorge. Saturday gets weekend shoppers, more tourists, and families."

"We'll need shift coverage. Can't leave the station unmanned."

"I'll take an extra shift," offered Danny Reeves from the end of the table. "My daughter's spending the day with my parents and then has a sleepover Saturday."

"Me too," another firefighter chimed in. "Happy to cover so others can do the fundraiser."

Steve looked around the table, genuinely moved by the immediate support. "You guys don't have to—"

"Yes, we do." Mark's voice was firm. "Sue's Pizza isn't just your ex-wife's restaurant, Steve. It's where we take our families for dinner. Where we celebrate promotions. Where half this town gathers for Friday night socializing. It matters to all of us."

"Plus, Sue's good people," Luke added. "Remember when she catered that fundraiser for the children's hospital two years ago? Did the whole thing at cost. This is payback."

Steve had forgotten about that. He'd been too wrapped up in his own carefully maintained distance to notice Sue's community involvement. But his crew remembered. The town remembered.

"Social media strategy." Mark was still planning. "We need to coordinate announcements. Let people know when and where we'll be collecting. Build awareness."

"I can handle that," Luke volunteered. "I'll create posts for the department's Facebook page. Maybe reach out to the local newspaper too—they love human interest stories like this."

"Keep it focused on community support," Steve said carefully. "This isn't about me or my history with Sue. It's about Laurel Ridge rallying behind a local business owner who's facing a crisis."

Mark's knowing look suggested he saw through that deflection, but he nodded. "Agreed. This is bigger than personal history."

They spent another twenty minutes hammering out details—shift rotations, equipment needs, messaging strategies, and business outreach. By the time lunch officially ended, they had a plan in place.

Steve cleared containers while his crew dispersed to various tasks—Luke heading to his computer to draft social media posts, Ray coordinating with the shift scheduler, and Mark making preliminary calls to verify intersection availability.

"You did good, suggesting this." Mark appeared beside Steve at the counter moments later, his voice low enough that others wouldn't hear. "Gives you a way to help without making Sue uncomfortable."

"That's the idea." Steve rinsed dishes, needing the mindless task. "She won't accept help from me directly. But she can't refuse help from the whole community."

"You know she'll figure out you organized it."

"Probably." Steve dried his hands on a dish towel. "She can be mad at me if she wants; I can handle it."

"She won't be mad." Mark leaned against the counter, arms crossed. "Frustrated, maybe. Confused about your motives, definitely. But not mad."

Steve wasn't so sure about that, but he appreciated Mark's optimism.

The afternoon passed in a blur of administrative tasks and permit applications. Steve drafted the official request for temporary use of public space, citing community outreach and charitable fundraising as the purpose. He included all the safety protocols Ray had outlined, contact information for their insurance carrier, and a detailed timeline for both collection days.

By three-thirty, he was pulling into the City Hall parking lot, manila envelope in hand.

His mother's office was on the second floor, marked by a placard reading "Gail Johnson, Finance Director." Steve knocked once and entered without waiting for a response.

Gail looked up from her computer, reading glasses perched on her nose. At fifty-four, she still had the same efficient energy that had defined Steve's childhood—the kind of woman who ran a household, managed a career, and volunteered on three church committees without ever appearing overwhelmed.

"Steven." She saved whatever document she'd been working on and removed her glasses. "This is a pleasant surprise. Everything okay?"

"Everything's fine." Steve set the envelope on her desk. "I need a favor. Expedited permit for a fundraiser this weekend."

Gail opened the envelope and scanned the application, her expression shifting from curious to understanding. "A Fill the Boot campaign for Sue."

"For the community," Steve corrected. "Sue's restaurant serves the community."

"Mm-hmm." His mother's tone was neutral, but her eyes were knowing. "And this has nothing to do with you wanting to help your ex-wife."

"It has everything to do with helping a local business owner in crisis. Which happens to be my job as fire chief." Steve sat in the chair across from her desk, feeling suddenly like he was sixteen again, explaining why he'd missed curfew.

"Your job is fire safety and emergency response." Gail set down the application. "Organizing fundraisers is above and beyond."

"Sue's Pizza matters to this town, Mom. You know that as well as I do."

"I do. And I think what you're doing is wonderful. I'm just making sure you're doing it for the right reasons."

Steve met his mother's gaze steadily. "I'm doing it because Sue needs help and won't accept it from me directly. This way, she gets support from the community she's served for years. It's the right thing to do."

"Watching her struggle must be killing you."

The observation landed with uncomfortable accuracy. Steve looked away, focusing on the framed photos on his mother's desk—family pictures spanning decades, including one from his wedding day.

"I failed her once," Steve said quietly. "Let my priorities get twisted until I lost what mattered most. I can't fix the past, but maybe I can do something useful now. Something that actually helps instead of just making me feel better about my guilt."

Gail was quiet for a long moment. When she spoke, her voice carried the gentle wisdom that had guided Steve through every major decision of his life. "You know she's going to realize you organized this."

"I know."

"And she might not appreciate it. Might see it as you overstepping or trying to fix things she didn't ask you to fix."

"I know that too. But I have to try, Mom. Even if it backfires. Even if she tells me to back off. I have to do something."

Gail leaned forward and smiled. "Then let's make sure this permit gets processed today. I'll walk it through the director's office myself."

"Thanks, Mom."

"Just—" She paused, choosing her words carefully. "Be prepared for this to get complicated. Sue's not the same woman you married, and you're not the same man she divorced. Whatever happens with this fundraiser, it's going to change things between you two."

Steve stood. "Things are already changing. The fire changed them. I'm just trying to make sure the change isn't all destruction."

He left City Hall with the permit approval process in motion and returned to the station to find his crew working on their plan. Luke had draft social media posts ready for review. Ray had finalized shift coverage. Mark had contacted the newspaper, and they were sending a reporter to interview Steve about the fundraiser.

Everything was falling into place with the kind of efficient coordination that made Steve proud of his team and grateful for their support.

Later, alone in his office while his crew settled into their normal routine, Steve pulled up the department's Facebook page and read Luke's draft announcement:

This Friday and Saturday, November 19-20, the Laurel Ridge Fire Department will be conducting a Fill the Boot fundraiser to support Sue Smith, who experienced a devastating fire at her place of business, Sue's Pizza, this past Sunday. All donations will go directly to helping this beloved local business owner. Join us at Main & Cedar or at the Route 19 junction. Every contribution makes a difference.

Simple. Professional. Focused on Sue.

Steve approved the post and watched it go live, knowing that by morning, most of Laurel Ridge would know what they were planning.

And would probably assume he'd organized it, no matter how carefully they'd phrased it to look as if it was a department initiative.

He wondered if Sue still refused to follow social media; it had never been her thing.

His phone sat on the desk, Sue's contact information just a few taps away. He could call her. Give her advance warning. Explain his reasoning.

Or he could trust that she'd understand when she found out. Trust that six years of distance had taught him something about respecting her and letting his actions speak for themselves.

Steve left the phone untouched and headed home, carrying the weight of decisions made and consequences still uncertain.

Friday would tell him whether he'd found a way to help Sue that honored her independence or whether he'd just started another fire between them.

Either way, the boots would be on the street corners, and Laurel Ridge would have its chance to show Sue that she'd never been as alone as she thought.

Chapter 11

Sue flipped another pancake on the griddle, watching the batter bubble and brown while Lindsey's animated voice filled their kitchen with the kind of energy only eleven-year-olds possessed before eight in the morning.

"—and Mrs. Phillips said I get to use the pottery wheel today. I've been waiting since last month. I was starting to think she forgot about me, but she didn't; she just saved me for last because—Mom, are you listening?"

"Pottery wheel. Mrs. Phillips didn't forget." Sue slid the pancake onto Lindsey's plate, adding it to the stack that was already drowning in maple syrup. "And you're excited because?"

"Because!" Lindsey cut into her pancakes with enthusiasm that suggested the question was ridiculous. "It's pottery, Mom. Like that movie we watched where the guy made the bowl for the girl he liked, and it was all romantic and stuff."

"That was a vase. And please don't recreate that scene in art class." Sue said as she poured batter for her own pancake.

"Mrs. Phillips would die." Lindsey giggled, then her expression shifted to something more thoughtful. "Are you still meeting with that electric guy today? The one Dad said was really important?"

Sue's hand paused over the griddle. "Mr. Clark? Yes, he's coming at ten."

"And then Uncle Graham at two?"

"Yep." Sue said as she transferred her pancake to a plate and joined Lindsey at the kitchen table. "You've been paying attention."

"It's important." Lindsey spoke with the seriousness of someone trying to be helpful. "Grandma says you're handling everything really good, even though it's hard."

"Grandma's biased. I'm just doing what needs to be done."

"That's what Dad always says." Lindsey took another huge bite, syrup dripping down her chin. "You guys are alike that way."

Sue chose not to examine that observation too closely. "Eat your breakfast. We need to leave in fifteen minutes."

They fell into companionable silence, the kind that came from years of Friday morning routines—pancakes, school drop-off, Sue heading to the restaurant while Lindsey headed to class. Except now, her restaurant sat damaged and empty, waiting for inspectors and contractors and the slow process of resurrection.

"The Christmas play auditions are next week at church," Lindsey said around her last bite of pancake. "Pastor Andrew said we're doing the nativity story, but with a twist. Whatever that means."

"Sounds interesting."

"I want to audition for Mary." Lindsey's voice went carefully casual, the tone she used when testing ideas she wasn't sure about. "Is that too big a part? Should I try for something smaller?"

Sue reached across the table and squeezed her daughter's hand. "You should audition for whatever part you'd like. I think you'd make a wonderful Mary."

"Yeah?"

"Absolutely." Sue stood and began clearing dishes. "Now go brush your teeth. I'll meet you in the car."

By the time they were driving toward town, Lindsey had moved on to dissecting her social studies project on West Virginia coal mining history and debating whether she should use poster board or make a diorama. Sue navigated the familiar mountain roads with the ease of someone who'd driven them daily for years while offering opinions on presentation formats while her mind simultaneously cataloged everything she had to do today.

Electrical inspection at ten. Structural evaluation at two, with Graham's construction crew coming to do the assessment that Steve would attend.

Steve. Sue still wasn't entirely sure how she felt about the arrangement—grateful for the expertise, wary of the proximity, and confused by the care embedded in every interaction.

"Mom, look." Lindsey pointed ahead as they approached the first traffic light on the edge of downtown. "Firefighters. Are they doing a training thing?"

Sue followed her daughter's gesture and saw two figures in full turnout gear standing at the intersection. They wore reflective vests over their bunker coats and held firefighters's boots in their hands.

Sue's foot eased off the gas as confusion rippled through her. What were they doing? It was Friday morning rush hour, not exactly prime time for training exercises.

The light turned red, and Sue pulled to a stop. Luke Benton approached her driver's side window with a wide smile, and she rolled down the window, questions forming on her tongue.

"Morning, Ms. Smith."

"Morning Luke, what's going on?"

"You don't know? We're doing a Fill the Boot fundraiser today and tomorrow. All proceeds will go to you."

The words hit Sue like a physical impact. She stared at Luke, at the boot in his hands, and at the handfuls of bills and coins already collected inside it.

"What?"

"A Fill the Boot campaign." Luke held up the boot so she could see the donations more clearly. "The whole department's participating. We've got crews at 3 different intersections collecting donations."

She tried to speak, to thank him, to ask who organized this, but no words would come. Her eyes burned with sudden tears she absolutely refused to shed.

"Mom?" Lindsey's voice was awed, excited. "They're raising money for you?"

"That's right." Luke grinned at Lindsey. "We figured your mom could use a little community support. Her restaurant is important to all of us."

"This is—" Sue finally found her voice, though it came out rough and unsteady. "I don't know what to say."

"You don't have to say anything." Luke's expression was genuinely kind. "Just our way of showing you the whole town's behind you. We're going to be out here all day today and tomorrow."

The light turned green. Luke stepped back with a wave, and Sue pulled forward on autopilot, her hands gripping the steering wheel.

"Mom, that was so cool!" Lindsey bounced in her seat with barely contained excitement. "Did you know they were doing this? How much money do you think they'll raise? Do you think Dad organized it? He probably did, right? He's always talking about community service and—"

"I don't know, baby." Sue's vision blurred again slightly, and she blinked hard to clear it.

But even as she said it, certainty settled in her chest. *Steve. This had Steve's fingerprints all over it.*

It was brilliant. Frustrating. Overwhelming.

And she had no idea how to feel about it.

"There's another one!" Lindsey pointed as they approached the Route 19 junction near the grocery store. Sure enough, 2 more firefighters stood in the intersection—Ray Miller and Danny Reeves this time—collecting donations from a steady stream of vehicles.

Sue drove past slowly through the green light, watching Ray smile as he waved at her.

"This is like the coolest thing ever." Lindsey was practically glowing. "Wait until I tell everyone at school. My mom's so important that the whole fire department is raising money to help her."

Sue's chest ached with a tangle of emotions she couldn't begin to sort through—gratitude and embarrassment and humility and something dangerously close to hope. All these people going out of their way to help. Not because she'd asked, but because they wanted to. Because Sue's Pizza mattered to them.

Because she mattered to them.

When they pulled up at Lindsey's school, Sue had to clear her throat twice before trusting her voice. "Have a good day, sweetheart. Enjoy the pottery wheel."

"I will!" Lindsey grabbed her backpack, then paused with the door half-open. "Mom? You should go thank them. The firefighters. They're doing this really cool thing."

"I'll—" Sue stopped and nodded. "I will."

"And Mom?" Lindsey's expression went serious in a way that reminded Sue her daughter was growing up faster than she wanted to acknowledge. "It's okay to let people help. You're always telling me that we're supposed to support each other and be there for each other. This is what that looks like, right?"

Sue's eyes burned again. "When did you get so wise?"

"Love you, Mom. Bye." Lindsey grinned, kissed Sue's cheek, and bounded out of the SUV toward the school entrance, where her friends were already gathering.

Sue sat in the drop-off lane, engine idling, while other parents came and went around her. She should drive to the restaurant. The electrical inspector would be there in less than two hours, and she needed to review her notes one more time, make sure she had all the documentation Mr. Clark might need.

Instead, she found herself thinking about Luke's smile, Ray's dedication, and the growing collection of donations in those boots. Thought about Steve organizing this entire effort—because it had to be Steve.

How did you thank someone for respecting your boundaries while simultaneously proving they still cared?

Sue pulled out of the school parking lot. Her hands seemed to move independently of conscious thought, steering toward Maple Avenue.

Toward the fire station.

She needed to know. Needed to hear Steve explain why he'd done this, what he hoped to accomplish, and whether this was about the restaurant or about something bigger that neither of them had been willing to name in six years of careful distance.

Sue drove through downtown. Past Martha's Diner and turning at the church with its white steeple reaching toward a gray November sky. Past familiar storefronts and businesses.

The fire station came into view—red brick and apparatus bay doors, American flag snapping in the wind above the entrance. Steve's truck sat in the parking lot beside the other department vehicles, confirming he was here.

Sue pulled into a visitor space and cut the engine.

Her phone showed 8:47 AM. The electrical inspector wasn't due until ten. She had time. Just enough to walk into that fire station and demand answers she wasn't sure she was ready to hear.

Her hand reached for the door handle, then stopped.

What should she even say?

Thank you for organizing something I didn't ask for but desperately need and appreciate.

Thank you for caring enough to help while respecting me?

Thank you for still being there after six years of me pushing you away because letting you close feels more dangerous than staying alone?

Through the station's glass front doors, she could see movement inside—firefighters going about their morning routines, completely unaware that outside in the parking lot, a woman sat frozen in her vehicle, caught between gratitude and fear, between the safety of independence and the risk of acknowledging she might not want to face everything alone anymore.

The clock on her dashboard flipped to 8:49.

Sue took a deep breath, grabbed her purse, and opened the car door before she could talk herself out of it.

Chapter 12

Steve's radio crackled to life, Ray's voice cutting through the morning quiet of his office. "Chief, we're at three hundred forty dollars at the Route 19 junction. Traffic's steady. People are stopping specifically to donate even if the light is green."

Steve keyed the mic, unable to suppress his smile. "Copy that, Ray. Keep me posted on the hour."

He marked the amount on his tracking sheet—$340 at Route 19, $287 at Main Street, and $310 at Cedar Avenue. They'd been collecting for less than two hours and had already surpassed what Steve had optimistically projected for the morning.

The firehouse hummed with energy this morning, a different quality than the usual preparedness tension. This was purpose combined with community connection—the kind of work that reminded Steve why he'd become a firefighter in the first place. Not for the adrenaline or the promotions, but for this: serving people who needed help.

Mark appeared in his doorway, still wearing his reflective vest over his uniform. "Just rotated back from Main Street. Seth's taking over.

You should see it out there, Steve. Cars are lining up and waiting to donate regardless of the stoplights. Mrs. Peterson from the craft store delivered cookies to each location. Earl said to tell you that he's putting in a matching donation at the end of the weekend."

"Earl Smith is matching donations? Good 'ole Earl," Steve set down his pen, genuinely happy. Sue's father had barely spoken to him since the divorce, maintaining polite but distant civility anytime their paths crossed.

Mark leaned against the doorframe. "Half the businesses on Main Street said they'll contribute. This is turning into something bigger than we expected."

Steve felt satisfaction mix with growing nervousness in his chest. The fundraiser's success was undoubtedly what he'd hoped for and what Sue needed.

"You did good organizing this. Stop second-guessing yourself."

"I'm not—"

"You are. I can see it." Mark crossed his arms. "Sue's going to find out you organized this. Probably already has. And when she does, she will see exactly what we all see—that you care about her and you found a way to help that respects her. That's growth, Steve. That's you being the man you should have been years ago."

Before Steve could respond, movement in the apparatus bay caught his attention. Through his office window, he watched Sue walk toward his office, her posture uncertain but determined.

His stomach dropped.

"Speak of the devil," Mark muttered, following Steve's gaze. "Want me to—"

"No." Steve stood, smoothing his uniform shirt with suddenly damp palms. "I've got this."

"Good luck, my man." Mark slipped out of the office, passing Sue in the hallway with a respectful nod.

Sue walked directly toward him, her eyes fixed on him with an intensity that made his mouth go dry. She entered his office without saying a word, closed the door behind her with deliberate care, and sat in the chair across from his desk.

Steve remained standing, uncertain whether sitting would make this easier or harder. Sue's face carried emotions he couldn't quite read—not anger, he didn't think, but something complicated that twisted between gratitude and confusion and maybe hurt.

"Hi," he said finally, when the silence stretched too long.

"Hi." Sue's voice was quiet, controlled. She folded her hands in her lap with the same precise care she'd used in closing the door. "I just saw Luke, Ray, Danny, and Adam. At two intersections. With boots in hand."

"Right." Steve's heart hammered against his ribs. "The Fill the Boot campaign."

"You organized it."

Steve moved around his desk and leaned against the front edge. "I proposed it to the crew. But they—"

"Don't." Sue held up one hand, stopping him. "Don't minimize this or make it sound like it was everyone's idea. I saw your hand-writing all over it the second Luke told me what was going on. You organized this."

Steve met her gaze steadily, seeing no point in deflection. "I was the one who initiated it. Yes. I helped organize it."

Sue was quiet for a long moment, her hands still folded in her lap, knuckles white with tension. "Why?"

"Because you deserve it. Because the restaurant matters to this community. Because—" Steve stopped, reconsidering his words. "Because

I wanted to do something useful instead of just standing on the sidelines watching you struggle."

"I'm handling it."

"I know you are. You're handling it with the same fierce independence and capability you handle everything else with." Steve kept his voice gentle, careful. "But that doesn't mean you should have to handle it alone."

Sue's jaw worked, emotions flickering across her face too quickly for Steve to catalog. "You should have told me. Before you started. You should have asked if I wanted this."

"Would you have said yes?"

Sue looked away, confirming what Steve already knew—she would have refused. Would have insisted she didn't need charity, didn't want special treatment, and could manage on her own.

"The crew jumped on the idea immediately," Steve continued when Sue didn't answer. "I hadn't even really thought this whole thing through before they jumped in feet first. They wanted to help because Sue's Pizza matters to them too. This isn't about you and me, Sue."

"Isn't it?" Sue's voice was soft, almost wondering. "Because it feels pretty personal, Steve. All of it. All that time and care you put into the folder you gave me. Offering to attend the inspection later today. Now this fundraiser. You keep saying it's professional, or it's about community, or about me, but—" She stopped, shaking her head. "I don't know what you want from me."

Steve's chest constricted painfully. He wanted to close the distance between them, wanted to take her hands and tell her exactly what he wanted—a second chance, forgiveness, the opportunity to prove he'd learned and changed and would never again prioritize career over family. But Sue wasn't asking for declarations. She was asking for honesty.

"I want you to accept help without feeling like you're compromising your independence," Steve said carefully. "I want the restaurant to reopen so Lindsey can watch her mom succeed and do what she loves. I want—" He paused, choosing truth over self-protection. "I want to do something good for you and try to make up for being the reason you're so self-reliant in the first place."

Sue's eyes widened slightly, surprise breaking through her controlled expression.

"I know I can't fix the past," Steve continued, words coming faster now. "I know I failed you during our marriage. I put my career and myself first, left you to manage everything alone, and taught you that depending on me meant disappointment for you. I can't undo that, Sue. But maybe... maybe I can at least try to be useful now. Try to support you in ways that respect this armor you've built around yourself because I gave you no choice but to build it."

Sue stared at him, and Steve watched her throat work as she swallowed hard. "You really organized all of this? The crew, the permits, the whole campaign?"

"I proposed it Tuesday after we talked at Martha's. The crew jumped in immediately. I asked my mom to expedite the city permit. But Sue, the response—that's all community... that's all people that love and care about you. Your dad's matching donations, by the way. Martha's providing free meals to the collection crews each day. Many local businesses are contributing directly. That's not me. That's Laurel Ridge taking care of one of its own."

"Because you mobilized them."

"Because they care. I just gave them a channel." Steve ran a hand through his hair, frustrated by his inability to make her understand. "You've spent years building something that matters here. Something bigger than just a restaurant. You created a gathering place and a community hub. When it burned, people wanted to help. They just needed organization and permission. That's all I provided."

Sue's hands finally unclenched in her lap. She looked down at them, at her bare ring finger where her wedding band used to sit, then back up at Steve with eyes that shimmered with unshed tears.

"The donations," she said quietly. "How much have you raised so far?"

"Over nine hundred dollars so far. And we've only been collecting for two hours. That's not including what some businesses have pledged already." Steve checked his tracking sheet. "At this rate, we're looking at least a couple thousand by the end of the weekend. Probably more."

"A couple thousand." Sue repeated the words as if they were in a foreign language.

"Mark just told me that several businesses on Main Street alone have said they will be contributing. And I've been getting calls from businesses in nearby towns wanting to contribute too. Word has spread fast."

Sue pressed her fingers to her temples, and Steve recognized the gesture—she was overwhelmed, trying to process information faster than her emotions could handle it.

"I need you to understand something," Steve said, his voice dropping lower. "This isn't about impressing you or winning points or proving anything except that you matter. To me, yes. But also to this entire town. You've given Laurel Ridge something precious—a place where people enjoy eating and love hanging out. Let us give something back."

"I don't run a restaurant for recognition or gratitude."

"I know. That's exactly why you deserve this." Steve finally allowed himself to move closer, crouching beside her chair so they were eye level. "Sue, you don't have to do everything alone. You can let people help and still be strong and independent. Still be exactly who you are."

Sue looked at him for a long moment, and Steve saw the walls she'd built start to crack—not crumble, but developing hairline fractures that let light through. "You really believe that."

"I do."

Sue nodded slowly, processing. Then she stood, forcing Steve to rise as well and step back to give her space. "Thank you. For organizing this. For mobilizing the community. For—" Her voice caught. "For caring."

The acknowledgment hit Steve hard, as if someone had thrown a baseball and hit him square in the chest. "You're welcome."

"I should go." Sue moved toward the door, then paused with her hand on the knob. "The electrical inspector is coming at ten. I need to be there."

"Right. Of course." Steve returned to his desk, needing a physical barrier between them. "I'll see you at two. For the structural assessment."

"Two o'clock." Sue opened the door, then turned back. "Steve?"

"Yeah?"

"Whatever money the fundraiser raises—I want it tracked. I want to know exactly which businesses contribute—" She stopped, struggling for words. "So I can properly thank them and the community. And acknowledge what you did."

"You don't need to acknowledge me for anything."

"Yes, I do." Sue's voice was firm. "And I will."

She left before he could respond.

Steve sank into his desk chair and stared at the tracking sheet covered in donation totals and check-in times. His radio crackled with another update from Luke—another $227 collected at Main, a steady stream of donations continuing.

Mark appeared in his doorway within seconds of Sue's departure. "Well?"

"She knows I organized it."

"And?"

Steve looked up at his friend, trying to sort through the complex tangle of emotions from the last fifteen minutes. "And she thanked me."

"Good. That's progress." Mark's expression was approving. "She's softening."

"Maybe. Or maybe she was just being polite because she knew we had an audience... which, by the way, I noticed all of you watching what was going on in this office while she was here... I imagine later today I'll get a good tongue-lashing from her."

"You don't actually believe that."

Steve didn't answer, because the truth was more complicated than belief or doubt. Sue had thanked him, yes. Had acknowledged his efforts and even seemed moved by them. But gratitude wasn't the same as forgiveness. Recognition wasn't trust. And Steve had no idea whether organizing a successful fundraiser proved he'd changed or proved nothing.

His radio crackled again. Ray's voice: "Chief, we just had someone drop off a check for five hundred dollars. Business owner from Beckley, who used to live here. He said Sue's Pizza was where his family ate every Friday for ten years before they moved. He heard about the fire and wanted to help."

Steve keyed the mic with hands that weren't entirely steady. "Copy that, Ray. Take a picture of his address on the check so Sue can send a thank-you card."

Five hundred dollars from someone who didn't even live in Laurel Ridge anymore. Because Sue had created something worth remembering. Worth protecting.

Steve added the donation to his tracking sheet and watched the total climb past a thousand dollars.

Sue would probably ask for updates when he arrived at the restaurant for the structural assessment later today. She would then maybe understand the scope of how much she meant to this community. She would have to confront the reality that she'd built something far bigger than she'd realized.

And maybe—just maybe—she'd also realize that Steve organizing all of this meant something more than professional courtesy or guilt-driven obligation.

Maybe she'd see what Mark saw, what the crew saw, and what Steve had been trying to show through every careful gesture the past few days: that he was a changed man.

Or maybe she'd just see a fire chief doing his job, and Steve would have to accept that some mistakes left scars too deep for any amount of community fundraising or kind gestures to heal.

Chapter 13

Steve stood beside Luke and Danny at the Route 19 intersection, watching his young firefighter accept donations with the kind of genuine enthusiasm that made him perfect for community outreach. The afternoon shift had been even busier than the morning—people donating in steady succession, some drivers specifically seeking out the collection points after hearing about it from friends or seeing social media posts online.

"Chief, at last count we're at thirty-two hundred dollars combined between all three locations," Luke reported. "And that's not counting business pledges or the matching donations."

Steve mentally noted the figure, still somewhat stunned by the community response. They'd surpassed every projection, every optimistic estimate.

A silver SUV pulled into the nearby parking lot, and Steve's attention shifted immediately when he recognized the vehicle. Sue emerged from the driver's side and opened the back hatch.

"Need help?" Steve called out, already moving toward her.

Sue looked up. "Actually, yes. I brought some things for the crew."

Sue pulled out a case of bottled water and set it on the pavement, then reached back in for a couple of bakery boxes that released the unmistakable aroma of fresh-baked goods.

"Muffins," she explained. "I called Shirley Gallagher at Taste of Heaven Bakery this morning to order a few dozen for the firemen. When she found out what they were for, she refused payment and donated them for the cause."

Steve lifted the case of water, following Sue toward where Luke stood with his collection boot. "You didn't have to do this."

"Yes, I did. Your crew is spending their day standing in traffic collecting money for me. The least I can do is make sure they're fed and hydrated."

Luke's face lit up when he saw them approaching. "Ms. Smith! This is amazing. We've had so many people—"

"I know." Sue set the boxes down on the nearby bench and opened the top one, revealing an assortment of muffins—blueberry, banana nut, and chocolate chip. "And I wanted to thank you personally. How's your sister doing? The last time I saw her at the restaurant, she mentioned starting nursing school."

"She's doing great. Just finished her first semester with all A's."

"That's wonderful. Tell her I'm proud of her." Sue handed him a muffin and then a bottle of water. "And thank you for this. For giving up your Friday to stand in traffic for me."

Luke's earnestness was genuine. "Your restaurant means a lot to me and my family. I have good memories of celebrating my high school graduation there, my sister's acceptance to nursing school, and my parents' anniversary last month. I just wanted to help you."

Steve watched Sue's throat work as she swallowed hard, emotion flickering across her face before she could contain it. "Your volunteering your time means more than you know."

Steve watched as Sue interacted with each of his crew members—including Danny in the conversation and asking about his wife and daughter.

This was why the community loved her. Not just because she ran a great restaurant, but because she genuinely cared about people.

"I'd like to visit the other location by the diner," Sue said as she began walking toward her SUV. "Could you carry the water for me?"

"Sure," Steve said and followed her to her vehicle.

They walked together down the street, Sue carrying boxes of muffins while Steve handled the heavier case of water. The November afternoon had warmed slightly, though clouds still hung low and grey over the valley. As they passed businesses and storefronts, several people called out to Sue—offering encouragement, expressing support, and sharing how much they missed her restaurant.

Sue responded to each person with warmth and gratitude, sometimes stopping to accept a quick hug or shake a hand.

"Sue!" An elderly woman emerged from the pharmacy, her face creasing into a wide smile. "Honey, I just heard about the fire. How awful!"

"Yes, it is, Mrs. Davidson. I'm working hard to get my restaurant reopened as soon as possible."

"Well, you let me know when you're open again. My bridge club enjoys coming to your restaurant every third Thursday of the month. I'm already craving your spinach artichoke dip."

Sue's laugh was genuine, unrehearsed. "I'll make sure we have extra ready for you when we reopen."

They continued down the street, and Steve found himself studying Sue in profile—the way she held herself with quiet confidence, the genuine warmth in her eyes when she greeted people, and the grace with which she accepted concern without dwelling on devastation.

She'd always been like this. Even when their marriage was crumbling, even when Steve was too wrapped up in himself and his career ambitions to notice, Sue had maintained this remarkable ability to make people feel valued and important.

He'd taken it for granted. He had assumed her warmth and love would always be there for him.

"Ray looks like he's enjoying himself." Sue said as she nodded toward where he stood at the intersection outside Martha's Diner.

As they approached, Steve watched a scene unfold that made his chest tighten. A young couple with a toddler stopped at the crosswalk, and the father lifted his daughter so she could drop coins into Ray's boot. The little girl's chubby fingers released the money with careful concentration, her face serious with the importance of her task.

"Good job, sweetie," Ray said warmly, his voice carrying across the intersection. "That's very kind of you."

The toddler beamed, and her parents thanked Ray before crossing the street.

Sue had stopped walking, watching the interaction with visible emotion. Steve set down the case of water and stood beside her.

"Did you see that?" Sue's voice was soft, almost wondering.

"I did."

"She couldn't have been more than two years old."

"Probably not." Steve watched Sue process the moment, saw the way it affected her—this tangible evidence of community care spanning generations.

Ray noticed them and waved, then jogged across the street during a break in traffic. "Sue! Chief. Perfect timing. I was just about to call for a water break."

"That's why we're here." Sue opened the bakery boxes, offering Ray his choice of muffin. "Thank you for this, Ray. For standing out here all day."

"It's my pleasure, ma'am." Ray selected a blueberry muffin. "I've had some real touching moments out here today."

"Like the toddler?" Sue asked.

"Like the toddler, yeah. But also—" Ray paused, his expression softening. "About twenty minutes ago, this elderly couple stopped. Must've been in their eighties. The husband pressed a hundred-dollar bill into my hand and said they've celebrated every anniversary at Sue's Pizza ever since you opened your doors. Said your restaurant is where they fall in love all over again every year."

Sue's eyes filled with tears she didn't try to hide. "Really?"

"That's what he said. His wife started crying while they were talking to me. She said she couldn't imagine Laurel Ridge without your place." Ray took a bite of muffin, giving Sue a moment to compose herself. "You're really something special, Sue. Today's proof of that fact."

Martha emerged from the diner carrying a folding table and a handmade sign reading "Support Sue's Pizza—Donations Welcome." She set up the table near the entrance.

"Figured I'd try to catch a little foot traffic," Martha called out.

Sue glanced at Steve, uncertainty flickering across her face, and then she walked to stand beside Martha at the table while Steve hung back.

What followed was one of the most moving displays of community solidarity Steve had witnessed in his career. People approached to donate, and some shared stories.

Stories of first dates at Sue's Pizza. Of birthday celebrations and graduation dinners. Of job promotions toasted over breadsticks and proposal celebrations over candlelight pasta. Of ordinary Tuesday nights that became extraordinary because they were spent at a place where everyone knew your name.

Sue listened to each story with full attention, accepted each donation with genuine gratitude, and somehow made every single person feel like their contribution mattered profoundly.

Steve watched her hug an older gentleman, who described bringing his grandchildren to Sue's Pizza every time they came to town to visit him. Watched her wipe away tears while a middle-aged woman recounted her daughter's engagement celebration there. Watched her laugh with genuine delight when a group of teenagers approached and explained how they had pooled their allowance money. And told her how they hoped she could open back up soon because it's the only place their parents allowed them to hang out together alone on a Friday night without their supervision.

And Steve understood, perhaps for the first time, exactly what Sue had accomplished. She hadn't just built a business. She'd created a repository for memories, a backdrop for life's significant moments, and a gathering place where community became tangible rather than theoretical.

He should have celebrated this with her years ago. He should've recognized the magnitude of what she was building instead of being so focused on himself and his own career. Should have been her partner in this achievement instead of someone who showed up late and left early, always with one eye on his radio and one foot out the door.

The regret tasted bitter.

Mark appeared beside Steve, observing the scene with the same appreciation. "She's something special."

"Yeah." Steve's voice came out rougher than intended. "She is."

"You know what's amazing? She's treating every single donor as if they just handed her a million dollars. I just watched Louella Fitch give her a dollar in quarters, and Sue thanked her like it was the most generous gift she'd ever received."

Steve nodded, unable to speak past the tightness in his throat.

By one-thirty, the crowd had thinned slightly, and Sue stepped away from Martha's table to where Steve and Mark stood on the sidewalk. Her eyes were red-rimmed but bright; her cheeks flushed with emotion.

"I can't believe this," she said, her voice thick. "All these people—"

"Love you," Mark finished simply. "That's what today is proving."

Sue pressed her fingers to her eyes, composing herself with visible effort. When she lowered her hands, she looked directly at Ray and Justin Collins, another firefighter, who had both moved to the sidewalk during a traffic lull.

"I need to say something to all of you." Sue's voice carried a particular quality of someone speaking from a deeply emotional place. "What you're doing today—what the entire department is doing—it's beyond anything I could have asked for or expected. You're giving up your time, standing in traffic, organizing this entire effort, and I—"

Her voice broke. She stopped, took a breath, and then continued.

"I don't have adequate words to express what this means to me. Not just the money, though that's incredibly generous. But the fact that you all cared enough to do this." Sue looked at each firefighter in turn—Ray, Justin, and Mark. "Thank you. From the bottom of my heart, thank you."

The firefighters mumbled modest responses—"It's nothing," "Our pleasure," "Happy to help"—but Steve saw how Sue's gratitude affected them, how it reinforced their own sense of purpose.

Then Sue turned to Steve, and something in her expression shifted.

"Steve. I know I thanked you this morning, but I need to say it again. You organized all of this—the fundraiser, the permits, the coordination with businesses. You mobilized an entire community because you thought it would help me."

"Sue—"

"Let me finish." She held up a hand, and Steve fell silent. "You did this without taking over the situation I'm in. Without making it about you or us or our complicated history. You found a way to help while respecting me. And I—" She stopped, her voice catching. "I'm grateful. And maybe a little bit... no, correction... I'm a lot amazed."

Steve's heart hammered against his ribs. "I just wanted to do something right for once."

"You did. You really did. And I want you to know that I see it. I see what you were trying to do, and I appreciate it more than I can express."

"You don't have to—"

"I do, though." Sue took a small step closer, closing the distance between them slightly. "Because for a long time, I convinced myself that the man I married was gone. That the Steve who used to stay up all night helping me plan the restaurant, who believed in my dreams before I fully believed in them myself—I thought that version of you didn't exist anymore."

Steve couldn't breathe. Couldn't speak. Could only stand there while Sue said things he'd stopped hoping to hear years ago.

"But this past week—" Sue gestured toward the fundraising table, toward the firefighters, toward the tangible evidence of Steve's efforts. "This week, I'm starting to wonder if maybe I was wrong. If maybe that Steve is still in there, just—different and wiser."

"I'm trying to be."

She nodded slowly, processing his words. Then she glanced at her watch, and her eyes widened. "It's almost two. Graham's crew will be at the restaurant soon."

"Right." Steve had completely lost track of time. "The structural assessment."

"I need to go." Sue took a step back. But something in her expression remained warm, open in a way it hadn't been since—since way before the divorce. "I'll see you there?"

"I'll be there."

Sue turned to leave, then paused. "Steve? Thanks again. Not just for today. For all of it. For trying."

She jogged toward her SUV, leaving him standing on the sidewalk outside Martha's Diner with three of his firefighters watching and his heart doing complicated things in his chest.

Mark appeared at his elbow. "Well. That was interesting."

Steve couldn't form words. He could only watch Sue as she jogged away.

"She just told you—in front of witnesses—that she's starting to see the man you've become. That's not gratitude talking, Steve. That's something else."

Steve knew exactly what Mark was suggesting. He knew the implications of Sue's words, the warmth in her voice, and the way she'd let her guard drop just enough to acknowledge that maybe he'd changed. Maybe he'd grown. Maybe he'd finally learned what mattered.

But knowing and trusting were different things. Sue might be starting to see him differently, but that didn't mean she'd forgiven him for the years of absence and neglect that had destroyed their marriage. It didn't mean anything except that today—for these few moments outside Martha's Diner—she'd let him see past her armor.

"I need to get to the restaurant," Steve said finally. "Structural assessment starts in a few minutes."

"Go." Mark clapped him on the shoulder. "And Steve? You did good today. Really good. Don't forget that."

Steve nodded and headed toward his vehicle.

Chapter 14

Graham stood on a ladder and aimed his flashlight at the ceiling joists above what used to be Sue's prep station. Lyle Bentley, the crew foreman, stood near him with a clipboard, making notes while Sue watched from the kitchen doorway, trying not to feel sick at the blackened walls and ruined equipment surrounding them.

"Load-bearing beam here looks solid," Graham said, tapping the exposed wood with his knuckles. "Heat didn't reach far enough to compromise structural integrity."

"What about the ceiling panels?" Sue asked, gesturing to where some sections looked as if they might just be damaged by smoke while other sections had fallen or hung at dangerous angles. "Do they all need to be completely replaced even if they look okay?"

"In my opinion... I'd replace every single last one," Lyle confirmed without looking up from his notes. His voice carried the matter-of-fact tone of someone who'd seen hundreds of fire-damaged buildings. "It won't affect the timeline much."

Steve stood near the back wall, observing. Sue noticed that he hadn't offered a single unsolicited comment since the assessment began fifteen minutes ago, only speaking when Graham or Lyle directed questions specifically to him about fire damage patterns.

Graham moved deeper into the kitchen, testing the stability of a support column with careful pressure. "Lyle, come look at this. The discoloration here—is that heat damage or water staining?"

Lyle joined him, and the two men consulted in low voices filled with construction terminology Sue only partially understood. She moved closer, trying to follow their conversation about load distribution and thermal exposure.

"Sorry," Sue interrupted. "Can you explain what you're concerned about?"

Graham straightened, his expression immediately apologetic. "Just being thorough. We're determining whether this is superficial or if the fire compromised the wood's internal structure."

"And if it's compromised?"

"Then we sister-beam it," Lyle said, as if that explained everything.

Sue looked at Steve without thinking. Steve met her gaze, and she saw him hesitate—clearly weighing whether answering would be helpful or overstepping.

"It means they'd attach a new beam alongside the existing one for additional support," Steve said carefully. "Reinforcement rather than replacement."

"Which would add time to the project," Sue concluded.

"A little." Graham was back to examining the column, running his hand along the surface. "But I don't think we'll need it. Lyle?"

Lyle produced a tool Sue didn't recognize and pressed it against the wood, checking readings on a small display. "Moisture content's normal. Structural integrity appears unchanged. Mark it for cleaning and sealing, but no reinforcement is needed."

Relief loosened something in Sue's chest. "So the main structure is sound?"

"The main structure is rock solid," Graham confirmed, grinning at his sister. "You picked a good building when you bought this place. The bones are strong."

They continued through the kitchen, Graham and Lyle methodically rechecking every beam, column, and support to be a hundred percent sure. Sue trailed behind them, asking questions whenever the technical language lost her, and found herself oddly comforted by Steve's quiet presence. He didn't insert himself into the assessment, didn't offer opinions she hadn't requested, but remained available—a resource she could access if needed without feeling like he was taking control.

"What about the electrical?" Sue asked as they moved toward where the fire had originated behind the prep station. The destruction here was the worst—blackened walls, melted wiring, and equipment reduced to twisted metal.

"Complete replacement required," Lyle said flatly. "Which you already knew from the inspector's report. But from a structural standpoint, the fire didn't penetrate deep enough into the walls to damage the framework. It's all surface-level destruction."

"Surface-level," Sue repeated, looking at the devastation that had shut down her entire business. "This is surface-level."

Graham's hand landed gently on her shoulder. "I know it looks bad. But from a construction perspective, this is actually good news. We're replacing damaged materials, not rebuilding the entire structure. A six-to eight-week restoration timeline is realistic."

"Could be less," Lyle added, making more notes. "If permits process quickly and we don't hit weather delays."

Steve shifted slightly, and Sue caught the movement in her peripheral vision. "You have a question," she said.

"Not a question," Steve said. "Just—Lyle, you'll want to check behind those wall panels before you commit to a timeline. Fire can travel through wall cavities in ways that aren't immediately visible."

Lyle nodded, already moving toward the area Steve indicated. "Good call. Let's pull back this section."

Graham helped Lyle remove a section of damaged wall panel, revealing the studs and insulation behind. They examined the space with flashlights, probing for hidden damage while Sue held her breath.

"Clean," Lyle announced after a thorough inspection. "Fire stayed contained to the surface. Insulation's intact."

"That's lucky," Graham said, glancing at Steve with respect. "Could've been way worse."

"The fire moved fast," Steve said as he turned his attention toward her, still keeping his tone professional. "But the quick response kept it from penetrating deeper into the structure. In another five minutes, and you'd be looking at a different situation."

Sue felt Graham's eyes on her, watching the interaction between his sister and his ex-brother-in-law with the kind of careful attention only siblings possessed. She ignored him, refocusing instead on Lyle's clipboard.

"So what's next?" Sue asked. "After today, I mean. What's the actual sequence of work?"

Lyle flipped through his notes. "Demo first. Strip out all damaged materials—wall panels, ceiling tiles, flooring in the affected areas, and ruined equipment. That's a week, maybe less if we get extra hands on it."

"My staff will help," Sue said immediately. "I've already arranged for them to do paid cleanup work. And I'll help as well."

"Perfect. That'll speed things up considerably." Lyle made a note. "Then electrical replacement, which has to happen before we can close up walls. Plumbing inspection while the walls are open also—that's just standard procedure. Then drywall, a new ceiling and floor, painting, and equipment installation."

"Six weeks minimum, sis," Graham added. "Eight if we're being conservative and accounting for inspection delays."

"But Christmas is seven weeks away... I'm really hoping to reopen by then," Sue said.

"Which is why we start demo Monday," Lyle said firmly. "No delays, no waiting around. The sooner we begin, the better your chances of hitting that Christmas deadline. I'll call in extra crew members if I have to, and you and your staff will be helpful as well."

Sue's phone buzzed in her pocket—a reminder she'd set this morning. School pickup in thirty minutes.

The men continued their discussion, moving into the dining room to assess smoke damage and ventilation requirements. Sue followed, half-listening to technical details about ductwork and HVAC systems while her mind cataloged everything she needed to coordinate: demo scheduling, equipment orders, staff assignments, and insurance documentation.

"The dining room's in decent shape," Graham said, running his hand along a window frame. "A few windows will need to be replaced. The smoke damage here is cleanable. Deep cleaning of the walls, floors, and furniture. But structurally? It's sound."

"That's something," Sue said, managing a small smile.

They spent another twenty minutes examining every corner of the dining room again, Lyle making notes while Graham tested various surfaces and fixtures just to be on the safe side. The conversation gradually shifted from technical assessment to logistics—delivery schedules, material suppliers, and subcontractor availability.

Steve remained mostly silent, offering input only when directly consulted, and Sue found herself grateful for his restraint. This was her project, her restaurant, and her decisions. But having his expertise available when she needed it—without the pressure of him taking over—felt like a balance she hadn't known was possible.

"I think we've seen everything we need," Lyle finally announced, clicking his pen closed. "I'll have a detailed report and estimate to you by tomorrow. I can drop it off at your house if you'd like."

"I'd appreciate that... and we can start demo Monday, correct?" Sue asked.

"Soon as you give us the green light."

Graham began gathering his equipment while Lyle made final notes on his clipboard. The assessment was wrapping up, and the technical work was complete. Sue felt the shift in atmosphere—from professional evaluation to the casual conversation that followed.

"You did good with the fundraiser, Steve," Graham said while packing up his tools. "The whole town's talking about it."

"We're pretty pleased with the response," Steve said, his eyes flickering to Sue.

"Pretty pleased? Steve, I heard those boots were filling up at record speed." Graham's admiration was genuine. "Sue, did you know your ex-husband organized the whole thing?"

"I know."

Graham's eyebrows rose, clearly surprised. "Yeah? What'd you think about that?"

Sue met Steve's gaze. "I think it was kind and thoughtful."

Steve glanced away.

"Dad's matching whatever the final total is. Said he couldn't let the fire department show him up." Graham said with a chuckle.

"Dad? He doesn't need to do that," she said.

"That's just Dad being Dad," Graham grinned.

Lyle cleared his throat diplomatically. "I'll walk the exterior perimeter one more time just to be on the safe side. Graham, do you wanna join me?"

"Sure thing." Graham followed Lyle toward the front door, throwing a knowing look at Sue that she pretended not to see.

And then it was just Sue and Steve.

Sue checked her phone again. "I need to get Lindsey from school. You're still picking her up this evening after you get off work, correct?"

"Yes. Of course."

She gathered her purse and jacket, suddenly aware of how carefully they were both maintaining distance and how the ease from outside Martha's had been replaced by professional courtesy.

"Thank you," Sue said, pausing near the doorway. "For being here today. For—" She gestured vaguely at the space between them. "For respecting boundaries."

"That's what you asked for."

"It is." Sue adjusted her purse strap, searching for words that would bridge the gap between gratitude and whatever else she was feeling. "Steve, would you mind locking up when Graham and Lyle are finished? I really need to go."

Steve's surprise was visible. "You trust me to lock up?"

"Yes. I do."

She left before Steve could respond.

Chapter 15

Sue pulled into her parents' driveway and parked beside Matt's truck. Anna Smith appeared on the porch, wiping her hands on her apron, her face lighting up the way it always did when her children came home.

"There's my girl," Anna said, pulling Sue into an embrace as soon as she stepped onto the porch. "How are you holding up, sweetheart?"

"I'm good, Mom." Sue leaned into the hug, feeling some of the week's tension ease from her shoulders.

"Where's my granddaughter?"

"With Steve, he had the weekend off from work." Sue followed her mother inside, where the warmth and wonderful aroma of pot roast wrapped around her like a warm quilt on a cold winter's day.

The house looked exactly as it had for decades—family photos covering the walls and Anna's quilts draped over furniture. Matt was already sprawled in the recliner watching a football pregame show, and Earl emerged from the kitchen carrying a bowl of mashed potatoes.

"Sue-bug," Earl said, using the nickname from her childhood. He set down the bowl and pulled her into a solid hug. "Love you."

"Love you too, Dad."

Graham appeared with a basket of Anna's homemade rolls, grinning. "Mom's outdone herself again, as usual. We've got pot roast, green beans, corn, mashed potatoes, rolls, and I saw at least two pies in the kitchen."

"Three," Anna corrected, ushering everyone toward the dining room. "Sue needs feeding. She's been working too hard all week."

They settled around the table that had hosted countless family meals—christenings and graduations, holidays and ordinary Sundays. Earl said grace, his voice steady and grateful, and Sue felt the rightness of being here, surrounded by people who'd loved her through every season of her life.

"So," Matt said, reaching for the pot roast. "Lyle came by the hardware store yesterday. Said the structural assessment went well. Six to eight weeks?"

"That's the estimate." Sue accepted the bowl of green beans from her mother. "We start demo tomorrow. My staff and I will be helping, which should speed things up."

"Smart thinking," Earl said. "Keep your employees earning a wage until you reopen."

"Martha's also giving some of them shifts at the diner," Sue added. "Between that and the cleanup work, everyone should stay afloat until we reopen."

Anna beamed. "That's wonderful, honey. You're taking such good care of your staff."

"Speaking of taking care of people," Graham said, loading his plate with mashed potatoes, "that Fill the Boot fundraiser was something else. I heard the count so far was over six thousand dollars, and that didn't include all the matching donations from local businesses that are still coming in."

Sue nearly dropped her fork. "Six thousand dollars?"

"Yep. I talked to Steve yesterday when I ran into him and Lindsey at the grocery store. Pretty impressive total so far if you ask me."

"Six thousand dollars," Sue repeated, trying to process the magnitude. "That's—that's incredible."

"It's the community showing how much they care about you," Anna said.

Earl cut his pot roast with careful precision. "Well, it's good that certain people could organize something helpful for once."

The comment landed in the middle of the table like a stone. Sue glanced at her father, recognizing the protective edge in his voice that sometimes emerged when Steve's name came up.

"Dad," Sue said carefully. "Steve did a good thing. A really good thing."

"I'm not saying he didn't." Earl kept his eyes on his plate. "Just noting that grand gestures are easy. It's the everyday showing up that matters."

"Earl," Anna's voice carried gentle reproach.

"I'm just saying what everyone's thinking." Earl looked up, his gaze finding Sue's. "This past week, I've heard a lot of talk around town. From what I've been told, Steve's been by the restaurant a few times, he organized that fundraiser, and Lyle mentioned he was at the structural assessment. And that's fine. That's helpful. But Sue-bug, you've been doing fine on your own for years. You don't need someone swooping in with big community projects or anything else to prove something."

"He's trying to help me, Dad."

"Is he?" Earl's tone wasn't harsh, just concerned. "Or is he trying to insert himself back into your life through the side door because the front door's been closed for years?"

Sue set down her fork, choosing her words carefully. "I think he's trying to do the right thing. Finally."

Matt and Graham exchanged glances while Anna reached for the rolls, her expression carefully neutral.

"Honey," Earl continued, his voice softer now, "I watched what you went through when your marriage ended. I watched you cry yourself to sleep multiple times over a man who kept putting himself and his job over his family. A man who missed Lindsey's dance recitals and school events and forgot a couple of anniversary dinners you had planned, if memory serves me right. A man who acted like you should just understand that his career was first and you and Lindsey were second."

"I remember, Dad." Sue's throat tightened.

"So forgive me for being skeptical when that same man suddenly becomes Superman, organizing fundraisers and showing up at structural assessments." Earl's eyes were kind but firm. "Leopards don't change their spots, Sue-bug. And workaholics don't suddenly become family men because a building caught fire."

"People can change, Dad. Can't they?"

Anna's hand covered Sue's on the table. "Of course they can, sweetheart. God specializes in redemption."

"Does He specialize in preventing daughters from getting their hearts broken twice by the same man?" Earl asked, then immediately looked apologetic. "I'm sorry. That was harsh."

"But not wrong," Sue admitted quietly. "I don't know what I'm doing, Dad. I don't know if Steve's really changed or if this is just—I don't know. A phase he's going through. A response to the crisis."

Graham cleared his throat. "For what it's worth, I've worked with Steve on several community projects over the past couple of years. The fire station renovation, the church fellowship hall expansion, and the community park repairs last summer, just to name a few. He's been reliable and present. He's not the same man he once was."

"That's a construction-type project," Earl pointed out. "Not family."

"True," Graham acknowledged. "But I'm just saying—he's changed."

Matt nodded. "He has. He coaches Lindsey's softball team and never misses a game, as far as I know. Helps with the church youth group camping trips. Volunteers at the community center." He paused. "I'm not saying he's perfect or that Sue should just forget everything that happened. But he's not the same Steve who you remember, Dad."

"Maybe he's just gotten better at hiding his selfishness," Earl said.

"Or maybe he's actually grown." Anna's voice was gentle but pointed. "Earl, you remember who you were when you were younger. Would you want people judging you now based on that version of yourself?"

Earl had the grace to look sheepish. "That's different."

"Is it?" Anna turned to Sue. "Sweetheart, it's okay to acknowledge that Steve's doing good things now. That he's trying. That he might have actually learned from his mistakes."

Sue pushed green beans around her plate. "It's scary."

"What is?" Anna asked.

"Letting myself believe he's changed. Because if I believe it and I'm wrong—" Sue stopped, the fear lodging in her throat. "I survived the divorce, Mom. But I don't know if I could survive being wrong about him again."

Earl's expression softened, his protective instincts clearly warring with his desire to support whatever decision Sue needed to make.

"Then don't rush into anything if you're wanting to try to be friendly with him or allow him back into your life more," Earl said finally. "Take your time. Watch his actions. Make sure whatever change you're seeing is real and lasting, not just a temporary response to the fire."

"But also don't close the door completely," Anna added. "Because sometimes grace means giving people room to prove they've grown. Even when it's scary."

Graham reached for seconds of pot roast. "What does Lindsey think about all this?"

Sue managed a small laugh. "Lindsey still believes her parents should get back together, live happily ever after, and give her a baby brother or sister. She's eleven and believes in fairy tales."

"Smart kid," Matt said with a grin.

"Biased kid," Sue corrected. "She loves her dad. Which is good. But it doesn't mean—" She stopped, not sure how to finish that sentence.

"It doesn't mean you have to love him again the way you once did," Anna finished gently. "Your relationship with Steve and Steve's relationship with Lindsey are two separate things. You can support one without forcing yourself into the other."

They ate in companionable silence for a few minutes, the tension gradually easing as conversation shifted to safer topics—Matt's plans to propose to his girlfriend at Christmas, Graham's new side project building a deck for the Methodist church in the next town over, and Anna's quilting circle's fundraiser for the local food bank.

But Sue's mind kept circling back to her father's words. Leopards don't change their spots. Was Earl right? Was she seeing a genuine change in Steve, or just temporary good behavior that would evaporate once the crisis passed?

She thought about Steve's careful respect during the structural assessment. His restraint in offering help without taking over. The way he'd organized the fundraiser specifically to honor her. The warmth in his eyes when she'd thanked him outside Martha's.

"Mom," Sue said during a lull in conversation, "can I ask you something?"

"Of course, honey."

"How do you know? When someone's really changed versus just pretending?"

Anna considered the question seriously. "I think you watch their actions when nobody's looking. When there's no benefit to them. When they make choices that cost them something but do right by others." She paused. "But mostly, I think you pray about it. Ask God to show you the truth and give you discernment. He's good at revealing what we need to see when we're ready to see it."

Sue nodded slowly, absorbing her mother's wisdom.

After dinner, while the men settled in the living room for football, Sue helped her mom clear the table. The kitchen work was familiar and soothing—the same tasks they'd done together for years, the same rhythm of working side by side.

"You're thinking awfully hard over there," Anna observed, handing Sue a serving dish to dry.

"I'm just—" Sue stopped, choosing honesty over deflection. "I think my heart might be softening toward Steve. Just a tiny bit. And that terrifies me."

Anna smiled, continuing to wash dishes. "Why does it terrify you?"

"Because if I let him back in and he hurts me again—" Sue's voice caught. "I barely survived divorcing him, Mom. He nearly destroyed me."

"Oh, sweetheart." Anna turned from the sink, her soapy hands dripping on the floor. "You're stronger than you give yourself credit for. You survived a divorce, you built a successful business, you're raising a beautiful daughter, and you've created a life you love. If—and that's a big if—Steve lets you down again, you'll survive that too. Because you're a survivor."

"I don't want to be," Sue admitted. "I want to be someone who doesn't have to survive. Who just gets to be happy."

"Those aren't mutually exclusive." Anna returned to the dishes. "And happiness doesn't mean never taking risks. Sometimes it means being brave enough to try again when you're not sure how it'll turn out."

Sue dried the serving dish with careful precision. "I'm not saying I want to get back together with him. I'm not saying that at all."

"I know."

"I'm just saying—maybe I'm not as angry anymore. Maybe I can see him as someone who made mistakes and hurt me and is genuinely trying to be a better person."

"That sounds like growth," Anna said gently. "For the both of you."

They finished the dishes in comfortable silence, and Sue found herself thinking about Steve picking up Lindsey this past Friday evening—how he'd arrived exactly on time, informed her of his plans for this weekend with Lindsey, and left without lingering or pushing for more conversation than she offered.

Small things. Consistent things. The everyday type of showing up that Earl said mattered.

Maybe both were true—the grand gestures and the quiet consistency. Maybe Steve was demonstrating both.

Or maybe Sue was seeing what she wanted to see because letting go of the anger was easier than holding onto it.

"Mom?" Sue folded the dish towel, hanging it on the oven handle. "What if I'm wrong? About his changing?"

Anna turned, her expression full of love and understanding. "Then you'll handle it. The same way you've handled every hard thing in your life—with grace and strength and faith that God will see you through."

Sue nodded, but the fear remained—a tight knot in her chest that wouldn't fully release.

They returned to the living room, where Earl and her brothers were debating a controversial call in the game. Sue settled onto the couch beside her mother, letting the familiar sounds of family wash over her.

But her mind stayed on Steve. On the fundraiser and the careful respect he showed and the way he'd looked when she'd said she trusted him to lock up the restaurant.

On the terrifying possibility that maybe—just maybe—Earl was wrong and people could change their spots after all.

And on the even more terrifying question of what she would do if Steve really had become someone worth trusting again.

Chapter 16

" —and then Luke came right up to our car with the boot full of money, Dad! You should have seen Mom's face. She looked like she was going to cry, but she smiled too, and then her mouth opened, but nothing came out at first—"

Steve's father chuckled from his seat at the head of the dining table, his weathered face creasing with amusement. "Sounds like you did a good thing, son, and made quite an impression on your daughter."

"It sounds like I did." Steve accepted the bowl of mashed potatoes from his mother, spooning a generous portion onto his plate before passing it to Dan.

"It was the best thing ever," Lindsey said, bouncing slightly in her chair. "All my friends at school were talking about it. Sarah Martinez said her dad donated, and so did Ben Cooper's mom, and Mrs. Phillips—you know, my art teacher—she said the whole teachers' lounge was talking about it, and they collected money too—"

"Breathe, princess," Steve said, though he couldn't suppress his smile.

The Johnson farmhouse dining room was full of warmth that Sunday afternoon. Sunlight streamed through the windows, glinting off the oak table that had hosted countless family dinners. Gail's ham sat at the center, surrounded by serving dishes—mashed potatoes, buttered corn, green beans with bacon, and a basket of rolls that were still warm enough to melt butter on contact.

"I'm just saying," Lindsey continued without missing a beat, "it was really cool. And Mom was surprised, but in a good way... I think."

Steve's mother caught his eye across the table, her expression carrying layers of meaning he'd learned to read over the years. Pride, certainly. But also curiosity and the particular brand of maternal concern that came from watching your child navigate complicated emotional territory.

"How much did you raise?" Dan asked, reaching for another roll. Steve's younger brother had arrived late from his shift at the timber mill, still wearing the exhaustion of a long day but present nonetheless because Sunday dinner was sacred in the Johnson household.

"Over six thousand dollars from the two-day collection." Steve cut into his ham, the fork scraping against the plate. "Not including business donations. Earl Smith alone is matching the full amount."

His father's eyebrows rose. "Really? Matching it?"

"That's what I've been told."

Tom Johnson set down his fork, his blue eyes studying his son. "That's mighty generous of Earl."

"Tom," Gail's voice carried a gentle warning.

"I'm just stating facts." Tom picked up his fork again. "Earl hasn't exactly been warm toward you since the divorce."

"He's Sue's father; the fundraiser has nothing to do with me," Steve said carefully, aware of Lindsey's presence.

Lindsey looked between the adults, her intuition picking up on the undercurrent even if she couldn't quite name it. "Grandpa Earl loves Dad. He's just...protective of Mom...at least that's what Mom says."

"That's exactly right, sweetheart," Gail said. "And that's what good fathers do—they protect their daughters."

Tom nodded slowly, his gaze still on Steve. "Yes, they do. All fathers love their children and want to protect them from being hurt."

Steve met his father's eyes steadily. "I agree."

Dan cleared his throat. "So, Sue... I hear she's hoping to reopen by Christmas."

"That's what she's hoping for. Graham and Lyle mutually agreed that the building's bones are solid. Surface damage mostly. They start demolition tomorrow."

"And Sue's handling it all okay?" Gail asked, passing the green beans to Lindsey. "I can't imagine how stressful this must be for her."

"She's managing." Steve thought about Sue standing in her damaged restaurant on Friday, the vulnerability in her voice when she'd told him she trusted him to lock up. "She's hired her staff to help with cleanup work so they can still earn wages. Martha's giving some of them shifts at the diner too."

"That sounds like Sue," Gail said softly. "Always taking care of her people."

"Mom's good at taking care of people," Lindsey said, her pride evident. "She's been calling customers to let them know when the restaurant might be open again... and she's been super crazy organized about all these appointments and meetings, and she's been working really, really late at night."

"Hmm, sounds like she's been busy, Lindsey," Tom said, his attention on Steve. "Just like your dad must have been spending time organizing a town-wide fundraiser while managing a fire department."

Steve felt heat creep up his neck. "The crew helped. It was a team effort."

"But you organized it," his father pressed. "You coordinated with City Hall for permits, scheduled the collection points, and managed the logistics. That was your leadership."

"I have resources. It made sense for me to use them."

"And no other reason?" Gail's question was gentle but pointed.

Steve set down his fork, knowing his mother wouldn't be satisfied with deflection. "I wanted to help. No, really... I had to help. Sue deserves support."

"But why'd you organize it, Dad?" Lindsey asked, her childlike directness cutting through adult nuance. "I mean, you're the fire chief, so I guess that makes sense... Mom's your ex-wife... you guys don't really talk much except about me, so... why'd you do all that work to help her?"

The dining room went quiet except for the distant ticking of the wall clock. Steve looked at his daughter, at her open expression and genuine curiosity, and felt the weight of responsibility settle on his shoulders. Whatever he said right now mattered. Would shape how Lindsey understood his motivations and maybe what she expected for the future.

"Because the right thing doesn't stop being right just because something's complicated," Steve said finally. "Your mom needed help. I was in a position to provide it in a way that respected her as a person. So I did."

"But you still care about her," Lindsey said. "Right?"

Steve's chest tightened. "Of course I care about her. She's your mom. And she's someone I—" He paused, aware of every adult eye on him. "Someone I'll always care about."

Lindsey smiled, the expression lighting her whole face. "I knew it. I told Sarah at school that you still love Mom even though you're divorced, and she said that was impossible, but I said love doesn't just stop, and—"

"Lindsey." Steve kept his voice gentle but firm. "Your mom and I have a lot of history. Complicated history. Caring about someone doesn't automatically fix everything that went wrong."

"But it's a start though, right?" Lindsey's optimism was undeterred. "Like, you caring enough to help with the restaurant and the whole fundraiser thing... that's you showing her you care. So maybe—"

"Maybe we should let the adults figure out adult things," Gail interrupted smoothly, "while you tell us more about this pottery wheel project at school you mentioned earlier."

Lindsey launched into an enthusiastic description of creating a bowl in art class while Steve caught his mother's knowing look.

"She's not wrong though," Dan said quietly, his voice pitched low enough that Lindsey wouldn't hear over her own narrative. "About you still caring."

Steve stared at his plate, at the half-eaten ham and cooling potatoes. "No. She's not wrong."

"So what are you going to do about it?" his father asked.

"Nothing." Steve met his dad's gaze. "Or rather, nothing more than what I'm already doing. Showing up. Helping when I can without overstepping. Proving to her that I'm not the same man who destroyed our marriage."

"And if Sue doesn't see it?" Tom asked.

The question lodged somewhere behind Steve's ribs, sharp and uncomfortable. "Then I accept it. Keep being the best father I can be to Lindsey, the best chief I can be to my department, and the best man

I can be to honor—" He stopped, swallowed. "To honor what we had, even if we can't have it again."

"That's growth, son. Real growth. I'm proud of you."

"Doesn't feel like much," Steve admitted.

"The most important growth rarely does," his father said. "It's the quiet kind. The kind nobody sees except the person doing it and God."

Lindsey's voice rose above their quiet exchange. "—and Mrs. Phillips said mine was the best in the class even though it's a little lopsided because—oh! I forgot to tell you guys. The Christmas play auditions are next week. I'm going to try out for Mary."

"That's wonderful, princess," Steve said, grateful for the shift to safer ground. "I think you'd be great."

"Will you come see the play?" Lindsey asked. "Both you and Mom?"

"I'll be there," Steve promised.

They finished dinner with talk of upcoming holiday events, the fire department's toy drive, and Dan's plans to join Steve's crew for a community service project at the elementary school next month. Gail brought out apple pie for dessert, and the conversation stayed light while they ate.

But when Lindsey excused herself to watch a movie in the living room, the adults lingered over coffee and the remains of pie.

"You're doing the right thing," Tom said without preamble. "Helping Sue, respecting her, being patient. That's the mark of a man who's learned something."

"I'm trying," Steve said.

"We can see that." Gail topped off his coffee from the pot on the table. "And I imagine Sue sees it too."

"I can only guess her dad doesn't," Steve pointed out.

"Earl will... he's a good man." Gail's voice carried certainty. "He loves his daughter. His coldness toward you is part of a parent's instincts because they've seen their child get hurt in the past. Not that I'm saying it's right, but all parents want to protect their children. He'll come around. It might take time, but he will."

"I get that, I do. And I deserve his distance, but I do miss being his friend. We once had a great relationship," Steve said quietly.

His parents exchanged a look, the kind of wordless communication that came from three decades of marriage.

"I really want to earn Sue's forgiveness and her trust. I miss her, and I miss what we used to have," Steve continued. "What if she never forgives me even though I'm trying?"

"Then you'll accept it and continue on," his father said simply. "You may regret and hurt for the rest of your life, but you'll survive. Because that's what men do when they've actually grown—they accept responsibility for their actions and their consequences without letting it destroy them."

Steve nodded, the words settling into the place where fear and hope tangled together in his chest.

"But I am not convinced that's how this ends," Gail added softly. "I've seen Sue at church, watched her when she thinks no one's looking. The way her eyes track you across the fellowship hall, the careful way she maintains distance like she's afraid of what might happen if she gets too close to you again. That's not indifference, Steve. That's self-protection."

"Which means she's still vulnerable," Dan said. "Still has feelings she's trying to protect herself from."

Steve wanted to believe it. Wanted to hold on to the hope that Sue's carefully maintained walls meant something still existed behind them worth guarding. But hope was dangerous. Hope could blind you to reality and set you up for devastation.

"I'm not going to push her," Steve said firmly. "Whatever happens, it happens on Sue's timeline. At her comfort level. With her explicit invitation. I'll just be thankful if we can be more civil... friends even."

"That's wise," Tom said. "But don't mistake patience for passivity. Sometimes love requires being brave enough to be honest about what you want."

"When the time is right," Gail added quickly. "Which isn't now. Not while everything's still so raw from this fire."

From the living room, Lindsey's laughter floated through the doorway, light and untroubled. Steve listened to it for a moment, that pure sound of childhood joy, and felt the full weight of what he stood to lose if he mis-stepped.

Not just Sue. But Lindsey's faith in love itself, in the idea that broken things could be mended and happy endings were possible.

"I need to get it right this time," Steve said quietly. "Not for me. For Lindsey."

"Then keep doing what you're doing," his father said. "Show up. Be steady. Let your actions speak louder than your words. And if all that happens is a friendship between you and Sue, then remember you're teaching Lindsey something valuable."

Steve finished his coffee and stood to help clear dishes, moving through the familiar rhythm of after-dinner cleanup. Dan washed while Steve dried, their synchronized movements speaking to years of shared Sunday dinners and unspoken brotherhood.

When Lindsey emerged from the living room, her movie finished, she was yawning and ready to head home. Steve gathered their coats while Gail packed leftovers into containers.

"Drive safe," his mother said, pulling him into a hug at the door. "And Steve? Trust God's timing. He's not finished with your story yet."

Chapter 17

The crash of metal reverberated through the damaged kitchen as Sue hefted another ruined piece of her kitchen onto the pile headed for the dumpster. Sweat trickled down her spine despite the November chill seeping through the open back door, and her shoulders ached from two hours of steady work, but she welcomed the burn in her muscles. This was progress. Tangible, visible, and undeniable progress.

"Sue, do you want me to grab that?" Graham called from across the kitchen, where he was examining the wall cavity behind the torn-out drywall.

"I've got it," she said as she adjusted her grip on the twisted metal shelving unit, maneuvering it through the maze of debris. Her work gloves were streaked with soot and ash, her old jeans sporting new tears at the knees, but she felt more grounded since that Sunday morning when she had learned her restaurant was on fire.

Carla appeared at her elbow, similarly dressed in work clothes and determination. "Let me help you."

Together, they carried the shelving unit outside to where a massive dumpster sat like a metal monument to destruction in the back alley. The November air hit Sue's overheated skin with welcome coolness.

"You doing okay?" Carla asked as they heaved the shelving into the dumpster with a satisfying clang.

"Better than I thought I'd be." Sue pulled off her gloves, wiping her forehead with the back of her hand. "This helps. Doing something instead of just thinking about everything that needs doing."

"Your brother's crew is impressive. They've cleared half the kitchen already."

"They know what they're doing." Sue surveyed the controlled chaos visible through the restaurant's propped-open doors. Her brother moved with confident efficiency alongside his crew members while three of Sue's employees helped under their supervision.

They headed back inside, where the rhythm of demolition continued—the scrape of pry bars against stubborn drywall, the clatter of debris hitting the floor, and the occasional grunt of exertion. Sue grabbed an industrial broom and began sweeping accumulated soot and fragments into a pile.

"Let's all take a quick water break," Graham announced, checking his watch. "Then we'll start on the ceiling panels."

Sue nodded and made her way to the cooler she'd packed that morning, pulling out bottled water, juice bottles, and iced tea.

"Here." She pressed a cold bottle of water into the hands of one of Graham's crew members—Jake, she thought his name was. "You've been working hard."

"Thanks, Ms. Smith." He accepted gratefully, downing half the bottle in long gulps.

She distributed drinks to the rest of the workers, moving through the space with the same efficiency she'd once used navigating a busy dinner rush. This was different labor, but the principles remained the same—anticipate needs, stay organized, and keep everyone functioning smoothly.

"Sue, quick question," Lyle called from near the kitchen's far wall. "We found some additional electrical damage behind this panel. Want me to document it for the insurance adjuster?"

"Yes, please. Photos and detailed notes." Sue crossed to examine what he'd uncovered. "Is it structural?"

"Cosmetic, but it'll add a little time to the electrical work."

"Okay. Make sure we get it all documented properly." Sue made a mental note to call her insurance adjuster later, then returned to her sweeping. The steady, repetitive motion calmed the anxious edge that wanted to resurface with each new challenge discovered.

By eleven o'clock, they'd started dismantling the ruined ceiling panels in the kitchen. Sue stood in the middle of what had been her domain—the place where she'd created hundreds of pizzas—and felt both grief and hope warring in her chest.

This space had represented her independence. Her ability to survive and thrive without needing anyone. Now it lay gutted and exposed, vulnerable in ways that made her acutely uncomfortable. Yet underneath the devastation, the bones remained strong. The foundation held. With work and time and help, it would be whole again.

Maybe stronger than before.

"That's good progress for the morning," Graham said, appearing at her side. His clothes were covered in construction dust and soot. "We're right on schedule. Better than, actually."

"Everyone's working hard," she said as she surveyed her employees with genuine appreciation. Carla was helping haul ceiling tiles. Two of her servers were sorting salvageable dishes from destroyed ones. Even her part-time delivery driver had shown up to help. "I'm grateful."

"They're here because they believe in you."

Before Sue could respond, the front door opened and a familiar silhouette filled the entrance, arms loaded with white paper bags bearing Martha's Diner's logo.

Steve.

Sue's stomach did something complicated that she refused to name.

"Hope I'm not interrupting," Steve said, maneuvering through the doorway with careful balance. "But I figured everyone might be hungry."

He carried what had to be a dozen bags, maybe more. Her first instinct was to question his presence, to wonder what agenda lay behind this gesture, but then she registered what he'd said.

Everyone. Not just her.

"Is that food?" Carla asked, appearing beside Sue. "Please tell me that's food because I'm starving."

"Martha's finest." Steve set the bags on one of the few undamaged tables in the dining room. "She put together sandwiches, chips, cookies, the works. Enough for the whole crew."

Graham appeared, followed by Lyle and the rest of the workers, all of them gravitating toward the promise of lunch with the universal enthusiasm of people who'd been engaged in physical labor. Steve began handing out bags, calling out sandwich types like he was working a lunch shift at the diner himself.

"Turkey and Swiss? Ham and cheddar? Roast beef?" He distributed bagged lunches with genuine warmth, accepting thank yous from Sue's employees and Graham's crew with the kind of gracious deflection that suggested he hadn't come here for praise.

Sue stood slightly apart, watching this unfold with emotions she couldn't quite sort. The gesture was thoughtful. More than thoughtful—it was considerate. Steve hadn't shown up with lunch for two, trying to create some intimate moment between them. He'd brought food for an entire work crew.

"Sue?" Carla appeared at her elbow, holding a bagged lunch. "Steve brought your favorite. Turkey with avocado."

"He remembered that?"

"Apparently."

Sue accepted the bag and tried to ignore how that small detail made her feel.

"Let's eat outside," Graham suggested, gesturing toward the side patio where outdoor dining tables still stood undamaged, their umbrellas closed but serviceable.

The group migrated toward the patio door, workers grabbing drinks from Sue's cooler to accompany their lunch. Sue followed, her lunch bag feeling heavier than it should in her hands, and searched for Steve in the crowd that was filling the outdoor space.

He'd already claimed a seat at one of the round tables and was unwrapping his sandwich.

She hesitated, caught between the available seats at different tables, before Carla's gentle hand on her back nudged her toward where Steve sat. She slid into the chair across from him.

"Thank you for this," Sue said as she unwrapped her sandwich.

"Seemed like the practical thing to do."

"Still. It was thoughtful."

He shrugged, the gesture modest. "Martha did the real work. I just played delivery guy."

Around them, conversation flowed with the easy camaraderie of people united in common purpose. Jake was telling some story about a renovation job gone wrong that had Graham and Lyle laughing. Carla chatted with one of her servers about scheduling shifts at Martha's

Diner. The delivery driver debated the upcoming basketball season with one of Graham's crew.

Sue ate her sandwich and watched Steve interact with this impromptu gathering. He answered questions about the fire department's upcoming toy drive with genuine enthusiasm. Listened to Lyle's concerns about a renovation project at his own home with patient interest.

Questions and thoughts circled through Sue's mind while she finished her sandwich and sipped her bottled tea. Across from her, Steve laughed at something Graham said, his face relaxing into an expression she remembered from their early years—before ambition and pride had hardened him into someone who measured every interaction by what it could gain him.

"You're being awfully quiet over there," Carla observed, leaning close enough that only Sue could hear. "Everything okay?"

"Just tired," Sue said, though that wasn't entirely true.

"Mm-hmm." Carla's skepticism was gentle but unmistakable. "Has nothing to do with your ex-husband showing up with lunches for everyone?"

Sue shot her friend a look that communicated exactly how unhelpful that observation was. Carla just smiled and returned to her conversation with the servers, leaving Sue to wrestle with thoughts that felt increasingly dangerous.

The lunch break stretched to forty-five minutes, everyone taking full advantage of the break time before diving back into demolition work. Steve collected trash, moving around the patio with quiet efficiency, refusing offers of help with the same modest deflection he'd used when accepting thanks for the food.

When the crew began drifting back inside, Steve caught Sue's eye across the patio. "I should get back to the station. I've got paperwork that won't do itself."

"Right. Of course," she said as she stood. "Thanks for the lunch. For thinking of everyone."

"You're welcome." Steve gathered the last of the trash bags. "You've made good progress today. The place is going to look great when it's done."

"Hopefully."

"You've got this, Sue. I've never known you to fail at something you set your mind to."

The compliment landed somewhere in her chest, warm and unexpected. Before Sue could formulate a response that wouldn't reveal how much those words affected her, Steve was heading toward his truck, offering waves and farewells to the crew members he passed.

Sue watched him drive away, his vehicle disappearing down Cedar Avenue toward the fire station, and tried to sort through the tangle of emotions his visit had stirred.

She should feel annoyed. She should protect herself from the dangerous softening she felt creeping through her defenses like spring thaw through winter ice.

Instead, she felt grateful and confused.

"You ready to get back to it?" Graham asked, appearing beside her with his tool belt slung over his shoulder.

"Yeah," she said as she pulled her work gloves back on.

She returned to the rhythm of demolition—hauling, sorting, sweeping, organizing—and let the physical labor occupy her attention. But as she worked, her mind kept circling back to Steve's easy presence at the patio table.

To the sandwich he'd remembered she liked after all these years.

To the way he'd fed an entire crew without making it about himself.

By the time Graham called an end to the workday at six o'clock, Sue's muscles screamed and her clothes were filthy, but the kitchen stood gutted and ready for reconstruction. Progress, steady and measurable.

After everyone had left, standing alone in her hollowed-out restaurant with the scent of ash and possibility hanging in the air, Sue thought about Steve sitting across from her at lunch. He had been comfortable and present in a way that shouldn't have felt so natural. She thought about how he'd looked at her—not with expectation or hope, but with something steadier and more patient. Like he was content just to show up and be helpful without demanding anything in return.

Maybe Steve really had changed.

Maybe the man who'd destroyed their marriage through selfishness and ambition had actually learned what mattered and was trying to prove it.

Sue locked the front door and walked to her SUV, exhaustion pulling at every limb. She sat in her vehicle with the engine running and pulled out her phone, thumb hovering over Steve's contact information for a long moment before she could convince herself to either call or put the phone away.

Finally, she typed out a simple message: *Thank you for lunch today. Everyone appreciated it, including me.*

Her thumb hovered over the send button. Sending the text felt like acknowledgment of more than just lunch—it felt like cracking open a door she'd kept firmly locked for self-preservation.

Sue hit send before she could overthink it further, then immediately regretted it and didn't regret it in equal measure. She set the phone in the cup holder and pulled away from the restaurant, trying not to watch for the telltale glow of a response on her phone.

She was halfway home when her phone chimed. She told herself not to look. She told herself it could be anyone—Carla or her mother or Martha checking in.

She stopped in the middle of the country road after checking to make sure no one was coming up behind her, and she grabbed her phone.

You're welcome. Happy to help.

Five words. Simple and direct.

She drove the rest of the way home, trying not to think about what it meant that she'd wanted him to respond or why his uncomplicated answer satisfied something she hadn't known she'd been looking for.

Chapter 18

Steve signed his name at the bottom of the incident report, the twentieth piece of paperwork he'd completed in the past two hours, when knuckles rapped against his office door frame.

"Come in."

Mark and Ray entered wearing civilian clothes—jeans, work boots, and plain t-shirts that had seen better days. Steve glanced at the wall clock. One fifteen on a Tuesday afternoon. Both men were officially off duty.

"Something wrong?" Steve set down his pen immediately cataloging potential problems. "You're supposed to be enjoying your day off."

"Ray and I are heading over to Sue's Pizza for a few hours. Figured we'd see if you wanted to join us," Mark said, leaning against the doorframe.

Steve looked from Mark to Ray, then down at the scattered paperwork covering his desk. Budget projections for next quarter. Equipment maintenance logs. Training schedule revisions. Nothing urgent. Nothing that couldn't wait.

"You're going to volunteer your time?" Steve asked, though the answer was obvious.

"Community service," Ray said. "Sue needs hands. We've got hands. Seemed logical."

Steve mentally ran through the station roster. Luke was on duty with Danny and two others. The engines were maintained. The equipment was checked. Everything was running smoothly without crisis or immediate need for command decisions. He'd only be a few minutes down the street if there was an emergency here.

"Give me five minutes to change," he said, already standing.

Moments later, Steve climbed into the passenger seat of the department's white pickup truck, with Mark behind the wheel and Ray claiming the backseat. The drive took less than five minutes.

They parked behind Graham's work truck and walked through the entrance into organized chaos. Sue stood on a ladder in the dining room, carefully prying loose a smoke-damaged ceiling panel while Carla steadied the ladder's base. Two of Sue's servers worked nearby, removing framed photos from walls and sorting them into keep and discard piles.

Sue looked down at them as they entered, her expression shifting from concentration to surprise. She wore work clothes—old jeans, sturdy boots, and a faded t-shirt—and her hair was pulled back in a ponytail. Dust streaked her cheek and exhaustion shadowed her eyes, but she'd never looked more beautiful to Steve.

"Mark? Ray? Steve?" Sue said as she descended the ladder. "What are you doing here?"

"Heard you could use extra hands," Mark said easily. "Thought we'd help out for a few hours."

Sue's gaze shifted to Steve, questions visible in the slight furrow of her brow.

"They showed up at the station," Steve explained. "Asked if I wanted to join them. Seemed like a good use of my afternoon."

"Shouldn't you be at work?" Sue asked.

"Community service work this afternoon. If the crew needs me, I'm minutes away."

"Well," she said after a moment's hesitation, "we're pulling all the ceiling panels and taking down anything mounted to the walls in here. Then we need to wash everything down that's staying. The windows over there," she gestured to four large windows overlooking Cedar Avenue, "are damaged and need to come out."

"We can handle the windows," Ray said, already assessing the work involved. "Mark, you wanna grab the tools from the back of the truck?"

"Sure." Mark headed back outside while Ray moved to examine the window frames, testing their stability with experienced hands.

Steve gravitated toward where Sue had returned to her ladder, reaching for another ceiling panel. He positioned himself to catch the panel as she loosened it.

"Be careful," Steve said. "Those edges are sharp."

Sue maneuvered the damaged panel toward him, and Steve accepted its weight, carrying it outside to the dumpster sitting in a parking space in front of the restaurant. When he returned, Sue was already working on the next section.

They worked in silence for several minutes, the dining room filling with the sounds of productive labor. Mark and Ray removed the windows with methodical precision. Carla and the servers began the long, cumbersome task of washing down soot-covered walls with industrial cleaner. From the kitchen, Graham's crew advanced through their own tasks.

"This is nice of you," Sue said finally, not looking down from her perch on the ladder. "All three of you. Showing up like this."

"We wanted to help." Steve positioned himself to receive the next panel. "Just three guys with spare time and a restaurant that needs work."

"Still." Sue lowered the panel into his waiting hands. "That was kind of you all."

Their eyes met for a brief moment before Sue turned back to her task.

"Remember when we first bought this place?" Sue asked after another few minutes of work. "These same ceiling panels gave us fits when we were installing them."

Steve did remember. He could recall with perfect clarity standing exactly where he stood now, a young man full of hopes and dreams, helping Sue install the very panels they were now removing. "You insisted we could do it ourselves instead of hiring professionals."

"We saved three thousand dollars doing it ourselves."

"We also almost killed each other in the process." Steve accepted another panel, his mind flooding with memories. "You dropped one right on my head."

"That was an accident," Sue protested, but he could hear the smile in her voice. "And you deserved it for not being in position like I told you."

"I was exactly where you told me to be."

"You were two feet to the left when I asked you to stand on the right."

"Same thing."

She laughed—actually laughed—and the sound hit Steve like a sucker punch. When was the last time he'd heard her laugh? Really laugh, not the polite chuckle she offered in public or the restrained humor she showed around him when Lindsey was present? This was genuine, unguarded, and achingly familiar.

"We were terrible at renovation work," Sue said, descending the ladder to move it to a new position. "I don't know what made us think we could transform an empty building into a restaurant."

"Stubbornness," Steve offered, helping her reposition the ladder. "And optimism. And the kind of naïve confidence that comes from being young and thinking love conquers all obstacles."

Steve mentally kicked himself for mentioning love.

But Sue didn't acknowledge the word. Instead, she climbed the ladder and resumed her work. "We got it done, though. Made something good."

"You made something good," Steve corrected. "This place is all you, Sue. Your vision, your heart, and your determination."

"You helped."

"In the beginning, maybe. Before I—" Steve stopped himself, unwilling to drag his past failures into this moment of unexpected ease. "Anyway. You built this. And you'll rebuild it even better."

Sue paused, ceiling panel in hand, and looked down at him with an expression he couldn't quite read. "I couldn't do it alone. The rebuilding, I mean. I need help. From Graham and Lyle and my employees and—" She stopped, seeming to wrestle with something before continuing. "And from people like you and Mark and Ray showing up because you want to."

The admission cost her something. Steve could see it in the careful way she held herself, in the emotions that flickered across her face before she could mask them. Sue had spent years proving she didn't need anyone, least of all him. Acknowledging that she needed help now—that she appreciated his help—represented a crack in the armor she'd maintained with militant discipline.

"You're welcome," Steve said simply, accepting the panel she handed down. "Anytime you need an extra set of hands, just ask."

"I'm not good at asking."

"I know. So maybe I'll just keep showing up until you get used to people offering a helping hand."

Sue met his eyes again, and this time she didn't look away quickly. "What if I never get used to it?"

"Then I'll keep showing up anyway."

Sue turned back to her work.

They worked through the afternoon, the dining room gradually transforming. Mark and Ray successfully removed all four windows. Carla and the servers were working on scrubbing the dining room walls for the second round to ensure no soot remained. From the kitchen, Graham's voice called out occasional updates on their progress with the electrical framing.

Around three-thirty, Sue descended her ladder and stretched, her back clearly protesting hours of overhead work. Steve resisted the urge to offer a shoulder massage and instead looked away.

"I need water," she announced, heading toward her cooler. "Anyone else?"

A chorus of affirmatives followed, and Sue distributed cold bottles. Steve accepted his gratefully, the November air providing inadequate cooling against the heat generated by physical labor.

"So," Sue said, leaning against one of the walls while everyone took an impromptu break. "Thanksgiving break starts tomorrow at Lindsey's school."

"Right," Steve said. "I'm working tomorrow, but she's welcome to hang out at the station if that helps you. I imagine you want to be here working."

"You sure? I don't want her to be a disruption."

"She's never a disruption. The crew loves having her around." Steve took another drink of water. "She can help Luke with equipment checks; one of the trucks is scheduled for washing and waxing, and she loves to help with that, or she can do homework in my office. Whatever keeps her entertained."

"That would actually be really helpful." Sue's relief was visible. "I really don't want her here in this mess."

"Drop her at the station whenever you want. I'll make sure she's fed and happy."

Sue nodded, seeming to consider something before speaking again. "What about Thanksgiving? Your family's doing dinner Thursday evening, right?"

"Six o'clock." Steve had been dreading this conversation, knowing logistics around holidays always carried the potential for awkwardness. "I'm working until five."

"My parents are doing noon. So Lindsey would be with us for lunch, then we'd need to get her to your parents' house by six."

"I can pick her up from your parents' place after I get off work."

"That's completely out of your way." Sue shook her head. "Your parents' farm is east of town. Mine is west. You'd be backtracking for no reason."

"It's not a big deal—"

"Steve. I'll drop Lindsey at your parents' house on my way home. It makes sense logistically."

Steve wanted to argue, wanted to take on the inconvenience himself rather than ask anything of Sue. But she was right.

"Okay," he agreed. "If you're sure you don't mind."

"I don't mind." Sue's expression softened slightly. "Co-parenting doesn't always have to be complicated."

"I agree."

They returned to work, Steve helping Sue finish the last section of ceiling panels while Mark and Ray moved to assist Graham's crew in the kitchen. The afternoon wore on with steady progress, the restaurant slowly shedding its damaged skin.

Around four-thirty, Steve's radio crackled to life at his hip. "Structure fire... 1247 Timber Road. Residential. Requesting all available personnel."

Steve's body reacted before his mind finished processing—years of training and instinct taking over. He was already moving toward the door, Mark and Ray materializing at his sides with the same automatic response.

"Sorry," Steve said to Sue, who'd frozen on her ladder at the radio call.

"Go," Sue said immediately, already descending. "Be safe."

He ran for the pickup truck, Mark already behind the wheel with the engine starting. Ray jumped in the back while Steve claimed the passenger seat, the vehicle moving before his door fully closed.

As they raced toward Timber Road, lights flashing and siren wailing, Steve's last glimpse of Sue was her standing in the doorway of her restaurant, watching them leave with an expression he couldn't quite name.

But her final words echoed in his mind: Be safe.

The truck rounded the corner, and Steve's professional mind took over, cataloging the smoke visible in the distance and the potential challenges ahead. But underneath the fire chiefs practiced assessment, a different part of him held onto those words like a tether.

Be safe.

Chapter 19

Steve's truck bounced over the familiar ruts in the gravel drive leading to his parents' farmhouse. His shift had ended at five, and he'd made the drive from the station in record time, eager to spend the evening with Lindsey and his family.

But as the farmhouse came into view, Sue's silver SUV parked near the barn made his pulse quicken.

He pulled in beside her vehicle, his hands gripping the steering wheel for an extra moment while he gathered himself. He'd been imagining this handoff all day—Sue arriving, dropping Lindsey off, maybe exchanging a few polite words.

He climbed out of the truck and headed toward the house, his stomach doing complicated things that felt suspiciously like nervousness. Through the living room windows, he could see movement and hear the muffled sound of voices. Lindsey's animated chatter rose above the others, punctuated by laughter.

Steve opened the front door and stepped inside.

"Dad!" Lindsey launched herself at him before he'd fully crossed the threshold, her arms wrapping around his waist with the kind of enthusiasm that made his heart squeeze. "You're finally here! We've been waiting forever!"

"It's been five minutes," Sue said from where she stood near the sofa, her voice carrying gentle amusement. She wore dark jeans and a cream-colored sweater that made her skin glow, her hair loose around her shoulders. "Your dad drove as fast as was safe, Lindsey."

"Safer," Steve managed, acutely aware of his mother and father watching from their chairs near the fireplace. Dan sprawled on the couch with a glass of what looked like apple cider. "Traffic was a little heavy driving through town."

"Grandma and Grandpa Smith's Thanksgiving was amazing," Lindsey said, still clinging to Steve but turning to include Sue in her narrative. "We had turkey and ham and Grandma's sweet potato casserole and three kinds of pie, and we played Monopoly for like two hours, and I won—"

"You bankrupted your Uncle Graham," Sue said. "That's not quite the same as winning."

"Close enough." Lindsey grinned. "And we watched the parade on TV, and Grandpa Earl let me help him carve the turkey even though Grandma said I was too young, but he said I was plenty old enough, and—"

"Breathe, Lindsey," Steve said, his hand finding the top of her head with affection. His eyes met Sue's, and they both grinned at the amusement in their daughter's exuberance.

"Sue was just telling us about the restaurant progress," Gail said from her chair, her voice warm. "Sounds like she's making good time on the reconstruction."

"Better than expected," Sue said, her attention shifting to Gail. "The new electrical work should be finished by Wednesday at the latest, and the replacement windows are being installed next week. Graham thinks we might actually make the timeline."

"That's wonderful, dear," Gail said.

Sue nodded. "I should let you all get to your dinner."

"You don't have to leave," Steve said.

The room went quiet. Even Lindsey stopped her energetic bouncing to stare at him.

"I mean—" Steve cleared his throat. "You could stay. For dinner. Mom always makes enough to feed half the county, and we'd—I'd—we'd all love to have you."

Sue's eyes widened, and Steve watched her process the invitation with visible uncertainty. "I couldn't impose—"

"It's not an imposition," Gail said immediately. "We'd be delighted to have you, Sue. You know you're always welcome here."

"Please stay, Mom!" Lindsey's enthusiasm shifted into overdrive. "Please, please, please! We can all have Thanksgiving together like a real family, and it'll be so much fun and—"

"Breathe, Lindsey," Sue said, but Steve heard the waver in her voice.

"I think it's a great idea," Dan added from the couch, his easy smile genuine. "It'll be nice to catch up."

Tom stood, and his expression was equally welcoming. "I'll just go set up another place at the table."

Sue looked from person to person, her internal debate visible in the way she worried her bottom lip. Steve recognized the gesture—she was weighing options, calculating risks, and trying to determine if staying would cross boundaries she'd carefully set in place.

"Come on, Mom," Lindsey said. "It's Thanksgiving. We're supposed to be together."

Sue's shoulders relaxed, and she nodded. "Okay. If you're sure it's not—"

"We're sure," Steve said, maybe too quickly, but he couldn't help the relief flooding his chest.

Lindsey bounced on her toes with renewed energy. "This is the best Thanksgiving ever!"

"Let's wash up for dinner," Gail said, already heading toward the kitchen. "Steve, you can help me get everything on the table. Sue, make yourself comfortable."

The next ten minutes passed in a flurry of organized chaos—food moving from kitchen to dining room and everyone finding their seats amid conversation and laughter.

Steve sat between his father and Lindsey, with Sue across the table between Dan and Gail. Not beside him, which was probably wise given the delicate nature of this unexpected gathering, but close enough that he could see her face clearly in the warm light of the chandelier.

"Let's say grace," Tom said.

They all joined hands—Steve's right hand finding Lindsey's, his left taking his father's calloused palm. Across the table, he watched Sue's hands disappear into Dan and Gail's grip, her head bowing as Tom began the prayer.

"Heavenly Father, we thank You for this food and for the hands that prepared it. We thank You for family—both the family we're born into and the family we choose. We thank You for second chances and new beginnings, for healing and hope, and for bringing us all together around this table tonight. Bless this meal and those gathered here. In Jesus' name, Amen."

"Amen," echoed around the table.

Steve released his father's hand but held Lindsey's for an extra moment, squeezing gently before letting go. When he looked up, Sue was watching him with an expression he couldn't quite interpret.

Then Gail started passing dishes, and the evening shifted into the comfortable rhythm of a shared meal.

"This stuffing is incredible," Dan said around his third helping. "Mom, you've outdone yourself."

"It's the same recipe I've used for thirty years, just with a slightly different ingredient," Gail said, but she looked pleased nonetheless.

"The secret's in the sausage," Tom added. "Your mother finally convinced me that name brand was superior to the generic brand I'd been buying."

"A rare admission of defeat," Steve said, earning a laugh from Dan and an affectionate eye roll from his father.

Lindsey had loaded her plate with more food than she could possibly eat, but she was making a valiant effort. She maintained a running commentary on everything from the cranberry sauce to the merits of mashed potatoes versus sweet potato casserole.

"Mom makes better rolls than Grandma Gail," Lindsey announced with the brutal honesty of youth. "No offense, Grandma."

"None taken," Gail said with a smile. "Your mom's rolls are legendary. I've been wanting her recipe for years."

"It's my grandmother's," Sue said quietly. "I could write it down for you if you'd like."

"I'd love that."

The conversations continued to flow naturally—talk of Lindsey's upcoming Christmas play audition, Dan's plans to take a hunting trip in late December, and Gail's latest quilting project for the church fundraiser. Steve found himself relaxing into the familiar comfort of family dinner, made better by Sue's presence across the table.

"So the restaurant really might reopen before Christmas?" Dan asked during a lull in Lindsey's narrative about her art class.

"That's the hope," Sue said. "My major concern is getting all the new kitchen equipment delivered and installed without any hiccups."

"You planning a grand reopening event?" Tom asked.

"I was thinking about hosting the church congregation for a private party on reopening day. Just something small and special. Then later that day, open the restaurant up completely to the community and have a bigger celebration."

"That's a wonderful idea," Gail said. "The community's been so invested in seeing you rebuild."

"Thanks to Steve," Sue said, and Steve felt her eyes on him. "The fundraiser made a huge difference for me financially."

Steve met her gaze across the table. "The community wanted to help. I just organized it."

"You did more than organize it," she said, and something in her voice made Steve's chest tighten. "You made it possible."

Lindsey looked between her parents, grinning.

"Dad's really good at helping people," Lindsey said. "That's what fire chiefs do, right, Dad?"

"That's one part of the job," Steve agreed.

"And you help Mom a lot lately," Lindsey continued, undeterred by subtlety. "Bringing lunch and helping and being all supportive and stuff."

"Lindsey," Sue's voice carried a gentle warning.

"What? I'm just saying Dad's been really helpful. You said so yourself last night when we were—"

"How about those pies?" Steve interrupted. "I saw a few in the kitchen."

"Pumpkin, apple, and pecan," Gail confirmed. "All homemade."

"Your pecan pie is almost as good as Grandma Anna's," Lindsey said, then seemed to realize the minefield she'd just walked into. "I mean—they're both really good. Just different. Like equally good but in different ways?"

Sue pressed her lips together, clearly fighting a smile. "Nice save."

The meal continued with easy conversation punctuated by Lindsey's enthusiastic interjections. Steve found himself watching Sue more than he probably should—the way she laughed at Dan's stories, the gentle way she corrected Lindsey's table manners, and the momentary sadness that crossed her face when Tom mentioned something about family traditions.

Around eight o'clock, Sue glanced at her watch and set down her napkin. "I should help clean up. It's the least I can do after you all fed me this incredible meal."

"Absolutely not," Gail said. "You're a guest."

"I'm still family," Sue corrected quietly, and Steve watched his mother's expression soften. "Please. Let me help."

"I'll help too," Steve said, already standing.

"Me three!" Lindsey bounded up with the energy of someone who hadn't just consumed her weight in turkey and pie.

They fell into the pattern of kitchen cleanup—Sue washing, Steve drying, and Lindsey putting away dishes whenever possible—with commentary on everything from the proper organization of Grandma's cabinets to her opinions on which Christmas songs were superior.

"Jingle Bells is silly," Lindsey announced, handing Steve a dried serving platter. "It's just about a sleigh. What's the meaning in that?"

"Not every song needs deep meaning," Sue said, her hands buried in soapy water. "Sometimes joy is enough."

"But Silent Night has both joy and meaning; that's what my music teacher said," Lindsey argued. "That's what makes it better... right?"

"Can't argue with that logic," Steve said, stacking the platter in his mom's china cabinet.

They worked together easily, and Steve was acutely aware of how right this felt—the three of them together in his parents' kitchen, doing something as mundane as dishes while Lindsey philosophized about Christmas carols. This was what he'd lost when his marriage fell apart. Not just Sue, but this. The ordinary moments in life.

"Remember when we did dishes in our first apartment?" Sue asked suddenly, her voice soft enough that Lindsey, distracted by organizing silverware, didn't seem to hear. "That terrible place on Meadow Street with a kitchen the size of a closet?"

"We could barely both fit in there at the same time."

"And the sink was so small we had to do dishes in shifts." Sue's expression held something wistful. "But we made it work."

"We were good at making things work back then."

Sue's hands stilled in the water, and for a moment they just looked at each other.

"Dad, where does this big spoon go?" Lindsey's question broke the moment, and Sue returned to scrubbing while Steve directed their daughter to the proper drawer.

By nine o'clock, the kitchen gleamed, and the three of them returned to the living room, where Tom and Dan were engaged in some debate about hunting regulations while Gail worked on her quilting.

"We are going to head home," Sue said, and Lindsey's immediate protest was cut short by Sue's firm look. "It's late, and you are leaving early in the morning to go Black Friday shopping with Grandma and Grandpa Smith, and I need rest so I can work hard at the restaurant tomorrow."

"But it's only nine," Lindsey argued. "That's not even late."

"It's late enough," Sue countered, already gathering their coats. "Say thank you and goodbye to your grandparents and uncle."

Lindsey made the rounds of hugs and thank yous while Sue expressed her gratitude as well. Steve automatically reached for his jacket.

"I'll walk you out," he said.

They stepped into the November night, stars brilliant overhead and the air carrying a sharp bite of the approaching winter. Lindsey skipped ahead to Sue's SUV while Steve walked beside Sue in silence.

"Thanks for inviting me to stay," she said when they reached her vehicle. "That was—it was really nice. Being together like that."

"I'm glad you stayed," Steve said. "It felt like—" He stopped, unsure how to finish that sentence without overstepping.

"It felt like family... don't be afraid to admit it."

Lindsey had already climbed into the passenger seat, her face pressed against the window as she waved enthusiastically at Tom, Gail, and Dan, who stood on the porch.

Sue opened her driver's door and paused before getting in. "Steve?"

"Yeah?"

"I'm glad you asked me to stay. I was honestly dreading going home to an empty house and pretending I was fine with spending Thanksgiving evening alone."

The admission hit Steve hard—the vulnerability in her voice, the honesty in her eyes, and the way she'd let her guard drop enough to tell him this.

"You shouldn't have to spend holidays alone," Steve said carefully. "You have people who care about you. Who want you around."

"Do I?" The question was soft, almost wondering.

Steve took a small step closer, close enough to see the uncertainty in her expression. "Yes. You do."

Sue held his gaze for a long moment, something unspoken passing between them that felt significant in ways Steve couldn't quite name. Then she smiled—small and genuine and achingly beautiful.

"Good to know. Goodnight, Steve."

"Night, Sue."

She climbed into her SUV and started the engine while Steve stepped back. Through the windshield, he could see Lindsey talking animatedly, probably already dissecting the evening's events.

Sue's vehicle pulled away, taillights disappearing down the drive toward the main road, and Steve stood watching until they vanished completely.

He turned back toward the house to find his entire family still standing on the porch watching him.

Steve climbed the porch steps slowly, bracing himself for whatever commentary was about to come.

But his mother just stepped forward and hugged him, her touch warm and understanding.

"That was a good thing you did tonight, son," Tom said simply.

Steve nodded, unable to trust his voice.

Dan slugged him in the arm and said, "Good job, Romeo."

Chapter 20

Sue stared at the laptop screen perched on the counter, her eyes scanning the specifications for commercial prep tables with the kind of intense focus usually reserved for reading legal documents. Around her, the restaurant hummed with productive energy—power tools whirring from the kitchen where Graham's crew worked, the rhythmic scrape of scrub brushes against wood as Carla and two servers cleaned tables and chairs.

"Option two has the stainless steel backsplash," Sue muttered to herself, clicking between browser tabs displaying equipment catalogs. "But option three includes the sink cutouts already configured."

From across the dining room, Carla looked up from where she was attacking a particularly stubborn soot stain. "You talking to yourself again?"

"It's the only way I get intelligent conversation around here," Sue shot back, earning a laugh from the servers.

"Rude." Carla dropped her scrub brush into a bucket and crossed to the counter, wiping her hands on her work jeans. "What are you wrestling with now?"

Sue turned the laptop so Carla could see the screen. "Prep tables for the kitchen. I need to order them today."

Carla leaned in, her practiced eye evaluating the options. "The backsplash on option two is nice, but we don't technically need it. Option three with the pre-cut sinks would save Graham's crew installation time."

"That's what I was thinking." Sue clicked to add option three to her digital cart. "One decision down. Approximately seven hundred to go."

"Dramatic much?"

"Have you seen this spreadsheet?" Sue gestured at the document open on a second screen—rows and rows of equipment needs, delivery schedules, and installation timelines color-coded in what looked like a rainbow threw up on Excel. "I'm currently juggling delivery windows for four ovens, two refrigeration units, and approximately seventeen miles of stainless-steel surfaces."

"You love this, and you know it. The organizing. The planning. The spreadsheets... all of it."

She couldn't argue. Despite the stress and the overwhelming nature of rebuilding an entire commercial kitchen, there was satisfaction in ordering new and updated equipment.

"Speaking of refrigeration," Carla said, tapping the screen. "What's happening with the walk-ins? You still debating options."

Sue pulled up another tab, this one showing industrial refrigeration units that cost more than her first car. "Both original units are completely shot. Fire damage on both of the compressors, smoke contamination in the cooling systems, and the electrical connections are toast."

"So we need two complete replacements."

"Yep," Sue confirmed. "The question is whether we go with the same sizes or upgrade."

"Upgrade how?"

Sue pulled up two side-by-side comparison images. "Our old units were eight by ten. We could replace them with the same dimensions, or—" she clicked to the second image "—we could go with a ten by twelve for each. Larger capacity, better organization, and more room for inventory during busy seasons."

Carla studied both options, her expression thoughtful. "Will the larger ones fit in the space?"

"Graham says yes."

"Cost difference?"

"Forty-two hundred dollars more than staying with the same size as our older models."

Carla whistled low. "That's significant."

"It is," Sue agreed. "But I can wing it financially. I'd have to tap into the business expense savings account, but it would genuinely improve our operational capacity—"

"You're talking yourself into the bigger ones."

"I'm talking myself into the bigger ones," Sue admitted.

"Then do it." Carla's voice was decisive. "If upgrading makes sense operationally, upgrade. The restaurant will benefit long-term."

Sue nodded slowly, her finger hovering over the order button before clicking with finality. "Done. Delivery scheduled for December fifteenth."

"Look at you, making big decisions before lunch."

"Speaking of lunch—" Sue checked her watch. "It's past eleven. Everyone should take a break. I packed sandwiches this morning."

Carla called out to the servers and stuck her head into the kitchen to inform Graham's crew. Within minutes, the entire group had migrated to the outdoor patio on the side of the building.

Sue retrieved the large cooler from her SUV and distributed sandwiches, chips, and bottled drinks. The November air was crisp but pleasant—a perfect fall day. The sun was warm enough to make eating outside enjoyable.

Sue settled at a table with Carla, eating her sandwich while her mind continued churning through decisions. "I'm thinking about paint colors for the dining room."

"Please tell me you're not going with beige. We've had that same color since the day you opened."

"I was actually considering something warmer. Maybe a sage green? With cream trim?"

Carla's eyes lit up. "I love that. Fresh but still cozy. Would go beautifully with those new light fixtures you ordered."

"And we need new curtains, obviously. The old ones are smoke damaged beyond saving." Sue pulled out her phone and started scrolling through fabric options she'd bookmarked. "Something in a natural linen, maybe?"

They were deep in discussion about window treatments when the sound of a vehicle pulling into the parking lot made Sue look up. Steve's fire department truck. Her stomach did that complicated thing it had been doing lately whenever he appeared unexpectedly.

He was wearing his official uniform—dark navy pants, a crisp white shirt with his chief's badge embroidered on the chest, and his radio clipped to his belt. Definitely not dressed for demolition work.

Steve walked to their table with steps that seemed almost hesitant, and Sue noticed the tension in his shoulders, the way his hand kept moving to his pocket before dropping back to his side. He was nervous about something.

"Hey," Steve said, his greeting encompassing everyone, but his eyes finding Sue's. "I didn't mean to interrupt lunch."

"You're not interrupting," Carla said easily. "Want a sandwich? Sue packed enough to feed an army."

"I'm good, thanks." Steve remained standing, shifting his weight in a way that amplified Sue's curiosity.

"Are you here for something specific?" She asked, trying to read his expression. "Is there a problem? Do you need to inspect something?"

"No, nothing like that." Steve cleared his throat. "Actually, I was hoping I could talk to you for a minute."

Carla stood immediately, grabbing her sandwich wrapper.

The servers followed her lead, leaving Sue and Steve alone at the patio table. Sue set down her half-eaten sandwich, her full attention on Steve, who looked increasingly uncomfortable.

"What's going on?" She asked. "You look nervous."

"I am nervous," Steve admitted. "I took the rest of the day off."

Sue's eyebrows rose. "You what?"

"Took the day off. I left Mark in charge at the station." Steve finally sat down across from her, his hands clasped on the table. "I know it's Friday and you're probably busy and Lindsey's with your parents shopping all day, but I was sitting at my desk this morning trying to focus on budget reports and inventory spreadsheets, and I just—I couldn't concentrate."

"Why not?"

Steve met her eyes directly. "Because all I could think about was you."

The admission hung between them, simple and devastating in its honesty. Sue's pulse quickened.

"I want to spend the afternoon with you," Steve continued, the words coming faster now, like he had to get them out before he lost his nerve. "It's a beautiful day. Perfect weather for getting outside and enjoying it. And I thought—maybe you'd want to take a break from the restaurant. Play hooky with me for a few hours."

She stared at him, trying to process what she was hearing. "Play hooky? Steve, you don't play hooky. You've probably never taken an unscheduled day off in your entire career."

"Which is exactly why I'm here." Steve's voice softened. "I'm trying to be different."

"But I'm working," Sue gestured vaguely at the restaurant behind them. "I have equipment to order and decisions to make and—"

"The construction crew has everything under control," Steve said. "Carla can handle any decisions that come up. You've been working nonstop. You deserve a break."

"I don't know." Sue felt torn between the practical voice that insisted she had too much to do and the impulsive part of her that desperately wanted to say yes. "What would we even do?"

"Go hiking." Steve's expression held something hopeful. "Beautiful views this time of year. We could just walk and talk and not think about restaurants or fires or anything complicated."

"Hiking? Where?"

"It's a surprise."

Sue opened her mouth to press for details when Carla appeared. "Go."

They both turned to find Carla standing nearby with her arms crossed.

"No arguments from you, Sue Smith," she continued, walking toward them with purpose. She grabbed the remains of Sue's lunch and other trash with efficient movements. "Just go. I'll lock the doors to this restaurant if I have to so you can't come inside and work, but honey, you are not allowed to work for the rest of the day. Go play hooky and act like you're a youngin' again."

Sue started to protest. "But the refrigeration unit order—"

"Already placed. Remember. I saw you click submit."

"The paint—"

"Can wait until Monday. Sue, the restaurant isn't going anywhere. Graham and his crew don't need you hovering. I can supervise just fine." Carla turned her attention to Steve, her voice taking on a warning edge. "Don't mess this up, or you'll have me to deal with."

"Understood," Steve said seriously.

Carla walked back toward the restaurant, leaving Sue and Steve alone again.

"So," Steve said carefully. "What do you think?"

Sue looked at him—really looked at him. Saw the vulnerability in his expression, the hope he was trying to hide, and the way his whole body seemed to be braced for rejection. He'd taken the rest of the day off work. For her.

"I need to change," Sue heard herself say. "I'm not hiking in work jeans."

Steve's expression transformed, surprise giving way to relief mixed with joy. "Really? You'll go?"

"Apparently." Sue stood, her decision made even though part of her brain was still protesting the irresponsibility of leaving when there was work to be done. "But I need details. How long of a hike are we talking about? What should I wear? Should I bring water? Snacks?"

"It's about a two-hour hike. Moderate difficulty. Wear layers—it's warm now but will cool off in the shade. I'll bring water and trail mix. Meet me at the fire station in an hour?"

Sue nodded, still processing that she'd agreed to this. "Fire station. One hour."

She walked to her SUV on autopilot, her mind spinning with implications. She was playing hooky from work. With her ex-husband. To go hiking to a mysterious location he wouldn't specify. This was impulsive and irresponsible and completely unlike her.

It felt terrifying.

It felt wonderful.

She climbed into her vehicle and sat for a moment, hands on the steering wheel, while she watched Steve drive away in his truck. Through the restaurant windows, she could see Carla giving her a thumbs up and a shooing motion.

She started the engine and pulled out of the parking lot, heading toward her house with a mixture of anticipation and nerves churning in her stomach.

She was going hiking with Steve.

Spending the afternoon with him.

Voluntarily.

Because she wanted to.

When had she started wanting to spend time with him again? When had the walls she'd so carefully maintained started feeling more like a prison than protection?

Sue pulled into her driveway fifteen minutes later and hurried inside, already mentally cataloging her closet for appropriate hiking clothes. She found her favorite leggings, layered a fitted athletic t-shirt under a fleece pullover, and laced up the hiking boots she hadn't worn in weeks.

In the bathroom mirror, she paused to really look at herself. Her cheeks were flushed—whether from hurrying or nerves, she couldn't say. Her eyes looked brighter than they had in weeks, maybe months. She looked like someone anticipating something good.

Sue grabbed a hair tie and pulled her hair into a ponytail, applied fresh deodorant, and added a swipe of tinted lip balm before stopping herself. This wasn't a date. This was just a hike. Two co-parents spending time together on a nice afternoon.

Except it felt like more than that.

She grabbed her small backpack, checked that her phone was charged, tossed in a couple of water bottles, just in case, and headed back out to her SUV. During the drive to the fire station, she spent the entire time trying to calm the butterflies that had taken up residence in her stomach.

Steve's truck was already there when she pulled into the parking lot. He'd changed into cargo pants and a thermal shirt under a fleece jacket. He was loading items into a hiking backpack when Sue approached.

"Perfect timing," he said, looking up with a smile that did complicated things to her pulse. "Ready for an adventure?"

Sue looked at him—at the genuine happiness in his expression—and felt something inside her shift and settle.

"Yeah," she said. "I'm ready."

Chapter 21

Steve's truck climbed the winding mountain road, taking curves with the kind of easy familiarity that came from driving them hundreds of times. Beside him, Sue sat with her window cracked, crisp air streaming through the cab while she watched the landscape roll past.

"You're really not going to tell me where we're going?" She asked, not for the first time since they'd left the fire station.

"Nope." Steve kept his eyes on the road, fighting a smile. "It's a surprise."

"I don't like surprises."

"Since when? You used to love surprises."

"That was before I learned that surprises usually mean something's on fire or broken or both."

Steve grinned. "Fair point. But I promise—no fires today."

Sue settled back in her seat, seemingly content to let the mystery unfold. The November sun filtered through trees still clinging to the last remnants of autumn color—gold and rust and deep burgundy against the evergreen pines. The past few days of unseasonably warm weather had melted most of the snow from the valleys, though Steve knew they'd encounter patches as they climbed higher.

"It really is beautiful up here," Sue said, her voice softer now. "I forget sometimes. Get so caught up in the restaurant and daily life that I forget how gorgeous these mountains are."

"Easy to do when you see them every day."

"Do you ever miss it? Living in the city, I mean. When you were at the academy in Charleston?"

Steve considered the question. "Every so often. The convenience, maybe. Bigger selection of restaurants. But I never seriously wanted to stay there."

They drove in comfortable silence for another few miles before Steve turned onto a narrower road, gravel crunching beneath the tires. When he made a right turn onto a dirt access road leading to the trailhead, Steve felt his pulse quicken with nerves.

This could go very wrong.

Sue straightened in her seat. Steve watched her process the familiar landmarks—the split oak tree marking the turn, the hand-painted wooden sign indicating the trail name, and the small parking area with space for maybe a dozen vehicles.

"Steve." Sue's voice changed. "This is—"

"I know." He parked and cut the engine. "I wasn't sure if I should bring you here. But it's always been my favorite trail, and I thought—" He stopped, uncertain.

Sue sat very still, her eyes fixed on the trailhead marker visible through the windshield. The silence stretched so long that Steve started to regret the entire plan.

"We used to come here all the time together," she finally said.

"Yeah. We did."

"Steve—"

"We don't have to hike it." Steve turned to face her fully. "If this is too much, we can go somewhere else. Anywhere else."

She looked at him. "You brought me to the place where you proposed."

"I brought you to a beautiful trail with incredible views that we used to hike all the time when we were younger."

They sat in the truck cab, the engine ticking as it cooled, while Steve mentally kicked himself for thinking this was a good idea. But then she opened her door and climbed out, moving toward the trailhead with purpose.

Steve grabbed his backpack and followed, catching up as she stopped at the wooden map display showing the trail route. Her finger traced the path they'd walked dozens of times years ago.

"Two miles to the waterfall," Sue said.

"You still want to do this?"

Sue turned to face him, and Steve saw determination in her expression. "I'm here, aren't I?"

They started up the trail, their boots finding purchase on the familiar packed earth. The path began with a gentle incline through a mixed hardwood forest, sunlight dappling through half-bare branches overhead. He let Sue set the pace, staying slightly behind to give her space to process whatever she was feeling.

The trail hadn't changed much. The same wooden bridge crossing the first creek bed. The same massive boulder they'd always stopped to rest against. Same marker indicating the halfway point.

"I've brought Lindsey here," Sue said suddenly, breaking the silence they'd maintained for nearly twenty minutes. "A few times over the past couple of years. She loves the waterfall. I come alone sometimes too... hike when Lindsey's in school."

"I didn't know that."

"Why would you?"

"True," Steve said as he navigated a rocky section of trails. "For what it's worth, I come here sometimes too. When I need to think."

Sue stopped walking and turned to face him. "You still hike this trail?"

"A couple of times a month, usually. More in summer." Steve met her eyes.

Sue turned and resumed walking. "All this time, we've both been coming to the same place separately."

"Seems that way."

They walked in silence again. The temperature dropped a little as they gained elevation, and Steve noticed patches of snow clinging to the shaded north-facing slopes.

"Cold?" Steve asked.

"A little. But it feels good. Fresh."

They reached a section where the trail narrowed. Steve went first, testing footholds and warning her about slippery spots. When they emerged onto a wider section, Sue came alongside him.

"You pointed out that oak tree once before when we hiked here," Sue said, gesturing to a massive tree whose roots created natural steps in the trail. "Said it was probably two hundred years old."

"Still is," Steve said with a grin. "Though now it's most likely about two hundred and fourteen years old, assuming my math was right the first time."

She surprised him with a laugh—genuine and unguarded. "Always so literal."

"Someone has to be. You're the creative dreamer. I'm the practical realist."

"Were," Sue corrected. "We were those things. Past tense."

"Are we not those things anymore?"

Sue considered this. "Maybe we still are. Just with more complications."

The sound of rushing water grew louder as they approached the final section of the trail. Steve's nerves returned with intensity as they climbed the last steep incline toward the waterfall overlook.

When they emerged at the viewing platform, Steve stopped to let Sue take in the view. The waterfall cascaded down a rocky cliff face in multiple tiers, water flowing in the afternoon sunlight. Massive icicles hung from the cliff edges where spray had frozen, creating crystal formations that caught and refracted light. The pool at the base of the waterfall churned white and cold.

It was as breathtaking as Steve remembered. It was as beautiful as it had been the day he'd brought Sue here the first time when they were dating years ago. Just as stunning as the morning he'd proposed with shaking hands and a heart full of certainty that she was his forever.

Sue walked to the railing, her hands gripping the weathered wood, and Steve watched her shoulders rise and fall with deep breaths. He joined her, both of them staring at the waterfall.

"It's beautiful," she said finally.

"It's my favorite spot."

"Mine too. Which makes it complicated."

Steve understood. This place held their best memories and their greatest hopes—all of which had crumbled under the weight of his ambition and selfishness.

"I come here to pray sometimes," Steve said. "When I need clarity or perspective or just to feel close to something bigger than my own mess."

"What do you pray about?"

"Depends on the day. Sometimes about work. Sometimes about Lindsey. Sometimes—" He stopped, unsure how honest to be.

"Sometimes about you and me?" Sue finished.

"Yeah. Sometimes about you and me."

Sue turned to face him then, and Steve saw tears threatening in her eyes. "Why are you doing this? Why did you bring me here? Why did you take time off work today?" Her voice rose slightly with each question. "What do you want from me?"

The questions were raw and demanding. Steve took his time answering, knowing this moment mattered more than any other since that Sunday morning when he'd run into a burning building to save her restaurant.

"I want a second chance," he said quietly. "I want the opportunity to prove that I've changed. I've learned what matters. That I can be the partner you deserve."

"I know it's asking a lot," he continued. "I know I have no right to ask for anything after how badly I failed us. I can't stop hoping that maybe—just maybe—we could find our way back to each other."

"You're serious."

"Completely serious," he took a small step closer. "I'm not asking you to forget what happened or pretend the past didn't matter. I'm asking if you'd be willing to try again. To see if what we had could be rebuilt into something even better."

Sue stared at him, emotions warring across her face. "Are you seeing anyone?"

The question surprised Steve. "What? No. I haven't dated anyone since the divorce."

"Not once?"

"Not once." Steve held her gaze. "What about you?"

Sue's expression shifted to something that might have been embarrassment. "No. I haven't either."

"Six years and neither of us has dated anyone else?"

"We're a mess," Sue said, but she was laughing now—slightly hysterical laughter that broke the tension. "You know that, right? We're both complete disasters."

"I know." Steve found himself laughing too. "We're thirty-four and thirty-six, divorced, still hung up on each other, and neither of us has managed to move on."

"It's pathetic."

"It's something."

Sue's laughter faded. "The spark between us never really went away, did it?"

"No. It didn't."

They stood looking at each other while the waterfall thundered behind them, filling the silence with steady white noise. Steve saw Sue working through something, her mind processing possibilities and risks.

"I'm scared," she finally admitted. "Terrified, actually. Of getting hurt again. Of letting you close enough to destroy me again."

"I know. I'm scared too."

"Of what?"

"Of disappointing you. Of falling back into old patterns. Of proving that people don't really change, and I'm still the same selfish workaholic who chose career over family."

Sue nodded slowly. "If we did this—and I'm saying if, not yes—there would have to be boundaries."

"Okay... what kind of boundaries?"

"Nothing crazy," Sue said quickly. "Just—we take it slow. Really slow. We communicate honestly even when it's uncomfortable. We have to consider Lindsey in every decision because this affects her more than it affects us."

"I agree with all of that."

"And if it's not working, if we're falling into the same problems that ruined us before, we have to be honest enough to admit it and stop before we cause more damage."

"Fair." Steve took another small step closer. "Anything else?"

Sue worried her bottom lip, thinking. "If we try and it fails, we have to be civil and functional for Lindsey's sake."

"We can do that." Steve paused. "Are you saying you're willing to try?"

"This is insane. But yes. I'm willing to try."

Relief flooded through Steve so intensely it made him dizzy. "Really?"

"Really. We're going to have to tell Lindsey something at some point."

"Eventually. But not yet. Not until we figure out what this is."

"Agreed." Sue glanced at her watch. "It's almost four. We should probably start heading back."

Steve nodded, recognizing the need to end this conversation before the weight of what they'd just decided became overwhelming. They'd climbed a mountain today—both literally and figuratively. Coming back down would require just as much care.

"Can I ask you something?" Steve said.

"Of course."

"Do you still love me?"

Sue's head whipped around so fast she nearly lost her footing. He reached out instinctively to steady her. She looked down at his hand on her arm, then back up at him.

He let go, unsure of what might come next, and took a small step back.

"I do. Even after everything you put me through, I still love you. That never went away."

He held out his hand to her—a gesture both momentous and simple. An offering. An invitation.

Sue looked at his hand, then up at his face. Slowly, she reached out and took it, her fingers sliding between his with a rightness that made his chest ache.

They stood like that for a moment at the waterfall overlook, where he'd once promised her forever. This time felt different—less about grand vows, more about quiet hope. Less about certainty, more about courage.

"Ready?" Steve asked.

"Yeah," Sue said. "Let's go."

They turned and started back down the trail, hands still joined, navigating the rocky path with careful steps. The descent would be easier in some ways, harder in others. Just like whatever came next for them.

Steve kept his eyes on the path, acutely aware of her hand warm in his, and wondered if they were brave, or foolish, or some uncertain mix of both.

Behind them, the waterfall kept its endless cascade—steady, unbothered, indifferent to human hopes and fears—just as it had been the day he'd proposed and every day since.

But ahead stretched something new: uncertain, fragile, and a little terrifying.

And for the first time in years, Steve let himself believe it might be possible.

Chapter 22

"Six gallons of the sage green and six of the tinted primer," Sue said, handing her brother the paint color sample she'd chosen.

Matt took the sample and examined it under the hardware store's fluorescent lights. "Nice choice. Should look good with the cream trim you mentioned."

"That's the plan." Sue leaned against the counter, watching as Matt disappeared into the back room for something. Her father emerged from the same direction, his reading glasses perched on his nose.

"Six gallons of paint and six of primer? Did I hear you correctly? Are you painting the whole restaurant or just the dining room?"

"Just the dining room. But I want extras in case we need touch-ups later." Sue pulled out her phone to double-check her measurements.

Earl nodded, already pulling up the paint formulas in the computer system. Even in semi-retirement, he couldn't quite let go of coming to work in the hardware store that he had been a part of daily since he'd been a young man. "Is Graham's crew doing the painting, or are you hiring that out?"

"My staff and I will do all the painting. I want Graham's crew to stay focused on the kitchen repairs."

"Smart." Earl began dispersing tints into open gallons of paint. "How's everything else going? Have you ordered new kitchen equipment yet?"

"All ordered." Sue smiled. "If everything stays on track, I'll be able to open back up before Christmas, just like I'd hoped for."

Matt had returned meanwhile and placed a closed gallon of paint in the mechanical shaker. The machine roared to life, and he raised his voice over the noise. "That's good news, sis. Glad everything is going well."

"Me too. Assuming nothing goes wrong. I'll have my restaurant reopened, and life can return to normal soon."

"Don't jinx your luck," Earl warned, though his eyes held warmth. He paused in his measuring to really look at his daughter. "You seem different today."

"Different how?"

"Happier." Earl returned to his work but kept glancing at her. "You've been working yourself to exhaustion for weeks, but today you look like you're actually enjoying yourself."

Sue felt heat creep up her neck. "I've been sleeping better."

"That's good," Matt said, pulling the gallon from the shaker and starting on the second. "You needed rest."

"I can see the finish line now," Sue continued. "The restaurant is actually going to reopen. All this work is leading somewhere instead of just feeling endless."

"But that's not all of it, is it?" Earl asked as he studied her with a paternal perception that had always made lying impossible.

Sue took a deep breath. She could deflect, change the subject, or offer some vague platitude. Or she could be honest.

"Steve and I are trying again."

"Trying again," Earl repeated. "As in… what?"

"As in seeing if we can rebuild what we had," she kept her voice steady and met her dad's eyes. "We're taking it slow. Being careful. But we're trying."

Earl walked around the counter to stand directly in front of her, his weathered hands finding hers. "Is that really what you want, Sue-bug?"

"It is." She said as she squeezed his hands, willing him to understand. "I know it's complicated. I know the risks. But yes, Dad. It's what I want."

He studied her face for a long moment, and Sue saw the war playing out behind his eyes—the protective father who'd watched his daughter's heart break warring with the man who wanted his child to be happy.

"You remember what I said before?" His voice was gentle but firm. "Leopards don't change their spots. Workaholics don't suddenly become family men."

"I remember." Sue felt her throat tighten. "But Dad, is that really how I should look at this? Isn't it better to believe in God and trust? You and Mom raised me to believe in forgiveness and second chances and redemption. Doesn't Steve deserve the same grace we'd extend to anyone else?"

Earl's expression shifted, surprise flickering across his weathered features. He was quiet for a long moment, his hands still holding hers.

"You're right," he said finally. "Faith means believing people can change, that God can work miracles in hearts and lives." He paused, then added, "But faith doesn't mean being foolish either. Be careful, sweetheart. Guard your heart even as you open it."

"I will." Sue pulled her father into a hug, feeling his solid presence the way she had since childhood when things felt uncertain. "I promise I will."

When she stepped back, Earl's eyes were suspiciously bright. "If he hurts you again—"

"Then I'll survive it," she said firmly. "The same way I survived the first time. But I have to try, Dad. I can't spend the rest of my life wondering what might have been."

Earl nodded slowly, then returned to his paint mixing. Matt caught Sue's eye and offered a small, encouraging smile before starting the shaker on another gallon.

For the next ten minutes, the industrial machines provided white noise while Earl and Matt systematically worked. Sue watched them, these two men who'd always been constants in her life, and felt grateful for their presence even if they didn't understand her choices.

When the last gallon finished mixing, Matt loaded everything onto a flatbed cart. "Let's get this up to the register and then out to your vehicle."

The three of them made quick work of ringing up the purchase and hauling everything outside to where Sue's SUV sat parked in front of the store.

"Shoot. I'll be right back—I forgot to grab you some paint-stirring sticks, Sue," Earl said as Matt and Sue started loading the gallons into her vehicle.

"You're doing the right thing," Matt said eventually. "For what it's worth."

"You think so?"

"I do. I always thought you and Steve were meant to be together, even when things fell apart. Sometimes, people need to grow separately before they can grow together. He's changed, Sue. Anyone with eyes can see that. And you're different too—stronger, more sure of yourself."

"I think we've both changed. I think we're better versions of ourselves now."

"You are," he said as he straightened and closed the tailgate with a solid thunk. "Just promise me you'll actually let yourself be happy. Don't sabotage it because you're afraid."

Sue nodded. "I'll try."

Earl emerged with a handful of wooden paint-stirring sticks and handed them to her. Then he stepped back, looking at his daughter with an expression that held both love and lingering concern.

"Drive safe," he said. "And Sue? I'm here if you need me. Always."

"I know, Dad. Love you."

"Love you too, Sue-bug."

Sue hugged both men, then climbed into her SUV and watched them walk back into the hardware store together—her father's hand on her brother's shoulder, both their heads bent in what was probably continued discussion of her announcement.

She sat there, engine idling, letting the conversation settle. Earl's concern was understandable. He'd seen her pain before, during, and after the divorce. He'd helped her pick up the pieces when her marriage had ended. Of course, he'd be cautious about her opening herself up to the possibility of hurt again.

Sue pulled out her phone, her thumb hovering over Steve's contact for just a moment before typing: *You free for lunch at Martha's?*

The response came within seconds: *Sure.*

Sue smiled and typed back: *Meet you there in ten?*

Three dots appeared, then: *See you there.*

She set the phone in the cup holder and pulled out of the parking space, her heart doing that complicated flutter it had been doing every time she thought about him lately. They'd texted a few times since Friday's hike, brief exchanges about Lindsey's schedule or mundane details about their days. They'd talked on the phone Saturday and Sunday evenings after he had gotten off work. Nothing deep or significant.

But asking him to lunch felt significant. It felt like taking another step forward into the unknown. It felt like she was actually dating her ex-husband.

"Dating my ex-husband," she said out loud.

She smiled as she drove through downtown Laurel Ridge toward Martha's Diner.

Chapter 23

Steve stood at the front window of the diner, watching Sue's silver SUV pull into the small parking area across Main Street. She climbed out, checked something on her phone, then looked both ways before crossing. The afternoon sun caught her hair, and Steve felt his chest do that thing it had been doing lately whenever he saw her—a combination of nervousness and anticipation that made him feel like a teenager again.

She spotted him through the window and smiled, raising one hand in a small wave. He returned it and then moved toward the door to greet her as she entered.

"Hey," Sue said, slightly breathless.

"Hey yourself," he said and then led her to a booth near the back. "Is this okay?"

"Perfect."

They slid onto opposite sides of the booth, and Steve was acutely aware of how normal this felt—like they'd done this a thousand times before. Which they had, of course, back when things were simple and uncomplicated.

Martha appeared almost immediately, coffeepot in hand and a smile on her face. "Well, look who's here. Together. At lunchtime. On a Tuesday."

"Hi Martha," Steve said.

"Martha," Sue greeted, her cheeks slightly pink.

"Coffee for both?"

"Please," they said in unison, then laughed at the synchronization.

Martha filled both their cups. "I'll give you a minute to look at the menu, then I'll be back for your orders."

She disappeared toward the kitchen, leaving them with menus they both knew by heart. Steve pretended to study his while watching Sue over the laminated edge.

"So," she said, setting down her menu. "I just bought the paint for the dining room at the restaurant."

"Really?"

"Yep. Six gallons of sage green and six of primer." Her enthusiasm was evident in her voice. "We can start painting tomorrow. The dining room is ready."

"That's great. Really great. How much longer until the health inspection?"

"Two weeks, hopefully. The electrical is still being worked on, but Graham is confident that should wrap up soon, and they'll work on all the plumbing next." Sue wrapped her hands around her coffee mug. "If everything goes smoothly, we might actually make it by Christmas."

"You'll make it," Steve said with certainty. "You've handled everything that's been thrown at you so far. A health inspection is nothing compared to what you've already accomplished."

She smiled at that. "Thanks. I needed to hear that today."

They fell into a comfortable conversation about the restaurant—the new walk-in refrigerators, the updated electrical system, and her vision for rebranding the restaurant with a fresh new look. Steve found himself genuinely interested in every detail, asking questions about things he knew nothing about just to keep her talking. There was something captivating about watching her discuss her work, seeing the passion and determination that had always been part of who she was.

Martha returned with her order pad. "What can I get you two?"

"Turkey club," Steve said. "With fries."

"I'll have the chicken Caesar salad. Extra dressing on the side."

"Coming right up." Martha collected the menus and headed back toward the kitchen.

Steve took a sip of his coffee, searching for the next topic. "Lindsey's birthday party is this Saturday."

"Her twelfth birthday." Sue's expression shifted to something between excitement and mild stress. "I cannot believe she's turning twelve. Time has passed so quickly. So far, ten of her friends are coming, plus both of our families."

"That's a lot of people."

"I know. Thank goodness she agreed to have the party at home; I really didn't want to make arrangements to rent a building or have her party somewhere else since we can't have it at the restaurant like usual," she pulled out her phone and scrolled. "I've got decorations, the cake's ordered from Taste of Heaven, and I'm doing finger foods. Mom's bringing ice cream and cookies, and your mom is bringing chips and drinks."

"What can I do to help?" Steve asked.

Sue looked up from her phone, surprise evident in her expression. "What?"

"I want to help. What do you need me to do?"

"I—" Sue seemed genuinely caught off guard. "Everything's mostly done. The pizzas are being delivered from The Pizza Place in Fayetteville, and I've got everything else covered."

"There has to be something I can do," Steve pressed. "Can I come early and help you decorate? Set up tables? Anything?"

She studied him for a long moment, and he wondered what she was thinking. "You really want to help decorate?"

"I really do."

"That would actually be really helpful. I was dreading trying to hang streamers and blow up balloons by myself."

"Consider it done." Steve felt absurdly pleased at being useful. "What time should I be there?"

"Party starts at two. Maybe come around eleven?"

"I'll be there at eleven." Steve paused, then added, "And I can pick up the cake. Save you a trip."

"Steve, you don't have to—"

"I want to." He held her gaze. "Please. Let me."

She nodded slowly. "Okay. The cake. Thank you."

"No thanks necessary."

Martha arrived with their food, setting plates down with practiced efficiency. "Anything else I can get you two?"

"We're good, thanks," Steve said.

They ate in comfortable silence for a few minutes, the diner's lunch crowd providing a pleasant background hum of conversation and clinking silverware. He found himself studying Sue between bites—the way she carefully arranged her salad before eating and the small smile that played at her lips when she caught him looking.

"What?" Sue asked.

"Nothing. Just—" he searched for words that wouldn't sound too heavy. "This is nice. Having lunch together."

"It is nice," she said as she speared a piece of chicken. "We should do this more often."

"I'd like that."

They continued eating, conversation flowing naturally from topic to topic—her upcoming choir practices for the Christmas play at church, the unusually warm November weather and the forecasted snow coming soon.

"Has Lindsey said anything to you about Thanksgiving?" Steve asked. "About all of us having dinner together at my parents house?"

"She's been floating on cloud nine ever since. She keeps asking when we're going to do it again."

"She's asked me a couple of times as well when she's called. What did you tell her?"

"That we'll see. That things are complicated." Sue set down her fork. "She understands more than we give her credit for, but she's also still young enough to believe in simple happy endings."

"Is that what we are?" Steve asked. "Complicated?"

"Aren't we?"

"I guess so." Steve finished his sandwich, wiping his hands on his napkin. "But maybe that's okay. Maybe complicated is better than what we were before."

"Politely distant?"

"Something like that."

Sue laughed at that—genuine amusement that made Steve grin in response. This was what he'd missed so much: easy laughter over lunch, comfortable conversation about nothing and everything, and the simple pleasure of spending time together.

"I should probably get back to the restaurant," she said eventually, though she made no move to stand. "Carla's supervising the afternoon work, but I should check in."

"And I need to get back to the station." Steve signaled Martha for the check. "Mark's been covering, but I've got paperwork that won't do itself."

Martha brought the check, and Steve grabbed it before Sue could reach for it.

"I can pay for myself," she protested.

"I know you can. But I'm paying."

Sue shook her head but didn't argue further. He left cash on the table—enough to cover the meal plus a generous tip—and they both slid out of the booth.

Martha intercepted them near the door, pulling Sue into a brief hug, then doing the same with Steve. "I'm glad you came in today... it made my day, and I expect to see you both again soon."

Steve looked at Sue, and she grinned.

"You will, Martha."

They stepped out onto Main Street, the afternoon air crisp and cool. Steve walked beside Sue toward the crosswalk.

At the curb, he held out his arm. "May I?"

Sue looked at his offered arm, then up at his face, something unreadable in her expression. Then she wrapped her hand around his forearm.

They crossed Main Street together, Steve acutely aware of her hand on his arm and the subtle scent of her perfume. When they reached her SUV, he opened her door, holding it while she climbed in.

"I'm glad you wanted to have lunch today."

"Me too."

He fought every instinct that urged him to lean in, to close the distance between them, to kiss her the way he'd been wanting to. Instead, he stepped back and closed her door gently, watching as she started the engine and backed out of the parking space.

He stood there until her SUV disappeared down Main Street, then walked to his own truck and climbed inside. For a moment, he just sat there, hands on the steering wheel, processing what had just happened.

It had been a simple lunch. Nothing dramatic or momentous. Just two people sharing a meal and easy conversation.

But it had also been everything.

Steve bowed his head, his hands still gripping the wheel.

"God," he said quietly. "I don't want to mess this up. Please—give me wisdom. Give me patience. Help me be the man she deserves, the man You want me to be. Guide me through this, because I don't trust myself not to ruin it again."

Chapter 24

"Mom! Mom, guess what?" Lindsey's backpack bounced against her shoulders as she sprinted across the elementary school parking lot, her ponytail streaming behind her.

Sue pushed off from where she'd been leaning against her SUV, noting her daughter's enthusiasm.

"I'm so excited!" Lindsey reached the vehicle and yanked open the passenger door, flinging her backpack onto the floor before climbing in.

"Seatbelt, Lindsey." Sue slid behind the wheel, starting the engine while Lindsey fumbled with the buckle. "What's got you so wound up?"

"Everything!" Lindsey finally clicked the seatbelt into place and turned to face her mom. "The tree lighting ceremony is this Friday, and everyone at school is talking about it, and Sarah said her family is going early to get good spots, and Ben's mom is making cookies, and Mrs. Phillips showed us pictures from last year's ceremony in art class today, and—"

"Lindsey... slow down, honey," Sue said, pulling out of the parking lot.

Lindsey sucked in an exaggerated breath, then continued without missing a beat. "I just really, really want to make sure we're going. You haven't forgotten, have you? Because I know you've been super busy with the restaurant and everything, but it's kind of really important and—"

"Lindsey." Sue reached over and squeezed her daughter's hand. "I haven't forgotten. We go every year. Why would this year be different?"

"Because everything's been different this year." Lindsey's voice lost some of its manic energy, settling into something quieter. "The fire... you've been so tired and working a lot, and I just thought maybe—"

"Hey, I'm sorry I've been distracted. But sweetheart, we are absolutely going to the tree lighting. It's tradition. We wouldn't miss it."

The smile that broke across Lindsey's face could have powered the town's Christmas lights. "Really? Promise?"

"Promise."

They drove through downtown Laurel Ridge, and Sue found herself caught up in her daughter's renewed enthusiasm as Lindsey pressed her face against the window, cataloging every new decoration that had appeared in town.

"Look! They put wreaths on all the lampposts on Main Street!" Lindsey pointed. "And there's garland around the poles too, with the red bows. Ms. Williams from the flower place must have done those."

Sue slowed the SUV as they approached the town square, where a large crowd of volunteers bustled around the massive tree that had been erected in the center of the space. The tree stood at least thirty feet tall, its branches still bare of decoration but magnificent in its natural state against the late afternoon sky.

"Oh wow, the tree is so big this year!" Ladders stood around the tree, and several people worked on stringing lights and hanging large ornaments in various colors. "Look at all the people helping. Is that Mr. Cooper? And Mrs. Morris!"

The tree lighting had been a Laurel Ridge tradition for as long as she could remember—longer, probably, stretching back through generations of families who'd gathered in this same spot to mark the beginning of the Christmas season.

"I love Christmas." Lindsey's voice held wonder. "Everything is so pretty and magical."

They continued past the square, passing businesses that had transformed their storefronts into winter wonderlands. Martha's Diner sported white lights outlining every window and a cheerful snowman display beside the entrance. The Book Nook had created an elaborate winter scene in its front window, complete with miniature carolers and a tiny snow-covered village. Even her dad's hardware store had gotten into the spirit with oversized candy canes flanking the door.

"Grandpa's decorations look good this year," Lindsey observed. "Better than last year."

Sue smiled, remembering her father's grumbling about excessive holiday displays while her mother had insisted on at least making an effort.

They reached the far edge of town, where businesses gave way to residential streets and mountain views. Sue prepared to turn onto the road leading toward home when Lindsey spoke again, her tone shifting from observational to carefully casual.

"So... I was thinking." Lindsey picked at the zipper on her jacket. "About Friday."

"What about Friday?"

"Well, you and I are going to the tree lighting." Lindsey's careful tone set off warning bells in Sue's mind. "... could Dad come too?"

"I don't know if your dad's working Friday evening. His schedule can be unpredictable."

"But if he's not working?" Lindsey pressed. "If he's free, could he come? With us? Like, all together?"

Sue glanced at her daughter, taking in the hope written across her young face. This wasn't just about the tree lighting.

"Why don't you ask him?"

Lindsey's head whipped around. "Really?"

"Really. Call your dad and see if he's free Friday evening. If he is, and if he wants to come, then yes. He can join us."

"Can we just go to the fire station? Like, right now? Please? It's not even four yet, and I know he's there because he told me yesterday his shift doesn't end until six today, and the fire station is right back through town, and it would only take a few minutes, and—"

"Yes, we can go to the station," Sue said, slowing the SUV, looking for a safe place to turn around.

"Yes!" Lindsey bounced in her seat, that manic energy returning full force. "Thank you, thank you, thank you!"

Sue turned around and headed back toward downtown.

Lindsey's excitement was contagious, and Sue found herself smiling as her daughter resumed her running commentary on the Christmas decorations, this time pointing out details she'd missed on the first pass through town.

As they neared the fire station, two bay doors stood open, revealing the gleaming red engines inside. A few firefighters moved around the trucks, performing maintenance checks.

Sue pulled into the visitor parking area and barely had the vehicle in park before Lindsey unbuckled and bolted for the open bay doors.

"Lindsey, wait—"

But her daughter was already gone, disappearing into the station with single-minded purpose.

Sue climbed out more slowly, taking a moment to smooth her wrinkled top. She was still wearing the jeans and casual top she'd thrown on that morning, her hair pulled back in a simple ponytail because she'd been painting the new trim work at the restaurant this afternoon before the school pickup.

She walked through the bay door into the familiar warmth of the firehouse. Voices echoed from deeper in the building—Lindsey's rapid-fire chatter rising above masculine laughter.

Sue followed the sound, rounding the corner into the common area where several firefighters had gathered. Luke sat at a table cleaning equipment, while Ray stood near the coffee pot. And there was Steve, looking slightly bewildered as Lindsey gesticulated wildly in front of him.

"—and there are wreaths on every lamppost and garland with red bows, and the tree in the square is huge, Dad, I mean really huge, like the biggest one ever, and there are so many people helping decorate it, and Mrs. Morris was there, and Mr. Cooper, and everyone's getting ready, and the whole town looks like something out of a Christmas movie, and—"

"Princess, slow down," Steve said, his hands settling on Lindsey's shoulders. "I can't understand half of what you're saying."

"Christmas!" Lindsey said, as if that explained everything. "The tree lighting is Friday, and everyone's so excited, and the decorations are everywhere, and it's going to be so beautiful, and—" She paused, finally taking a breath. "Will you come with us?"

Steve's eyes found Sue's over Lindsey's head. The question in his expression was clear, and Sue smiled.

"Come with you where?" Steve asked, his attention returning to their daughter even as his awareness of Sue remained palpable.

"To the tree-lighting ceremony, Dad! Friday night! Mom said I could ask you, and so I'm asking—will you come? With us?"

Around them, the other firefighters had gone conspicuously quiet, pretending interest in their various tasks while obviously listening.

Steve's gaze returned to Sue. "Would that be okay with you?"

Sue stepped closer. "It would. If you're free."

"I'm off duty by four."

"It starts at seven," Lindsey said. "But we should go early because it gets crowded, and we want good spots and—"

"How about this," Steve interrupted gently. "I could pick you both up around five. We could have dinner at Martha's first, then head to the square with plenty of time before the ceremony starts."

"Sounds like a plan," Sue said. "Martha's at five, tree lighting at seven."

"Yes!" Lindsey threw her arms around his waist, squeezing tight.

Steve hugged their daughter back, his eyes still on Sue. The smile on his face made her stomach flip.

Luke appeared at the edge of Sue's vision, his friendly grin directed at all three of them. "The tree lighting's a great tradition."

"Wouldn't miss it," Steve confirmed, finally releasing Lindsey but keeping one hand on her shoulder. "It's one of my favorite nights of the year."

"Mine too!" Lindsey's enthusiasm showed no signs of dimming. "Except maybe Christmas Eve and Christmas Day and my birthday and—"

"We get it," Sue said with a laugh. "You have many favorite days."

Ray approached with his characteristic quiet presence, nodding at Sue. "Good to see you, Sue. Restaurant coming along?"

"Better every day. We start painting the walls in the dining room tomorrow."

"That's good to hear. It sounds like you're moving right along. I'm off next Monday and may stop by and lend a hand if that's alright with you."

"I'd love it if you came to help, Ray."

Sue turned her attention back to Steve and said, "We should let you all get back to work. I'm sure you have things to do."

"Nothing that can't wait," Steve said, as he naturally fell into step beside her as they headed back toward the bay. Lindsey skipped ahead, her mission accomplished and her joy evident in every bouncing step.

They emerged into the late afternoon light. The November sun hung low on the horizon, painting everything in shades of amber and rose. Sue turned to face Steve.

"Friday then," she said.

"Friday. I'll pick you both up at five."

"We'll be ready."

They stood looking at each other while Lindsey climbed into the SUV. The moment stretched, comfortable and charged at once.

"This is our first public outing as a family," Steve said quietly. "As... whatever we are now."

"I know." Sue resisted the urge to step closer, aware of potential eyes watching from inside the station. "Are you okay with that?"

"More than okay." His hand twitched at his side, as if he wanted to reach for her but was restraining himself. "I want people to see us together, Sue. Want them to know I'm trying to be the man you deserve."

"You're already that man, Steve."

His expression shifted to something so tender it made her breath catch. Before either of them could say anything else, Lindsey's voice carried through the open window.

"Mom! Are we going, or are you and Dad just going to stand there staring at each other all afternoon?"

Heat crept up Sue's neck. "I'm coming."

She turned toward her vehicle, but Steve's voice stopped her.

"Sue?"

She looked back.

"Thank you. For letting me be a part of this. For giving me another chance to do this right."

Sue nodded, not trusting her voice, and walked to her SUV.

Lindsey was texting furiously, her fingers flying across the screen. "Sarah's going to flip when I tell her Dad's coming with us. She said her parents might even go together, but they're not, like, together-together anymore, so it's not the same thing, but still—"

"Lindsey."

Her daughter looked up, phone lowering slightly. "Yeah?"

"This doesn't mean..." Sue searched for the right words. "Your dad and I are trying to figure things out. I don't want you to get your hopes too high about—"

"Okay," Lindsey interrupted, her voice surprisingly mature. "I get it. But Mom?" She set her phone down completely, turning to face Sue with an expression far older than her years. "You guys still love each other, right?"

"Of course we do, but love is complicated sometimes when moms and dads are divorced."

They drove for several minutes; the landscape shifting from town to countryside as they headed toward home. Sue waited patiently for

Lindsey to speak again; she could tell something else was brewing in her daughter's mind.

"Mom?" Lindsey's voice was softer now, thoughtful. "What are you going to wear?"

Sue glanced at her daughter, confused by the abrupt shift. "Wear when?"

"Friday. To dinner and the tree lighting." Lindsey's expression turned calculating. "You should wear that dark red sweater. The one Grandma Anna gave you last Christmas. It looks real pretty on you, and it'll match the whole Christmas thing."

"When did you become a fashion consultant?"

"I'm almost twelve. I know stuff." Lindsey grinned. "So, will you wear it?"

"Maybe."

"That's a yes." Lindsey returned to her phone, satisfied. "I'm wearing my red sweater with the reindeer on it. The sparkly one."

Sue smiled, turning into their driveway. As she parked and climbed out, helping Lindsey gather her school things, she caught herself thinking about that red sweater and about Friday evening.

Inside the house, Lindsey immediately disappeared upstairs to her room, phone pressed to her ear as she called what was probably the first of many friends to share the news. Sue stood in the quiet kitchen, her coat still on, and let herself enjoy the peace and quiet and think about Friday evening.

Steve arriving at five o'clock to pick them up. The three of them walking into Martha's Diner together, sliding into a booth like they'd done hundreds of times years ago. Dinner conversation flowing easily while Lindsey chattered between them. Then the short walk to the town square, where neighbors and friends would gather, where hot chocolate and Christmas carols filled the air. They'd stand together waiting for that magical moment when thousands of lights transformed an ordinary tree into something transcendent.

Her phone buzzed in her pocket. A text from Steve: *Thanks for stopping by earlier; it meant a lot to me.*

Sue typed back: *I'm glad you're coming with us.*

Three dots appeared, disappeared, and appeared again as Steve responded, and then finally: *I want to be everywhere you are. Friday's just a start.*

Sue stared at the message, her heart doing complicated things behind her ribs.

Chapter 25

99 —and then Mrs. Phillips said my voice was perfect for the soprano part, which is so cool because Sarah really wanted it, but I guess I'm just better at high notes and she's better at lower stuff anyway, so it worked out, and we get to wear these red scarves, and—"

Steve watched his daughter's animated gestures, her hands moving in time with her rapid-fire narrative, and felt something in his chest expand. Across the table, Sue caught his eye and smiled.

"Lindsey, slow down, honey," Steve said gently, reaching for his water glass. "You're going to pass out before we even get to the tree lighting."

Lindsey paused mid-gesture, sucked in an exaggerated breath, and grinned. "I'm excited! It's my first time being old enough to sing at the tree lighting—"

"What songs are you singing?" Sue asked, her hand moving to cover Lindsey's where it rested on the checkered tablecloth.

"'Silent Night,' 'Joy to the World,' and 'The First Noel.'" Lindsey ticked them off on her fingers. "We've practiced for weeks. Mrs. Phillips says we sound good."

"I'm sure you do," Steve said. "Your mom's been teaching you well with all those choir practices at church."

"Lindsey's got natural talent. That's all her, not me."

Martha appeared beside their table, coffeepot in one hand. "How are we doing over here? Everyone ready to order?"

"I want the chicken parmesan," Lindsey announced immediately. "With extra garlic bread. And can I have a cherry Coke?"

"You absolutely can." Martha's pen moved across her order pad. "Sue?"

"I'll have the pot roast with mashed potatoes and green beans."

"Good choice. Steve?"

"Grilled chicken sandwich with fries. And more coffee, please."

"Coming right up." Martha collected the menus but lingered for a moment, her expression softening. "It's really good to see you three together like this. Real good."

Around them, the diner buzzed with Friday evening activity—couples on date nights, families grabbing dinner before the tree lighting, and regulars occupying their usual spots at the counter. Christmas lights twinkled in the windows, and a small artificial tree sat on the counter near the register, decorated with ornaments that looked handmade.

"I like us being together like this," Lindsey said, her voice dropping to something more serious than her usual exuberance.

Steve met Sue's eyes again, saw her throat work as she swallowed. The moment stretched between them, heavy with things neither seemed ready to say in front of their daughter.

"I like it too, sweetie. It's nice," Sue said, her gaze still locked on Steve's.

Lindsey beamed, apparently satisfied with this acknowledgment, and launched into another topic. "So tomorrow's my birthday party... I'm still super excited, and everyone's coming—Sarah and Ben and Emma and all my friends. It's going to be a blast."

"I'm looking forward to it," Steve said, exchanging a glance with Sue.

"Your dad's coming early tomorrow, Lindsey, to help me set up," Sue said.

"Wait, what? Really?"

"Really," Steve confirmed. "Figured your mom could use help hanging streamers and blowing up balloons."

His daughter's mouth fell open slightly, her eyes widening with delight. "You're going to help decorate? Like, actually help set up for my party?"

"Of course. It's your birthday." Steve kept his voice casual. "Can't have your mom doing all that work by herself."

"This is the best!" Lindsey bounced in her seat. "Both my parents setting up my party together. Just like..." She trailed off, seeming to catch herself.

"Just like old times?" Sue finished gently.

Lindsey nodded, suddenly looking younger than her almost-twelve years.

Steve reached across the table, his hand finding Lindsey's. "Some old times are worth revisiting."

"Some are," Sue agreed quietly, and when Steve looked at her, he found her watching him with an expression he couldn't quite name but desperately wanted to understand.

"You two are really acting weird..." Lindsey said, looking back and forth between her parents.

Martha returned with their drinks. "Food'll be out in about five minutes. Kitchen's running smooth tonight."

Lindsey immediately grabbed her cherry Coke, taking a long sip through the straw. "This is so good. Mom never lets me have soda at home."

"Because you turn into a tornado when you have too much sugar. I'm making an exception for tonight."

"And tomorrow?"

"Don't push your luck."

Steve sipped his coffee, content to watch them banter with the easy affection of a mother and daughter. This was what he'd missed during the past six years—these ordinary moments that weren't ordinary at all, but precious and irreplaceable.

"So the electrical is finished at the restaurant?" Steve asked.

"Completely done. The inspector signed off this morning. And they installed the new flooring in the kitchen today—commercial-grade tile that's supposed to be indestructible."

"What color?"

"Soft gray with dark grout lines. Very modern but still practical." Sue pulled out her phone, swiping through photos. "See? It looks wonderful."

Steve leaned across the table to view the screen. The flooring did look impressive—clean lines and professional installation that would serve the restaurant well for years to come.

"That's great progress," he said. "What's next?"

"Install the ceiling in the dining room and get it painted. Ceiling installation in the kitchen starts Monday." Sue's fingers moved across her phone screen, pulling up what looked like a detailed timeline.

"Graham thinks we might actually be ready for the health inspection by December fifteenth."

"Really?"

"Yep. It's almost too good to be true." Sue set her phone down. "Everyone's been working so hard, and nothing else has gone wrong, so maybe... maybe we'll actually make my Christmas deadline."

"You will," Steve said with certainty. "You've handled everything perfectly."

Sue's cheeks colored again at the praise. "I had a lot of help."

"You coordinated all that help."

"You're a superhero, Mom," Lindsey said as she stirred her Coke with her straw. "Fixing the restaurant, you sing in the church choir, you planned my birthday party, and you put up with me. That's like, so many things."

Sue laughed. "You're not something I 'put up with,' sweetheart. You're my favorite thing."

"Even when I'm being annoying?"

"Especially when you're being annoying. That's when you're most yourself."

Steve watched them together, mother and daughter sharing this easy moment, and felt gratitude wash over him. Sue had done an incredible job raising Lindsey largely on her own. Their daughter was kind, confident, and full of joy—all reflections of Sue's patient guidance and unconditional love.

"Remember Lindsey's first tree lighting?" Steve asked suddenly.

Sue's expression shifted to something nostalgic. "She was so little. We bundled her up in that pink snowsuit with the hood that made her look like a tiny marshmallow."

"And she cried when the lights came on and the whole town started cheering," Steve continued, the details coming back in vivid color. "We had to leave early."

"But then we drove around town looking at Christmas lights for an hour until she fell asleep in her car seat," Sue finished.

"I don't remember that," Lindsey said, looking between her parents.

"You were a newborn," Sue said. "That was a good night."

"It was," Steve agreed, holding Sue's gaze.

"Tell me another one," Lindsey said.

"The year you were three... you insisted on wearing your Halloween costume. It was a pink dress with lots of lace. All you kept wanting to do was touch that tree," Steve said. "You kept trying to climb over the barrier to get to the ornaments."

"Your dad had to hold you the entire ceremony to keep you from escaping," Sue added with a laugh. "You were so determined."

Martha arrived with their food, plates balanced with practiced skill. The aromas of roasted chicken, seasoned pot roast, and garlic bread filled their corner of the diner. She set each plate down with a flourish.

"Anything else I can get you folks?"

"We're good, thanks, Martha," Steve said.

"Enjoy." Martha said as she patted Sue's shoulder.

Steve cut into his chicken sandwich, the grilled meat perfectly seasoned and the bread toasted exactly right. Across from him, Sue savored her pot roast while Lindsey attacked her chicken parmesan with enthusiasm.

"This is so good," Lindsey mumbled around a mouthful of food.

"Manners," Sue said automatically.

"Sorry." Lindsey swallowed. "But seriously, it's good."

They continued eating, and Steve found himself noticing small details—the way Sue tucked her hair behind her ear when she leaned forward to cut her meat, the way Lindsey's enthusiasm extended even to her eating style, and the comfortable way their booth felt like a small island of family in the busy diner.

"Tell us about the fire department's preparations for tonight," Sue said, her attention on Steve.

"We've got two engines on standby at the station, and I'll have radio contact with Luke and Danny, who'll be circulating through the crowd. Mark's handling traffic control on Main Street." Steve sipped his coffee. "Mostly it's just making sure we're ready if anything happens, which it probably won't. But with crowds this size, we take precautions. Last year we estimated around eighteen hundred people. Could be more tonight, given the weather forecast is calling for continued snow through the night—perfect for a tree lighting ceremony."

Lindsey reached across the table suddenly, grabbing both Steve's hand and Sue's hand, holding them simultaneously. Her small fingers squeezed tight.

"I'm so happy," Lindsey said simply. "I love us all being together."

Steve's throat tightened. He looked at Sue and found her blinking rapidly, clearly fighting tears.

"We love it too, sweetheart," Sue managed.

"So much," Steve added, his voice rougher than intended.

Lindsey held their hands for a long moment before releasing them to return to her dinner. But the warmth of that simple gesture lingered, creating a tenderness that settled over their table like a blessing.

They finished their meal with easy conversation about Lindsey's upcoming Christmas break from school, Sue's plans for the restaurant's reopening celebration, and Steve's schedule for the following week. Every topic flowed naturally into the next, creating a tapestry of shared life that felt both familiar and new.

When Martha brought the check, Steve grabbed it and got up to pay at the register. When he returned to the table, Sue and Lindsey were already standing, bundling into their coats. Steve helped Sue with hers, his hands briefly touching her shoulders, and felt her lean back slightly into the contact before stepping away.

They walked outside into the December evening. The temperature had dropped a little more, and snow was falling softly; their breath formed clouds in the crisp air. Main Street glowed with Christmas lights, every lamppost and storefront contributing to the festive atmosphere.

"Ready?" he asked.

Lindsey stepped between them, grabbing both their hands. "Ready!"

Chapter 26

"Silent night, holy night..."

Sue's throat tightened as Lindsey sang her short solo part, her clear soprano voice rising in the air. The risers positioned near the town square's gazebo held twenty-three children bundled in coats and scarves.

Beside her, Steve's shoulder pressed against hers—steady and warm Around them, the crowd stood shoulder-to-shoulder, parents craning necks to spot their own children while the scent of hot chocolate, coffee, and roasted candied nuts drifted from vendor booths scattered throughout the square. Strings of white lights crisscrossed overhead, transforming the town square into something out of a storybook. The massive Christmas tree stood dark and waiting, its branches heavy with unlit bulbs that would soon blaze to life.

"All is calm, all is bright..."

Mrs. Chalmers stood in front of the risers, her hands conducting with gentle precision. Lindsey's eyes found theirs in the crowd, and her smile widened mid-verse before she refocused.

"She's incredible," Steve murmured.

"She is." Sue said. Pride swelled in her chest, mixing with something bittersweet—awareness of how quickly time was passing, how soon Lindsey would be a teenager, then grown.

The final notes of "Silent Night" hung in the cold air before dissipating like the children's breath. Applause erupted around them, and Sue joined in, her gloved hands making muffled sounds against each other.

Mrs. Chalmers raised her hands for quiet, then counted the choir into their next song.

"Joy to the world, the Lord is come..."

The tempo picked up, and Sue watched Lindsey's face transform with the shift—pure joy radiating from her as the familiar words tumbled out. Several of the younger children bounced on their toes, their enthusiasm barely contained by the need to stand still on the risers.

Steve's hand found Sue's, his fingers threading through hers with the same ease they'd managed at dinner. Sue's pulse quickened, but she didn't pull away. Instead, she squeezed back, acknowledging what they both knew—that this moment mattered.

The choir finished "Joy to the World" to more enthusiastic applause, then launched immediately into "The First Noel." Sue found herself singing along quietly. Beside her, Steve did the same, and she caught herself smiling at his slightly off-key voice.

When the final chord faded, the applause was deafening. Mrs. Chalmers beamed at her students, then gestured for them to take a bow. The children complied with varying degrees of coordination—some bowing deeply, others waving at parents, and a few simply standing there looking overwhelmed by the attention.

Mayor Thompson approached the microphone set up near the tree, his portly frame bundled in a heavy coat and red scarf. The children began filing off the risers, dispersing into the crowd to find their families. Sue watched Lindsey navigate the steps carefully, then break into a run the moment her feet hit solid ground.

"That was so cool!" Lindsey threw herself at Sue first, then Steve, her cheeks flushed from cold and excitement. "Did you hear us? Were we good? Mrs. Chalmers said we nailed it, but I wasn't sure if—"

"You were perfect," Steve said, pulling her into a proper hug. "Every note."

"Really?"

"Really," Sue confirmed. "Your solo part in 'Silent Night' gave me chills."

Lindsey's face split into a grin that rivaled the twinkle lights overhead.

Mayor Thompson's voice boomed through the sound system. "Good evening, Laurel Ridge! What a beautiful performance from our talented young people!"

Applause rippled through the crowd again. Lindsey hopped from foot to foot anticipating the tree lighting, still radiating energy despite the cold.

"I want to take a moment," the mayor continued, "to thank everyone who made tonight possible. Our volunteer decorating committee, the vendor booth operators, our local businesses that sponsored the event, and of course, Fire Chief Johnson and his crew for ensuring everyone's safety tonight."

"Laurel Ridge is more than a town," Mayor Thompson continued, his voice taking on a more serious tone. "It's a family. And like all families, we support each other through challenges and celebrate together in moments of joy. This year has tested some of us, but it's also shown us the strength of community, the power of neighbors helping neighbors, and the blessing of faith that sustains us through all seasons."

"Now," Mayor Thompson continued, his tone brightening, "before we light this magnificent tree, I'd like to invite Pastor Andrew Whitman to offer a blessing."

Pastor Andrew stepped forward, his face calm and welcoming in the glow of string lights.

"Let us pray," Andrew said simply.

Around them, the crowd settled into respectful quiet. Sue bowed her head, feeling Steve's hand tighten around hers.

"Heavenly Father," Andrew's voice carried across the square, "we thank You for this community, for the gift of friendship and fellowship, for the blessing of seasons that remind us of Your faithfulness. As we light this tree tonight, we're reminded that You are the Light of the World—the light that darkness cannot overcome. Bless this gathering, protect those traveling home tonight, and help us carry the joy and peace of this season into every day of the coming year. In Jesus' name, Amen."

"Amen," echoed across the square.

Mayor Thompson returned to the microphone. "All right, Laurel Ridge—let's count down together! Ten... nine... eight..."

The crowd joined in, voices rising in unison. Lindsey grabbed both Steve's and Sue's free hands, creating a chain between the three of them.

"Seven... six... five..."

Sue looked at the dark tree, then at Lindsey's upturned face, then at Steve watching both of them with an expression that made her heart skip.

"Four... three... two... ONE!"

The tree exploded into light.

Thousands of bulbs blazed simultaneously—warm golden white cascading from top to bottom, transforming the evergreen into something magical. The crowd gasped collectively, then burst into applause and cheers. Children shrieked with delight, and somewhere behind Sue, someone started singing "O Christmas Tree."

Lindsey squeezed both their hands hard. "It's so pretty!"

"It is," Steve agreed, but he was looking at Sue when he said it.

The tree's lights reflected in his eyes, and she found herself thinking about how many tree lightings they'd attended together, how many they'd missed during their separation, and how precious this one felt because they'd chosen to be here together.

The band that had been set up near the gazebo launched into "Deck the Halls," and the crowd's energy shifted from reverent awe to celebration. Children began running between adults again, their earlier restraint abandoned now that the main event had concluded.

"Mom! Dad!" Lindsey tugged their hands. "Can I go with my friends? Please? Sarah, Ben, and Emma are all meeting by the dance floor, and we want to hang out, and there's going to be dancing and everything, and—"

Steve scanned the square, a questioning look on his face.

Lindsey pointed toward a cleared area near the gazebo where a temporary wooden platform had been erected. Already, several couples were swaying to the band's music. "I'll be right there. We'll stay together the whole time, I promise."

Sue studied the location—visible from almost anywhere in the square, well-lit, and close to the vendor booths and adult supervision. "You have your phone?"

"Yes."

"And you'll text either your dad or me if you leave that dance floor?"

"Yes, Mom."

"And you'll stay with your friends? No wandering off alone?"

"I know the rules." Lindsey's tone held affectionate exasperation. "Can I go now?"

Steve pulled out his wallet, extracting a twenty-dollar bill. "For hot chocolate or snacks. Share with your friends."

Lindsey's eyes widened. "Really?"

"Really. Have fun."

"Thank you!" Lindsey hugged them both quickly, then took off running toward the dance floor.

Steve and Sue stood watching until Lindsey reached her friends and dissolved into the group with animated gestures that probably recounted every moment of the choir performance.

"She's going to be exhausted tomorrow," Sue said.

"Her? I doubt it." Steve said with a laugh as his hand found hers again. "Wanna get something warm to drink?"

"Coffee sounds perfect."

They walked toward the nearest vendor booth, weaving through families and groups of teenagers. The line was manageable—maybe a dozen people waiting ahead of them. Sue noticed several familiar faces turn to watch them pass, saw the knowing smiles and subtle nods that acknowledged what Sue and Steve's presence together meant.

"I think Lindsey's picking up on things," Steve said quietly, his voice barely audible over the band's rendition of "Jingle Bell Rock."

"You noticed that too?" Sue glanced up at him.

"Yep." Steve's expression held amusement mixed with concern. "We're not exactly being subtle, I'm afraid."

"No, we're not." Sue thought about Lindsey's observations, her pointed comments, and the way she kept looking between them with poorly concealed hope. "She's going to start asking more questions."

"Probably." They moved forward as the line advanced. "How do you want to handle that?"

Sue considered the question carefully. "Honestly... I think she's smart enough to know something's going on between us, and I'm thinking she's getting to that age where the truth matters."

"So we tell her we're... what? Dating? Working things out?"

"Both, maybe?" Sue struggled to find the right words. "We're figuring things out together. Taking it slow. We answer whatever question she's asking with honesty."

Steve nodded slowly. "I like that. She's old enough to understand that relationships take work and that adults can make mistakes and learn from them."

"It's actually a good opportunity," Sue said, warming to the idea. "To show her what a healthy relationship can look like. That love doesn't mean everything's perfect, but that people who care about each other can work through tough things together."

"Look at you, turning our complicated situation into a parenting lesson." Steve's tone was fond. "You're really good at this, you know."

"At what?"

"Being a mom. Taking every situation and finding the growth opportunity, the teaching moment. Lindsey's lucky to have you."

Heat crept up Sue's neck despite the cold air. "We're both lucky. She's an amazing kid."

"Because of you." Steve's voice carried absolute certainty. "I wasn't there for most of the hard years. You shaped her into who she is."

"You're here now," Sue said quietly. "That matters."

They reached the front of the line. The vendor—a woman she recognized from the Baptist church across town—greeted them with a warm smile.

"What can I get you folks?"

"Two coffees, please," Steve said. "Cream and sugar for both."

"Coming right up."

Sue started to reach for her wallet, but Steve's hand on her arm stopped her. "I've got it."

"You paid for dinner."

"And I'm paying for coffee." His tone was gentle but firm. "Let me take care of this, Sue."

She relented, watching him hand over bills and accept the two steaming cups. He passed one to her.

"Thanks."

"You're welcome."

They wandered away from the booth, sipping their coffee and letting the warmth seep into their cold hands. The band had shifted to slower songs now, and more couples filled the dance floor—some Sue recognized, others likely visitors from neighboring towns.

"Look," Steve said, nodding toward where Lindsey and her friends clustered at the edge of the dance floor. They were watching older teenagers dance, giggling behind their hands at some private joke.

"She's so grown up," Sue said. "When did that happen?"

"Suddenly." Steve's expression held the same bittersweet awareness Sue felt. "One day she was our baby, the next she's almost a teenager."

They stood watching their daughter laugh with her friends and watching the community celebrate around them.

The band started a new song—something slow and romantic that Sue recognized but couldn't name. Several couples on the dance floor drew closer together, swaying gently.

"Dance with me," Steve said.

Sue's head whipped toward him. "What?"

"Dance with me." He set his coffee cup on a nearby trash can lid, then took hers and did the same.

Sue stared at his offered hand, her heart hammering against her ribs.

"Lindsey will see," she said.

"Good." Steve's voice was steady. "Let her see her parents choosing each other and choosing to try."

Sue placed her hand in his.

Steve drew her toward the dance floor, finding a spot near the edge where they could still see Lindsey and her friends. His arm came around her waist, and Sue's hand rested on his shoulder. They began swaying to the music, their movements tentative at first, then gradually relaxing into the familiar rhythm they'd once known.

"I've missed this," Steve murmured, his breath warm against her ear.

"Dancing?"

"Being close to you. Having the right to hold you. Feeling like we belong together."

Sue's throat tightened. "We're not there yet. Not all the way."

"I know." His hand spread warm across her lower back. "But we're getting there. One step at a time."

They turned slowly, and Sue caught sight of Lindsey watching them with barely contained excitement, elbowing Sarah and pointing in their direction.

"People are staring," she said.

"Let them."

"Martha's going to have a field day with this."

"I'm sure."

"Lindsey sees us."

"I noticed."

Sue smiled. "Your mom called me yesterday."

"Did she?"

"Mmm. Wanted to know what I was bringing to your parents' Christmas dinner."

Steve pulled back slightly to look at her. "I didn't know you were coming to Christmas dinner."

"I didn't either until yesterday." Sue met his eyes. "I told her I'd be there."

Something shifted in Steve's expression—joy mixed with relief mixed with hope. "I'm glad."

"Me too."

They continued swaying, the band transitioning seamlessly into another slow song. Sue let herself sink into the moment—the warmth of Steve's arms, the security of his presence, and the rightness of being held by him again after so many years of careful distance.

"Sue," Steve's voice was rough.

"Hmm?"

She lifted her head from his shoulder, finding his face closer than expected. Their breath mingled in the cold air, and Sue's pulse kicked up.

"I love you. I never stopped. Not during the divorce, not during all these years apart. I've loved you every single day, and I'm tired of not saying it."

Sue's eyes burned. "Steve—"

"You don't have to say it back. I just needed you to know. I needed you to understand that this isn't casual for me; it isn't just about convenience or nostalgia. I love you, Sue. I love your strength and your stubbornness and the way you love Lindsey fiercely. I love—"

"I love you too. I tried so hard not to, tried to protect myself by staying angry, but it never worked. I've always loved you."

Steve's hand came up to cup her face, his thumb brushing her cheek. "Yeah?"

"Yeah."

He leaned in slowly, giving her time to pull away, time to protest, and time to remember they were in the middle of the town square with hundreds of witnesses. Sue didn't move.

Their breath mingled. His lips were inches from hers. Sue's eyes fluttered closed.

"You gonna kiss her or not, Dad?"

Sue's eyes flew open. Steve froze.

Lindsey stood there, surrounded by her entire group of friends, all of them giggling madly. Her hands were on her hips, her expression one of exaggerated impatience, but her eyes sparkled with mischief and joy.

Heat flooded Sue's face. Steve's hand dropped from her cheek, but his arm stayed firm around her waist.

"Lindsey Elizabeth," Sue managed, her voice strangled somewhere between mortification and laughter.

"What?" Lindsey's attempt at innocence was undermined by the grin she couldn't quite suppress. "You've been staring at each other all night and standing really close, and now you're dancing, and now you want to kiss each other... so just do it already!"

"Yeah, Mr. Johnson!" one of Lindsey's friends called out. "Kiss her!"

The other children dissolved into giggles. Several nearby adults had turned to watch, barely suppressing their own smiles.

Sue looked up at Steve, expecting to find him as embarrassed as she felt. Instead, his eyes held laughter and something bolder—challenge, maybe, or simply determination.

"Well," he said, his voice pitched loud enough for Lindsey to hear, "your daughter makes a compelling argument."

"Steve—" Sue's warning died as his mouth curved into a smile.

"Unless you object?"

"I don't object," she said.

Steve's smile widened. Then he dipped his head and kissed her.

It was soft and sweet—a gentle press of lips that lasted maybe three seconds. But it carried the weight of six years of separation, of love that had survived despite everything, and of hope for a future they were brave enough to choose together.

When Steve pulled back, applause erupted around them—not just from Lindsey's friend group, but from nearby couples on the dance floor, from families watching at the sidelines, and from Martha, who'd apparently materialized with perfect timing.

Sue buried her face in Steve's shoulder, her cheeks burning. But she was smiling.

"I hate you right now," she mumbled against his jacket.

"No you don't." His arms tightened around her. "You love me. You just said so."

"I'm reconsidering."

"Too late. No take-backs."

Lindsey appeared beside them, still grinning. "So does this mean you're back together?"

Sue lifted her head to look at their daughter. "It means we're working on it."

"But you kissed! In public! In front of everyone!"

"We did," Steve confirmed. "Because your very loud commentary didn't leave us much choice."

"You were taking forever." Lindsey bounced on her toes. "I was just helping."

"That's one way to describe it," Sue said dryly.

"That was so romantic! Like something from a movie!" Sarah said.

"Right?" Lindsey beamed. "My parents are the best."

"You're all adorable, and I love you," Sue said, but she was laughing. "Now go back to your friends before I die of embarrassment."

"Okay, okay." Lindsey hugged them both quickly. "But just so you know—I'm really happy. Like, really, really happy."

"We know, sweetheart," Steve said. "Now go have fun."

Lindsey bounced away with her friends, already rehashing the entire scene with animated gestures.

Sue and Steve continued dancing on the edge of the dance floor, the band playing and the lights twinkling overhead.

"That went well," Steve said.

Sue laughed—a real laugh that came from her belly and made her shoulders shake. "We're never going to live this down."

"Nope." Steve grinned. "Martha's probably already texting everyone who wasn't here. The whole county will know by morning."

"Your parents. My parents. The entire church congregation." Sue shook her head. "This is going to be interesting."

"Interesting is one word for it." Steve's hand found hers again. "Regret it?"

Sue looked at him—at the hope and vulnerability in his eyes, at the man he'd become, at the future spreading out before them, uncertain but possible.

"Not even a little bit," she said.

And she meant it.

Chapter 27

" —and then Sarah tried to do a cartwheel, but she totally wiped out and landed in the snowbank, and we were all laughing so hard—"

Sue smiled from her position near the kitchen island, watching Lindsey exaggerate wildly while recounting some schoolyard drama to Emma and Ben. Purple and silver streamers cascaded from the vaulted ceiling of her living room, twisting between clusters of metallic balloons that caught the afternoon light filtering through the windows. Outside, snow fell, coating the trees and meadow in fresh white that made everything look like it belonged inside a snow globe.

Her home had been transformed. The dining table groaned under platters of finger foods—mozzarella sticks, chicken tenders, fresh vegetables with ranch dip, and chips with salsa. Pizza boxes from The Pizza Place in Fayetteville sat open on the counters.

Sue watched as Anna and Gail worked in tandem, refilling bowls, wiping spills, and anticipating needs before they arose.

"Remember Lindsey's second birthday?" Anna said, arranging cookies on a platter. "When she insisted on wearing that princess costume and refused to take off the crown even to eat cake?"

Gail laughed. "I do. Steve finally had to sneak it away while Sue tried to clean all the cake off her face and hands and out of her hair."

"And she cried for that crown the entire time until she got it back," Anna added, shaking her head fondly.

The casual way they shared memories made Sue's throat tight. She'd missed this. The blended family gatherings, the way holidays felt fuller when both sides came together, and there was no tension between herself and Steve.

From the dining area, male voices rose in debate. Sue glanced over to find Steve, her father, Tom, and her brothers gathered near the windows, gesturing at something outside. Dan had joined them, apparently weighing in on whatever discussion was happening.

"—can't be more than six inches," Matt was saying.

"More like eight," Earl countered. "Look at how it's sitting on the railing."

"Either way, it's perfect packing snow," Steve said. "Lindsey's been begging to go sledding all morning."

"She's not going outside until after her friends go home." Sue called over.

Steve caught her eye, winked at her, and grinned. "Yes, ma'am."

Heat crept up Sue's neck at his tone—playful and warm.

Anna squeezed her shoulder, and when Sue looked up, her mother's eyes held knowing warmth.

"He's trying," Anna said quietly.

"Yes."

"And you're letting him." Anna's voice carried approval. "I like this, sweetheart."

Sue nodded.

In the living room, Lindsey and her friends had abandoned the snack table in favor of a game that involved a lot of shrieking and running around. Sue watched her daughter's flushed, happy face and felt gratitude wash over her so intensely it was almost overwhelming.

"Sue?" Gail appeared beside her, holding a fresh pitcher of lemonade. "Where should I put this?"

"The dining table is fine." Sue said as she moved to clear space.

"Can I say something?" Gail asked, her voice pitched low enough that only Sue could hear.

Sue braced herself. "Of course."

"Thank you." Gail's hand found Sue's arm.

"For what, Gail?"

"For giving my son another chance. You're truly a remarkable woman. I'm deeply grateful and blessed. That's all."

Sue hugged her quickly, feeling Gail squeeze back. When they separated, both women were blinking rapidly.

"Okay, no crying at a birthday party," Gail said, laughing. "What else needs doing?"

"Actually, I think we're ready for cake." Sue checked her watch. "It's almost three."

"I'll get the candles ready," Anna said, already moving toward the counter where the birthday cake sat in its pink and purple glory. Taste of Heaven Bakery had outdone themselves—two tiers decorated with edible flowers and Lindsey's name written in elegant script across the top.

Steve materialized at her side. "Cake time?"

"Cake time." Sue looked up at him, catching the way his gaze softened when it landed on her. "Want to help me get everyone gathered?"

"Always."

They moved through the house together, Steve corralling the men while Sue herded Lindsey's friends toward the dining area.

Once everyone had squeezed into the space around the dining table, Sue stepped back to let Steve place the cake in front of Lindsey. Anna lit the twelve candles while Gail dimmed the lights, and then the room erupted into "Happy Birthday."

Lindsey's face glowed in the candlelight, her smile so wide it looked like it might split her face. When the song ended, she closed her eyes, clearly making a wish, then opened them to look at both Sue and Steve.

"Will you help me?" she asked.

She glanced at Steve and found him already moving to Lindsey's left side while gesturing for Sue to take the right. Together, they leaned in, each placing a hand on Lindsey's shoulders.

"On three," Steve said. "One, two, three—"

They blew in unison, and all twelve candles flickered out. Applause and cheers filled the room, and Sue looked across their daughter to find Steve watching her with an expression that made her knees weak.

Sue straightened, blinking against the burn in her eyes. When she risked a glance around the room, she found both her parents and Steve's parents smiling, Dan grinning like he knew something wonderful was happening, and her brothers watching with grins.

"Time for presents... we can eat cake later!" Lindsey announced, and her friends erupted with excitement.

The living room became chaotic as gifts were opened—books, art supplies, jewelry, gift cards, and various items that made Lindsey squeal with delight. Sue photographed each moment, capturing Lindsey's expressions as she tore through wrapping paper, cataloging which friend gave what so thank-you notes could be written later.

Steve moved through the room with his own phone, angling for different shots. At one point, he caught Sue's eye and jerked his head toward the hallway. She followed, finding him waiting near the guest bedroom with two wrapped boxes.

"You said we should wait until after she opened the friend gifts. Is now good?"

"Now's perfect," she said.

They returned to the living room to find Lindsey examining a new journal Emma had given her, already planning what to write in it first.

"Lindsey?" Sue said. "Your dad and I have something for you. Want to come here?"

Lindsey practically launched herself off the floor, scrambling over discarded wrapping paper to reach them. "What is it? What is it?"

"Open them and find out," Sue said, laughing.

Lindsey grabbed the larger box first, tearing into the paper with enthusiasm that sent shreds flying.

"No way," she breathed, holding up a brand-new guitar—acoustic, with a sunburst finish that caught the light beautifully. "Is this... is this real?"

"Your mom said you've been wanting to learn," Steve said. "And we thought—"

"It's so pretty and—" Lindsey looked between them, clearly overwhelmed. "Thank you!"

"There's more," Sue said, nodding at the smaller box.

Lindsey set the guitar carefully aside and opened the second package. Inside, she found an envelope. Her hands shook slightly as she pulled out the contents.

"Concert tickets?" She read the print, then read it again, then looked up with eyes gone enormous. "Tickets to see Lauren Daigle? In Charleston? In February?"

"For you and four friends," Sue said, smiling.

"I'm going to see Lauren Daigle live." Lindsey's voice had gone faint. "I'm actually going to be in the same room with Lauren Daigle."

Lindsey threw herself at both of them simultaneously. "Best. Birthday. Ever. Thank you, thank you, thank you!"

Over Lindsey's head, Sue met Steve's eyes. The joy in his expression matched her own.

Lindsey pulled back, already turning toward where her friends watched. The shrieks that followed could probably be heard in the next county. Lindsey's friends swarmed her, everyone talking at once about the concert and the guitar and how lucky she was, and could they please, please, please be one of the friends she took to Charleston?

"Well done," Earl said quietly, appearing at Sue's side. "That's going to be a memory she carries forever."

Sue glanced at her father, noting the softness in his expression as he watched Lindsey. "We wanted it to be special."

"It is." Earl looked at Steve, then back at Sue. "I'm proud of you two."

The simple acknowledgment meant more than a flowery speech would have. Sue squeezed her father's arm, grateful beyond words.

"Picture time!" Anna announced, wielding her camera. "Everyone gather around Lindsey!"

What followed was a flurry of activity as Anna directed various groupings—Lindsey with her friends, Lindsey with Sue, Lindsey with Steve, Lindsey with both parents, Lindsey with grandparents, and Lindsey with aunts and uncles. Then the whole extended family, with Lindsey in the center holding her new guitar while everyone else clustered around.

"Say cheese!" Anna called.

"Cheese!" everyone chorused.

The camera flashed. Sue felt Steve's hand settle on her lower back, warm even through her sweater. She leaned slightly into the contact, caught between the camera's lens and Steve's solid presence, and thought that if they could freeze this moment forever, she would.

Cake and ice cream were served soon after, and eventually the doorbell rang around four-thirty—the first parent arriving to collect their child. Sue answered to find Mrs. Martinez bundled in a heavy coat, snowflakes caught in her dark hair.

"Come in, come in," Sue said, ushering her inside. "We're just finishing up."

By a little after five, the last of Lindsey's friends had been collected, leaving just family. The living room looked like a wrapping paper explosion, the dining table needed clearing, and the kitchen desperately needed cleaning.

"That was so fun!" Lindsey flopped onto the sectional, her new guitar cradled in her lap. "Best birthday ever."

"I'm glad, sweetheart." Sue began gathering used plates, but her mother intercepted.

"Gail and I will handle this," Anna said firmly. "You've been on your feet all day."

"Mom—"

"No arguments." Gail appeared with a trash bag already half-full. "Tom and Earl are loading the dishwasher. Matt and Graham are taking care of the leftovers. Dan's breaking down boxes. We've got this covered."

Sue wanted to protest but found herself too tired to muster much resistance. She sank onto the sectional beside Lindsey, who immediately curled into her side.

"Mom?"

"Hmm?"

"Can I ask you something?"

"Always."

"Sarah invited me to sleep over at her house tonight." Lindsey looked up, hope written across her face. "Can I go? Please?"

Sue's immediate instinct was to say yes, but then she remembered. "Honey, it's your dad's weekend. You're supposed to go home with him."

"Oh." Lindsey's face fell. "I forgot."

Steve appeared from the kitchen, drying his hands on a dish towel. "What's going on?"

"Lindsey wants to know if she can sleep over at Sarah's house tonight," Sue explained. "But I told her it's your weekend."

Steve looked at their daughter. "Do you want to go to Sarah's?"

"Yeah."

"It's fine. It's your birthday weekend, so why not?"

Lindsey scrambled up. "Really? I can go?"

"Really.."

"Thanks, Dad!" Lindsey hugged him, then Sue. "I'm gonna go pack!"

She thundered up the stairs toward her bedroom, leaving Sue and Steve alone in the living room. The sounds of a family working in the kitchen and dining room filtered around them: voices, running water, and the clink of dishes.

Steve set the dish towel aside and sat on the sectional where Lindsey had been. "Well, I guess my evening's free now."

Sue turned to look at him. "Looks that way."

He reached for her hand, his thumb brushing across her knuckles. "I have an idea."

"What kind of idea?"

"The kind that involves just the two of us. There's this restaurant in Lewisburg—a fancy place. I heard it's really romantic. White table-cloths, candlelight, the works. I could call and make a reservation, and we could drive out there, make an evening of it."

Sue's heart did that skip-flutter thing it had been doing increasingly often around Steve. "That sounds wonderful."

"Yeah?"

"Yeah. But..." Sue glanced down at her casual sweater and jeans and thought about the effort required to get dressed up after hosting a children's party all afternoon. "Can I make a counterproposal?"

"Always."

"After today, I'd rather not get all fancied up and drive an hour to sit in a restaurant." Sue met his eyes. "What if we just stayed here... just made dinner together with whatever I have in the fridge?"

Steve's smile widened slowly. "That sounds perfect."

He squeezed her hand. "Honestly? I'd rather have you in jeans in your kitchen than dressed up in some restaurant where I have to share you with a bunch of strangers."

"Mom! Dad!" Lindsey's voice carried from upstairs. "Can someone help me find my overnight bag?"

"Coming," Steve called back, but he didn't immediately move. His eyes stayed locked on Sue's, his thumb still tracing patterns on her hand.

"I'm holding you to that fancy dinner in the future though... I'm not letting you off the hook."

"Deal," Steve said with a grin.

Chapter 28

Steve pulled his truck into Sue's driveway and cut the engine. The porch lights glowed warmly against the darkening evening. His pulse kicked up as he climbed out and headed for the door.

The house smelled of birthday cake and pizza. The Christmas tree in the corner was still lit. He found Sue in the kitchen, cabinet doors open, staring at the shelves with an expression that suggested she'd lost whatever she was looking for.

"Everything go okay with dropping Lindsey off at Sarah's?"

"Smooth as could be." Steve moved closer, noting the tired set of Sue's shoulders. "You okay?"

"I don't even feel like cooking," she said as she closed one cabinet and opened another, her movements carrying the restless energy of someone too drained to actually do anything productive. "I'm trying to figure out what I have that doesn't require much effort."

Steve stepped around her and opened the refrigerator. The middle shelf held leftovers—a foil-covered dish that looked like a casserole, half a platter of vegetables, and a large pizza box. He pulled out the pizza box and lifted the lid.

"How do you feel about party leftovers?"

Sue's laugh came out relieved. "That'll work."

"You've been on your feet all day hosting a dozen twelve-year-olds. I think we're allowed to take the easy route." Steve set the pizza on the counter while Sue turned on the oven. "I'll grab us some plates."

They moved around each other with ease—Steve getting plates and cups while Sue found napkins; him setting the table while she transferred pizza slices onto a baking sheet to warm. When Steve went to the pantry for chips, he found them right where he remembered, and the familiarity of that small detail hit him harder than it should have.

This had been his pantry once. His kitchen. His home. He'd walked out of here six years ago with boxes of his belongings and a marriage in ruins, certain he'd destroyed the best thing in his life beyond any hope of repair.

"Steve?" Sue's voice pulled him back. "You okay?"

"Yeah." He grabbed the bag of chips and closed the pantry door.

They set the dining room table together. Through the windows, he could see the snow still falling. The world outside looked peaceful and insulated, like they existed in a bubble separate from everything else.

The oven timer dinged. Sue retrieved the pizza while Steve filled their glasses with ice water, and then they sat next to each other at the table that had once been theirs together.

For a while, they ate in comfortable quiet punctuated by easy observations about the party.

"Did you see Lindsey's face when she opened the guitar?" Sue asked, smiling at the memory.

"I thought she might pass out." Steve took another bite of pizza.

They continued like that—swapping stories about party moments, laughing over the craziness of too many kids in one space, and marveling at how quickly Lindsey was growing up. The conversation flowed naturally, the kind of easy back-and-forth they'd mastered years ago when life was simpler and their marriage wasn't broken.

But gradually, Sue's smile faded into something more thoughtful, her gaze distant as she pushed chips around on her plate without actually eating them. He watched her struggle with something unspoken and saw the moment she decided to voice it.

"Can I ask you something?" Sue set down her napkin, turning toward him.

"Anything."

"Do you understand why our marriage fell apart?"

He set down his slice of pizza, appetite vanishing.

"Yes. I destroyed it. My ambition, my obsession with proving myself at the fire department, and my complete failure to see what mattered until it was too late."

Sue nodded slowly, her expression unreadable.

"I was so tired, Steve." Sue's voice wavered slightly. "So exhausted trying to hold our life together by myself. The house, the bills, the restaurant, Lindsey—all of it fell on me while you were married to your job."

"Sue—"

"Let me finish." She held up a hand. "Please."

Steve swallowed hard and nodded.

"I would wake up at five in the morning to get bills paid, clean the house, and get Lindsey ready for daycare so I could go to the restaurant. I'd work all day, pick her up, make dinner, and do bath time and bedtime alone because you were at the station. Then I'd do laundry or do whatever else needed to be done or fix whatever needed fixing around the house, and by the time I collapsed into bed, you still weren't home most of the time. I know you had to be at the station 2 days on and 2 days off; that was the schedule back then. But you kept taking on more. Extra shifts, extra trainings, and more certifications. You were at the station even on your days off—volunteering, working out, doing whatever it was that kept you from us."

Sue's hands twisted in her lap. "And when you were home, you were exhausted or distracted or already planning the next certification or training that would keep you away. I kept thinking if I could just hold on a little longer, if I could just be stronger, if I could just need you less—"

Her voice broke. Steve's hands fisted on the table, every instinct screaming to reach for her, but he forced himself to stay still. To listen. To bear witness to the pain he'd caused.

"I got so mad at you," Sue continued, her eyes bright with unshed tears. "So angry. Because I was the one taking care of everything. This house that we'd bought together and fixed up together—I maintained it alone. The restaurant. Our daughter—I raised her alone while you were in the next room or at the firehouse or wherever ambition took you."

"I'm sorry." The words felt pathetically inadequate. "Sue, I'm so—"

"I got tired of trying." Sue's voice steadied, though tears now tracked down her cheeks. "Tired of fighting for your attention. Tired of begging you to take time off. Tired of feeling like I ranked somewhere below your job and your ego. So I filed for divorce because I figured I was already doing everything on my own anyway, and at least without you there I wouldn't keep hoping you'd show up."

The truth of it gutted him. Steve had spent years telling himself Sue had given up on him too easily, that if she'd just communicated better or been more patient, they could have worked it out. But sitting here listening, he understood with brutal clarity that Sue hadn't given up at all.

She'd survived.

"You're right. About all of it. I failed you in every way that mattered."

"I'm not trying to make you feel guilty—"

"You should. Sue, everything you just said is true. I was so convinced that providing for you meant working harder, climbing higher, and proving I could give you security. But what you needed was me. Present and engaged. Actually participating in the life we'd built instead of using our life as fuel for my ambition and ego."

Sue wiped her cheeks with the back of her hand. "I know you thought you were doing the right thing."

"That doesn't make it right." Steve's hands ached to reach for her. "I can't take back those years. Can't undo the damage or erase the loneliness you felt. But Sue—" He paused, gathering courage. "What changed? What made you even consider giving me another chance?"

Sue was quiet for a long moment, her gaze fixed. When she finally looked up, her expression held something Steve couldn't quite name.

"A lot of things," she said slowly. "Seeing you show up to help with the restaurant reminded me of the man I married—the one who'd roll up his sleeves and work beside me. Our hike last week, when we talked, helped me believe you'd genuinely changed."

"But?"

"But the real turning point happened last Sunday night." Sue pushed her chair back and stood.

She disappeared into the living room, returning moments later with her Bible—worn leather cover and pages marked with countless slips of paper. She sat back down and opened it carefully, flipping through until she found what she was looking for, then turned the book toward him.

"Read this," she said quietly.

Steve looked down at the page, his eyes finding the highlighted verse in Ezekiel that she was pointing to.

"I will give you a new heart and put a new spirit in you," he read aloud, his voice unsteady. "I will remove from you your heart of stone and give you a heart of flesh."

The words settled into his chest, heavy with meaning he was only beginning to understand.

"I'd been praying for peace," Sue said. "Asking God to show me if forgiving you—if trusting you again—was foolish or faithful. And then I read that verse, and it just... stopped me cold."

Steve turned to look at her, finding her watching him with an expression that made his throat tight.

"I realized God wasn't asking me to rebuild what was broken," Sue continued. "He was offering to create something entirely new. In both of us. Forgiving you wasn't about excusing the past or pretending the hurt didn't happen. It was about letting God soften what had hardened inside me."

"Sue—"

"I didn't give you another chance because I suddenly trusted you completely," she said, her voice steady now despite the tears still on her cheeks. "I gave you another chance because I trusted God to guide my heart. To show me whether this was restoration or just wishful thinking."

Steve looked at her, this woman who'd survived his failure and somehow found the courage to risk being hurt again. The faith it must have taken to open that door completely, to let him back into her life—he couldn't fathom it.

"I don't deserve you," he managed.

"Maybe not." Sue's lips curved into something that wasn't quite a smile. "But maybe that's the point. None of us deserves grace, Steve. We receive it anyway."

The weight of her words pressed down on him—the profound gift she was offering, the trust she was extending despite every reason not to. Steve felt something crack open inside his chest, some final wall he'd been holding up crumbling under the force of her generosity.

They sat in silence, the only sounds being the soft tick of the clock on the wall and the whisper of snow against the windows. Steve looked at the Bible still open between them on the table.

He reached for her hand.

She didn't pull away.

Their fingers intertwined, and Steve felt the first hot slide of tears down his own face—grief for what he'd broken, gratitude for what she was offering, and hope for what they might become.

"Thank you," he whispered.

Sue squeezed his hand, her thumb brushing across his knuckles in a gesture of comfort that made his chest ache.

They sat like that as evening deepened into night, hands clasped, sitting close together, the Bible open on the table before them bearing witness to something sacred unfolding in the quiet of Sue's home.

Neither spoke. Words felt insufficient for the magnitude of what had just passed between them—confession and absolution, honesty and grace, the terrible beauty of two broken people choosing to believe that God could make them whole.

Chapter 29

"*Great is Thy faithfulness, O God my Father...*"

Sue's voice blended with the other choir members, the familiar hymn rising toward the vaulted ceiling of Laurel Ridge Community Church. From her position behind the pulpit at the front of the church, she could see the entire congregation, people she'd known for years.

Her gaze found Steve sitting beside Lindsey in the fourth pew, right side. Tom, Gail, and Dan flanked them on one side, while her mom, dad, and brothers occupied the space on the other. Both families together in one row. The sight made her throat tight even as she continued singing.

Steve's eyes met hers, and he smiled.

"*Morning by morning new mercies I see...*"

Lindsey leaned against Steve's shoulder, her hand clasped in his. She watched her daughter—their daughter—looking content and happy.

The hymn ended. Sue and the other choir members filed down from behind the pulpit, returning to their seats in the congregation.

She sat down beside Steve. His hand found hers immediately, fingers threading together.

Pastor Andrew approached the pulpit, his Bible already open in his hands. "Good morning, church family," he said, his warm voice carrying through the sanctuary.

"Good morning," the congregation responded.

"What a beautiful way to start our worship this morning. Thank you to our choir for leading us in praise. Let's open our service with prayer."

Heads were bowed throughout the sanctuary. Andrew's voice carried over them, thanking God for bringing them together, asking for open hearts to receive His word, and lifting members of the congregation who were struggling with illness or hardship.

"In Jesus' name we pray, Amen."

"Amen" echoed through the church.

"Please turn with me to the Gospel of John, chapter fifteen, verses one through eight. This will be our scripture reading for today."

The rustle of turning pages filled the church. Sue opened her Bible to the passage as Steve shifted to share it with her.

Pastor Andrew began reading, his voice clear and measured: "I am the true vine, and my Father is the gardener. He cuts off every branch in me that bears no fruit, while every branch that does bear fruit he prunes so that it will be even more fruitful..."

Sue's eyes tracked the words as Andrew read, the familiar passage taking on new weight after last night's conversation with Steve. The imagery of pruning—painful but necessary for growth—resonated in ways it never had before.

"Remain in me, as I also remain in you," Andrew continued. "No branch can bear fruit by itself; it must remain in the vine. Neither can you bear fruit unless you remain in me."

He finished reading the passage, then looked up from his Bible at the congregation.

"This morning, I want us to consider what Jesus means when He says, 'Remain in me.' It's not just about staying in one place. It's about being so deeply connected, so rooted in Christ, that we draw our very life from Him—the way a branch draws life from the vine."

"We live in a culture that glorifies independence," Andrew continued, his hands gesturing to emphasize his point. "We're taught to be self-sufficient, to need no one. But God's design is different. He created us for connection—to Him first, and then to each other. The branch doesn't strain to produce fruit through sheer willpower. It simply remains attached to the vine, and the life flowing through that connection produces fruit naturally."

Beside her, Steve's thumb traced circles on the back of Sue's hand. She glanced at him and found him already looking at her with a hopeful expression.

Andrew was talking about spiritual dependence on Christ, but Sue heard echoes of what she and Steve were learning—that trying to do everything alone had nearly destroyed them both. Maybe restoration meant learning to remain connected, to draw strength from shared roots rather than isolated independence.

The sermon continued, moving through scripture with Andrew's characteristic blend of scholarly insight and practical application.

After the sermon, they stood for the closing hymn. Steve released Sue's hand to pick up the hymnal. Sue shifted closer so they could share, their shoulders pressed together, her voice blending with his as they sang.

"Blessed assurance, Jesus is mine! O what a foretaste of glory divine..."

She could feel the rumble of Steve's voice, could smell the faint scent of his cologne, and could see from the corner of her eye the way Lindsey watched them with barely contained delight.

The hymn ended, and Pastor Andrew raised his hands in benediction.

"May the Lord bless you and keep you. May He make His face shine upon you and be gracious to you. May He turn His face toward you and give you peace. Go in grace to love and serve the Lord."

"Amen," the congregation responded.

The sanctuary filled with the sounds of people gathering belongings and greeting neighbors. Sue turned to collect her Bible and purse, but Steve's hand on her arm stopped her.

"Sue?" His voice was low enough that only she could hear. "Can I ask you something?"

"Of course."

"Usually on Sundays, I have dinner with my parents, and you spend the afternoon with yours, and Lindsey goes with one of us." Steve glanced at their daughter, who was already chattering with her grandmother Anna. "What if we just... didn't do that today? What if the three of us spent the day together instead?"

"Just us?"

"Just us. We could grab lunch somewhere, or even go back to my place and have lunch, maybe drive up to Hawks Nest, just... be together." Steve's expression held hopeful uncertainty. "If you want."

"Well... all of that sounds fine... but what if we just go eat somewhere and then go back to my place and watch movies or even go sledding?"

"Can we, Dad?" Lindsey had clearly been eavesdropping. "Please? I vote for sledding!"

Sue looked at her daughter's eager face, at Steve's careful hope, and at the future taking shape in front of her that she was brave enough now to reach for.

"Sounds like a plan then," Steve said.

They made their way down the aisle with the rest of the congregation, Sue between Steve and Lindsey, moving slowly through the crowd. Several people stopped them—members asking about the restaurant's progress, friends commenting on Lindsey's choir performance Friday night at the tree lighting ceremony, and Martha catching Sue's eye and giving her an exaggerated wink that made Sue's cheeks heat.

At the door, Pastor Andrew and Lily greeted each person as they exited. When Sue reached them, Lily pulled her into a quick hug.

"Beautiful hymn this morning," Lily said. "The choir sounded wonderful."

"Thank you." Sue stepped aside so Steve could shake Andrew's hand.

"Good to see you, Steve," Andrew said. "Lindsey tells me you got her a guitar for her birthday."

"We did." Steve's hand found the small of Sue's back as he spoke. "She's already driving us crazy practicing."

"I am not!" Lindsey protested, but she was grinning. "I'm getting really good!"

They moved outside into the cold December morning. The temperature had dropped overnight, and their breath formed clouds in the air. Most of the congregation hurried toward the parking lot, too cold for the usual lingering conversations. A few hardy souls headed toward the fellowship hall behind the church, where coffee and cookies waited.

She spotted both sets of parents gathered near the sidewalk, clearly waiting for them. Earl had his arm around Anna, both bundled in heavy coats. Tom and Gail stood nearby, speaking with Dan.

"I should tell them," Steve said quietly.

"We should tell them," Sue corrected.

They approached together, Lindsey bouncing ahead to announce the change in plans before they could.

"Guess what? Mom and Dad and me are spending the whole day together! Just us!"

Anna's face lit up. "Well... now that sounds like fun."

"I apologize; I know this will throw a kink in our normal Sunday routine, but Sue and I are just going to spend the day together, the three of us," Steve said, directing his words to both sets of parents.

Earl looked at Steve for a long moment, and Sue held her breath. Then, her father's expression softened into something approving.

"You don't need to apologize for wanting to spend time with your family, son," Earl said, and the casual use of 'son' made Steve grin.

"You go enjoy your family," Gail said, pulling Sue into a quick hug. "You three go enjoy your day."

Tom clapped Steve on the shoulder. "Drive carefully, son. Roads might be slick."

They said their goodbyes—Anna insisting Sue text her later, Tom making Lindsey promise to show him her guitar progress next time she visited. Then it was just the three of them walking across the parking lot toward Steve's truck.

"Shotgun!" Lindsey called, then paused. "Wait, does Mom get shotgun now since you guys are, like, together again?"

"You can have shotgun," Sue said, laughing. "I'll survive one car ride in the back seat."

"No, you won't." Steve's hand found hers again. "Lindsey, climb in the back. Your mom sits up front."

"But I called shotgun!"

"And I'm overruling shotgun." Steve opened the passenger door for Sue. "New family rule—your mom always gets the front seat when I'm driving."

Lindsey grumbled good-naturedly as she scrambled into the back seat. Sue slid into the passenger seat, the familiar smell of Steve's truck wrapping around her—coffee, leather, and something distinctly him that made her chest warm.

Steve climbed into the driver's seat and started the engine. The radio came on softly, playing something instrumental and peaceful. He backed out of the parking spot, checking mirrors while Lindsey immediately started scrolling through her phone to find restaurant options.

"There's that new barbecue place in Fayetteville," Lindsey announced. "Sarah said it's really good. Or we could do pizza? Or that Italian place Mom likes?"

"We had pizza yesterday," Sue reminded her.

"So? Pizza is always good."

Steve's hand found Sue's across the center console, his fingers threading through hers. She looked at their joined hands, then at Lindsey chattering in the back seat, then at Steve's profile as he navigated out of the parking lot.

Sunday stretched ahead of them. No obligations and no schedules. Just the three of them together.

"Barbecue sounds good to me," Steve said, glancing at Sue. "If that works for you?"

"Perfect," Sue said, and meant it about so much more than lunch.

He turned onto Main Street, leaving the church behind.

Lindsey leaned forward between the seats. "Can we drive through town the long way? I want to see all the Christmas decorations again."

Steve squeezed her hand, and when she looked at him, his smile held the same thing she was feeling—joy uncomplicated by fear or regret, simple and pure.

He drove through Laurel Ridge's decorated streets, Lindsey pointing out every decoration she thought was cool, Steve driving slowly so they could take it all in.

Lindsey's phone buzzed. "Sarah wants to know if I'm going to youth group on Wednesday after school."

"Yes," Sue said.

"Can Dad come pick me up after?"

Steve glanced in the rearview mirror. "Sure."

"And then maybe we could all have dinner after?" Lindsey's voice carried such hope it made Sue's chest ache.

"Maybe," Sue said carefully.

"That's a yes!" Lindsey crowed.

Steve's thumb traced circles on Sue's palm. "Is it?"

Sue looked at him—really looked at him. At the man who'd failed her and owned it, who'd changed and proved it, who'd been given grace and received it with humility. At the man she'd loved and lost and was learning to love again in a new way.

"Of course," she said.

Chapter 30

Steve climbed back into his truck, arms loaded with his duffel bag stuffed with snow gear and a change of clothes. The engine was still running, keeping Sue and Lindsey warm while he'd dashed up to his apartment. Snow continued falling in thick, lazy flakes. After eating lunch, they'd stopped at his apartment to grab a few things before heading to Sue's.

"Got everything?" Sue asked.

"Gloves, snow pants, extra jeans, dry shirt—the works." Steve said as he set his bag in the back seat, then settled behind the wheel.

Steve's hand found hers as he navigated out of the parking lot, his thumb brushing across her knuckles in a gesture that was becoming delightfully familiar.

Laurel Ridge looked like something out of a Christmas card—white-blanketed roofs, icicles hanging from eaves, and Christmas décor all around. The afternoon light had a particular quality of winter days when snow is falling, everything soft and muted and peaceful.

"How much snow do you think we've gotten?" Lindsey pressed her face against the window, her breath fogging the glass.

"Six inches, maybe seven." Steve took the turn onto Pine Ridge Road carefully. "Perfect packing snow too. Not too wet, not too dry."

"Perfect for sledding," Lindsey said, bouncing slightly in her seat. "And tobogganing. And tubing. And snowmen. And snow angels. And—"

"And everything else you can possibly think of," Sue finished, laughing. "We get it. You're excited."

Steve caught Sue's eye, saw the happiness there mixed with something more tender. They both knew what Lindsey really meant—not just the snow day itself, but the three of them together, doing family things like they used to when Lindsey was small.

The truck climbed the winding road toward Sue's house, passing through the neighborhood where modest homes sat on generous lots with mountain views. Steve had driven this route thousands of times during their marriage and knew every curve and dip. The familiarity of it settled something in him, like coming home after a long absence.

Steve turned onto the driveway, and the house came into view, the steep roof now looked heavy with snow. The front yard sloped gently down toward the woods, but the real attraction was the back—a hillside perfect for sledding that ended in a flat area before the tree line. Steve had spent hours out there with Lindsey when she was little, pulling her back up the hill on her sled while she giggled and begged for "one more time, Daddy, please?"

He pulled into the driveway and parked in front of the garage. The house looked warm and inviting, Christmas lights twinkling along the porch railing despite the afternoon hour, wreaths hanging on the windows.

"Lindsey and I will go change into our snow gear. Steve, the garage code is—" Sue said, unbuckling her seatbelt.

"Still 1204?" Steve asked, remembering. Lindsey's birthday, December fourth.

"Yep, still the same. The toboggan should be on the right side near the back, hanging on the wall. Lindsey's sled is—"

"On the right side near the workbench," Lindsey supplied. "And the tubes are in the big plastic bin under the window."

"Got it. I'll get everything ready. You two take your time."

They climbed out into the falling snow. Sue and Lindsey headed up the front porch steps, while Steve walked toward the garage. The code panel glowed as he punched in the familiar numbers. The garage door went up, and Steve stepped into the garage.

It was organized in that particular way Sue had always maintained—everything in its place, labeled bins stacked neatly on metal shelving, and tools hanging on pegboards.

He found Lindsey's sled first—a bright purple plastic number with handles and a pull rope. Then the tubes, inside a large storage bin exactly where Lindsey had said. Steve set them by the door leading to the backyard.

Then he turned back to the right side of the garage for the toboggan. It hung there, about six feet up, suspended on heavy-duty hooks. The wood was weathered but well-maintained, the red and yellow painted stripes faded but still visible. He reached up and lifted it down.

They'd bought this toboggan during their first winter together as a married couple. Steve could still remember the day—shopping at a sporting goods store in Beckley, Sue insisting they needed the "good" kind that would last, Steve laughing at her practicality even as he'd loved her for it. They'd used it constantly that winter, flying down this very hillside until they were breathless with laughter and cold.

When Lindsey was a toddler, they'd taken her out with them, all three piled on the toboggan—Sue in front holding her, Steve in back holding Sue, steering them down the hill while Lindsey shrieked with toddler delight.

Steve ran his hand along the smooth wooden slats, feeling the grain beneath his gloved fingers.

"Steve?" Sue's voice came from the doorway to the house. "Did you find everything?"

Steve turned, the toboggan still in his hands. Sue stood there in snow pants and a heavy purple winter coat, her hair pulled back in a ponytail, warm gloves already on. She looked beautiful.

"You still have our original toboggan," he said

"I do. Lindsey and I still use it during the winter."

Sue opened the back door and looked outside to see Lindsey already running through the snow. She turned to him as he slipped on his snow pants and gloves and smiled, "Come on. We've got a hill to conquer."

Steve grabbed the sled and toboggan while Sue took the tubes.

"Finally!" Lindsey said.

"Think you can carry this?" Steve asked as he handed Lindsey her sled.

"I'm twelve, Dad. I can carry lots of things."

The backyard spread before them—a white expanse, untouched snow, perfect and pristine. The hill wasn't terribly steep, but it was long, running a good hundred yards before leveling out near the tree line. Perfect for sledding.

"Who's going first?" Steve asked.

"Me! Me!" Lindsey was already dragging her sled toward the top of the hill.

Sue laughed, following her daughter while Steve brought up the rear with the toboggan.

They reached the top of the hill, and Lindsey immediately positioned her sled at the edge. "Watch this!" She threw herself onto it stomach-first and shoved off.

The sled shot down the hillside, Lindsey's delighted screams echoing across the yard as she picked up speed. She hit a small bump about halfway down and went briefly airborne, landing with a soft whump in the snow before continuing to the bottom.

"That looked fun," Sue said, shading her eyes to watch as Lindsey tumbled off the sled at the bottom, laughing.

"Your turn," Steve said.

Sue set both tubes down, but instead of sitting in one of them right away, she looked at Steve with a mischievous expression. "Race you."

"What?"

"You heard me. Race. Last one to the bottom has to pull both tubes back up."

Steve grinned, grabbing the second tube. "You're on."

They positioned themselves side by side at the top of the hill, Sue settling into her tube while Steve did the same. At the bottom, Lindsey had turned to watch, cupping her hands around her mouth to shout encouragement.

"On three?" Sue asked.

"On three," Steve agreed.

"One," Sue counted.

"Two," Steve added.

"Three!" they shouted together and pushed off.

The tubes spun as they descended, picking up speed quickly. Steve heard Sue laughing—real, genuine, unbridled laughter—and the sound of it made him laugh too, even as his tube hit a patch of faster snow and spun him backward.

The world became a blur of white. Steve's tube hit a small rise and bounced, sending him slightly off course. Beside him—or behind him, or ahead; he'd lost track—Sue's laughter continued, bright and clear.

They reached the bottom almost simultaneously, Sue maybe half a second ahead, both tubes sliding to a stop in the flat area before the trees. Steve tumbled out of his tube, dizzy and laughing, to find Sue already on her feet doing a victory dance.

"I won!" She raised her arms in triumph. "You have to pull both tubes up!"

"That was barely a win," Steve protested, but he was grinning.

"A win is a win." Sue helped him up, her gloved hands gripping his. "Fair and square."

Lindsey jogged over, her sled dragging behind her. "That was so cool! Can we all go down together on the toboggan next?"

"Sure," Sue said. "But first, your dad has some tubes to pull up the hill."

Steve grabbed both tube ropes, slinging them over his shoulder. "You're enjoying this too much."

"Maybe a little." Sue's eyes sparkled with mischief and joy, and Steve thought he'd drag a dozen tubes up that hill if it meant seeing her this happy.

The three of them trudged back up, Steve hauling the tubes, and Lindsey talking nonstop about how fun everything was and how they should do this every weekend and maybe they could build a jump at the bottom of the hill, and wouldn't that be so cool?

At the top, Steve positioned the toboggan. "Okay, who's in front?"

"Me!" Lindsey claimed the front position, sitting down and gripping the curved front of the toboggan.

Sue settled in behind their daughter, her legs on either side of Lindsey, arms wrapped around her middle.

Steve climbed on last, his much longer legs bracketing both Sue and Lindsey, his arms reaching around Sue to grip the sides of the toboggan. The position put him pressed against Sue's back, close enough to smell her shampoo, to feel her warmth even through layers of winter clothing.

"Everybody hold on," Steve said, his voice close to Sue's ear.

"Go, go, go!" Lindsey chanted.

Steve pushed off with his boots, and the toboggan started moving, slowly at first, then faster as gravity took over. The three of them leaned as one when Steve steered, and Lindsey squealed with delight.

The toboggan flew down the hillside, faster than either the sled or the tubes, picking up momentum that made his stomach swoop. Lindsey's laughter mixed with Sue's, the pure joy of it infectious.

They hit the bottom and kept sliding; the toboggan gliding smoothly across the flat snow until friction finally slowed them to a stop. Nobody moved for a moment, all three of them breathing hard, faces flushed with cold and exhilaration.

"Again!" Lindsey twisted around to look at her parents. "Can we go again? Please?"

"Definitely," Sue said, already starting to climb off. "But this time, your dad's in front. I want to steer."

"You want to steer?" Steve raised an eyebrow.

"I want to steer."

At the top of the hill, they repositioned—Steve in front, Lindsey in the middle, and Sue in back.

"Ready?" Sue asked.

"Ready," Steve and Lindsey chorused.

Sue pushed off, and they were flying downhill again.

They spent the next hour going up and down that hill—sometimes all together on the toboggan, sometimes in pairs, sometimes in individual races on the sled and tubes. Lindsey went down backward on her sled and immediately regretted it, dizzy and laughing at the bottom. Sue and Steve raced on the tubes three more times, Sue winning twice and Steve once.

The snow continued falling, adding to the accumulation, making each run slightly different as the paths shifted and changed.

After what must have been their twentieth trip down the hill, Steve found himself at the bottom with Sue watching as Lindsey twirled around in the snow trying to catch snowflakes with her tongue.

"She's going to sleep well tonight," Sue said.

"We all are."

"Worth it though."

"Absolutely worth it."

They stood together, watching Lindsey twirl.

"Steve?"

"Yeah?"

"It's been a good day. I wouldn't trade this for anything."

Steve turned to face her fully. "Neither would I."

He stepped closer, reaching up to brush a snowflake from her cheek. His glove was wet and cold, but Sue leaned into the touch anyway.

A snowball hit him square in the back.

Steve whirled to find Lindsey, grinning like the Cheshire cat.

"Got you!" she said.

"Oh, you're in trouble now," Steve said, already packing snow into a ball.

It hit Lindsey in the shoulder, making her yelp with laughter and immediately start packing more ammunition. She backed up, trying to create distance while throwing snowballs as fast as she could form them.

"Now you've done it," Sue said, but she was laughing, already creating her own snowball. She threw it at Lindsey, hitting her in the leg.

"Two against one? That's not fair!" Lindsey protested, but she was giggling too hard to sound convincing. She retreated toward a large drift of snow, using it as a shield while she stockpiled ammunition.

What followed was chaos. Lindsey pelted them from behind her snowy fortress while Steve and Sue flanked her from opposite sides, all three of them laughing and dodging and throwing as fast as they could pack snow.

"Truce!" Lindsey finally called, holding up her hands. "Truce! I'm outnumbered!"

"Do we accept her truce?" Steve asked Sue, who was breathing hard from laughing and throwing.

"Never!" Sue grabbed a handful of snow and threw it at Steve instead of Lindsey.

It hit him in the chest, exploding in a puff of white. Steve stared at Sue in mock betrayal. "That's treason."

"That's strategy," she said as she backed away, another snowball forming in her hands.

Steve advanced on her slowly, deliberately, packing his own snow-ball with exaggerated care. "You realize this means war."

"Bring it, Fire Chief."

They circled each other while Lindsey watched from her snowdrift, grinning at her parents' antics. Sue threw first, but Steve dodged, the snowball sailing past his shoulder. He countered immediately, and Sue tried to dodge it, but her boot caught in the deep snow.

She went down with a startled yelp, landing on her back in the soft powder.

"Sue!" he said as he rushed over, falling to his knees beside her. "You okay?"

She started laughing, making a snow angel with her arms. "I'm fine. The snow's soft."

He joined her in laughter, relief mixing with lingering adrenaline from the chase. "You scared me."

"Sorry." Sue stopped moving her arms, looking up at him. Snowflakes caught in her eyelashes and melted on her flushed cheeks. Her hat had come askew, and her ponytail was a mess, and Steve thought she'd never looked more beautiful.

He leaned in closer, drawn by something magnetic and inevitable. Her hand came up to grip his jacket, and then the distance between them disappeared.

He kissed her there in the snow at the bottom of the hill, gently and sweetly and full of promise.

When they broke apart, Steve rested his forehead against hers.

"Hey gorgeous," he whispered.

"Hey handsome," Sue whispered back, smiling.

"Helloooo... I'm sitting over here bored!" Lindsey's voice carried across the distance, filled with exasperated amusement. "That's kind of rude."

They both started laughing. Steve stood up and helped Sue to her feet. They brushed snow off each other's coats while Lindsey trudged over.

"You know what we should do now?" Lindsey asked.

"What's that?" Sue asked as she straightened her hat.

"Build snowmen. In the front yard."

Steve and Sue exchanged glances. "Sounds good to me," Sue said.

They gathered their equipment and trudged back up the hill, around the side of the house, to the front yard. The snow in the front was untouched, pristine, and deep, perfect for snowman construction.

"Okay," Steve said, surveying the yard. "Three snowmen. Big, medium, and small. Family style."

"I call making the small one!" Lindsey immediately started rolling a snowball.

"I'll take medium," Sue said, beginning her own base.

"Which leaves me with the big one." Steve bent down and packed snow into a tight ball. "Good thing I've got muscles."

"Oh, please," Sue said, but she was grinning.

They worked together in companionable silence broken by occasional comments—Lindsey asking for help to lift the middle section of her snowman, Sue requesting their assessment of whether her proportions were right, and Steve recruiting both of them to help him roll the massive base of the largest snowman into position.

The front yard gradually transformed into a winter tableau. Lindsey's snowman ended up slightly lopsided but charming, with a carrot nose. Sue's snowman was near perfect, elegant almost, decorated with a silk scarf she hadn't used in years. Steve's snowman was impressive in its size, towering over the other two, with stick arms raised in what might have been a wave or a cheer.

"Wait, we need a picture." Sue pulled out her phone.

Lindsey positioned herself in front of the three snowmen, grinning widely. Sue snapped several photos, then called Steve over. "Your turn. Stand with her."

Steve draped his arm around Lindsey's shoulders, both of them mugging for the camera while Sue laughed and took what must have been a dozen pictures.

"Okay, now all of us," Lindsey said. "Mom, come here."

"But who'll take the picture?"

"Selfie mom. Duh." Lindsey grabbed the phone and positioned herself in front of their snow family.

They huddled together—Steve on one side, Sue on the other, and Lindsey in the middle holding the phone at arm's length.

"Say cheese!"

"Cheese!" they chorused, and Lindsey snapped the photo.

She checked the screen and grinned as snow continued falling.

"I'm getting cold," Lindsey admitted finally, her teeth starting to chatter slightly.

Sue immediately shifted into mom mode. "Inside. Now. Before we all get hypothermia."

Chapter 31

Sue's fingers fumbled with the zipper on her snow pants, numb from the cold. Beside her in the mudroom, Steve was peeling off his snow gear while Lindsey hopped on one foot trying to remove a boot that seemed determined to stay on.

"Here, let me help." Steve steadied their daughter with one hand while tugging the stubborn boot free with the other.

Lindsey's sock-covered foot emerged, and she immediately started working on the second boot. "That was the best day ever!"

Sue finally got her zipper down and stepped out of her snow pants, grateful for the warmth of the house. She gathered the wet outerwear and draped everything over the drying rack Steve had pulled out from behind the door.

"Hot chocolate, Lindsey?" Sue asked as she moved toward the kitchen.

"Yes!" Lindsey padded after her in thick wool socks. "With marshmallows?"

"With marshmallows."

Sue pulled milk from the refrigerator while Lindsey retrieved mugs from the cabinet.

"Can I help?" Steve asked, hovering near the island.

"Just sit and relax." Sue poured milk into a saucepan and set it on the stove. "I think you've earned a break."

Steve settled at the kitchen table, his long legs stretched out in front of him. She could feel his gaze following her movements as she measured hot chocolate mix into one of the ceramic mugs and spooned coffee grounds into the coffeemaker.

The milk began to steam, and Sue poured it carefully over the hot chocolate mix, stirring until the mixture turned silky brown. She added a generous handful of mini marshmallows to Lindsey's mug and slid it across the island.

"Perfect." Lindsey wrapped both hands around the mug, inhaling the chocolate-scented steam. "Thanks, Mom."

The coffee maker hissed and gurgled, and soon Sue was pouring two cups. She carried both to the table and sat down across from him, cradling her mug between her palms.

Lindsey joined them at the table, pulling out the chair beside Sue. "I'm hungry. Like, actually starving."

"Me too. We burned a lot of energy playing in the snow today." Sue said as she ran through the options she had in the refrigerator. "I could make—"

"You sit. I'll fix dinner." Steve interrupted.

"Seriously?"

"What are we thinking? Sandwiches? Soup?" he asked as he stood and walked toward the refrigerator. He pulled open the door and surveyed the contents.

"Both!" Lindsey said immediately. "Peanut butter and jelly sandwiches and soup."

"Sounds good to me." Steve located the bread on the counter and the peanut butter and jelly in the pantry. "Sue, where do you keep the soup now?"

"Cabinet next to the stove. Second shelf."

Steve found two cans of vegetable soup and set them on the counter, then pulled out a pot. "Lindsey, do you wanna help with sandwiches?"

Lindsey bounced up from her chair and washed her hands at the sink.

Sue watched them work together—Steve opening the soup cans and pouring the contents into a pot while Lindsey lined up bread slices on the counter. They moved around each other with surprising coordination.

"Not too much jelly on mine," Steve called over his shoulder.

"I know how you like it, Dad." Lindsey's tongue poked out slightly as she concentrated on getting the jelly layer just right.

Sue sipped her coffee as she enjoyed the easy banter between father and daughter.

Lindsey finished the sandwiches and cut them diagonally, then arranged them on three plates. Steve ladled soup into bowls, steam rising in fragrant curls. They brought everything to the table and settled in with Lindsey between them.

"This is so good," Sue said after her first spoonful of soup. The vegetables were soft, the broth savory and warming.

"Canned soup is underrated," he said. "Quick, easy, and hits the spot after a day in the snow."

Lindsey took an enormous bite of her sandwich, chewed, and then launched into a story about her art class. "So Mrs. Phillips is having us make winter scenes using construction paper and cotton balls for snow, and we get to use glitter if we want, but only a little bit because last time Bobby dumped the whole container on his project and it got everywhere, and I'm thinking about making another one with our backyard and the sledding hill and maybe putting little people on sleds going down. Think that's a good idea?"

"I think it's a great idea," Steve said.

"That's what I thought." Lindsey said. "Oh, and in social studies we're doing this project on traditions, and I picked Christmas traditions in the mountains as my topic, so I need to talk to Grandma Anna and Grandpa Earl about what Christmas was like when they were little."

"I'm sure they'd love that," Sue said. "You could call them tomorrow after school."

"Or maybe I could go visit them?" Lindsey looked hopeful. "I haven't spent time at their house in forever."

"We'll see. It's only been a few days since you were at their house," Sue made a mental note to check with her parents.

The conversation continued through the rest of the meal, Lindsey dominating most of it with her usual enthusiasm. She talked about her friends at school, about a book she was reading for English class, and about her part as Mary in the upcoming Christmas play at church.

"Speaking of which," Sue said, "you have Christmas play practice this week. Tuesday and Thursday evening from six to eight."

"I forgot!" Lindsey's eyes lit up.

"I can pick her up from practice and bring her home both nights," Steve offered.

"Are you sure?"

"Positive."

They lingered at the table even after the food was gone, talking about nothing important and everything important all at once. Sue relaxed into the conversation.

Eventually Lindsey yawned, covering her mouth with her hand. "Can we watch a movie? Please?"

Sue checked the time on the microwave. Seven-thirty. *Not too late for a movie, especially on a Sunday when tomorrow is a school day and Lindsey will likely fall asleep halfway through, anyway.*

"Something short," Sue compromised. "A Christmas special, maybe?"

"Yes!" Lindsey was already heading for the living room. "I saw that the old Rudolph cartoon is on tonight."

Steve started gathering dishes, and Sue joined him, both of them rinsing dishes, loading the dishwasher, and wiping down the counter. They finished cleaning and moved to the living room, where Lindsey had already commandeered the remote and was scrolling through various streaming channels. The Christmas tree lights twinkled in the corner, and the room felt cozy despite its size.

"Dad, can you light the fireplace?" Lindsey asked without looking away from the television screen.

"Sure thing." Steve knelt in front of the gas fireplace and clicked the ignition. Flames sprang to life behind the glass, adding another layer of warmth to the room.

Sue settled onto the sectional, tucking her legs beneath her. Lindsey immediately curled up beside her, head resting on Sue's shoulder. Steve hesitated for just a moment before sitting on Sue's other side.

The familiar opening of Rudolph the Red-Nosed Reindeer filled the room—the narrator's voice, the stop-motion animation, and the songs Sue had known since childhood. Lindsey knew all the words, singing along softly with "Silver and Gold."

Sue let herself sink into the moment. With the fire crackling softly and the cartoon playing, Lindsey felt warm and solid against her side, and Steve's presence beside her equally solid and comforting. This was what happiness felt like—not grand gestures or dramatic declarations, but simple togetherness at the end of a perfect day.

Steve shifted slightly, and Sue felt his arm slide along the back of the sectional behind her shoulders. She leaned back into him, and his arm settled more firmly around her.

On screen, Rudolph was navigating the Island of Misfit Toys. Lindsey's breathing had slowed, and Sue realized their daughter was falling asleep quicker than she expected.

"She's out," Steve whispered.

"She had a big day." Sue kept her voice equally quiet. "We all did."

"Best day I've had in years."

Sue turned her head slightly to look at him. The firelight cast shadows across his face, softening the lines around his eyes, making him look younger. Or maybe it was the happiness she saw there that made the difference.

"Me too," she admitted.

Steve's free hand found hers where it rested on her lap. Their fingers intertwined, and Sue felt the rightness of it settle deep in her bones.

The cartoon continued, but Sue wasn't watching anymore. She was too aware of Steve beside her, of the warmth radiating from his body, and of the gentle pressure of his thumb tracing circles on the back of her hand.

Steve leaned down and pressed a soft kiss on the top of her head.

Sue closed her eyes and smiled. Everything about this moment felt right—the weight of Lindsey sleeping against her, Steve's arm around her, the fire warming the room, and snow falling softly outside.

Chapter 32

" —and then Lindsey told Mrs. Phillips that her winter scene needed more glitter because real snow sparkles, and Mrs. Phillips actually agreed with her." Sue laughed, unwrapping her sandwich from Martha's Diner. "Our daughter has become an art critic at twelve."

Steve grinned from behind his desk, his own lunch spread across the cleared space between incident reports and budget spreadsheets. The fire station hummed with quiet afternoon energy—crew members moving through equipment checks, the distant sound of someone washing Engine Two in the bay, and radio chatter providing a constant low backdrop.

Sue had surprised him twenty minutes ago, appearing in his office doorway with two bags from Martha's and an expression that still made his heart skip. They'd fallen into this simple rhythm over the past few days—stolen lunches when his schedule allowed, quick coffee dates between her restaurant work and his shift work, phone calls that stretched late into the evening until one of them finally admitted they needed sleep.

"She gets that confidence from you," Steve said, taking a bite of his roast beef sandwich.

"Please. That's all you." Sue pointed her pickle spear at him. "You're the one who taught her to stand up for what she believes in."

"I taught her stubbornness?"

"I prefer 'conviction.'"

Steve's chest warmed. These moments—casual, domestic, and comfortable—felt like coming home after years of wandering. Sue sat in the chair across from his desk, her legs crossed, one foot swinging slightly as she ate. She'd come straight from the restaurant, wearing her work jeans and an old soft blue t-shirt that brought out the color in her hazel eyes. Her hair was pulled back in a loose ponytail, a few strands escaping to frame her face.

"How's the reopening prep going?" Steve asked, reaching for his water bottle.

"Good. Better than good, actually." Sue's face lit up the way it always did when she talked about the restaurant. "The new ovens arrived this morning. Graham's crew is installing them tomorrow. We're finally painting the dining room today after being delayed. Carla's been training the staff on the updated menu. We're testing the online ordering system Wednesday."

"You're really doing it. Opening Saturday."

"I'm really doing it. Because of you. Because you helped make it possible."

"You did this, Sue. Your determination, your vision—"

"Our partnership," she interrupted gently. "Don't diminish what you contributed, Steve. You showed up and helped every chance you could. That meant everything."

Steve reached across the desk, palm up. Sue placed her hand in his, their fingers intertwining with ease.

The office phone rang.

Steve grimaced. "Sorry. I should—"

"Go ahead." Sue released his hand, returning to her sandwich.

Steve lifted the receiver. "Fire Chief Johnson."

A woman's voice, professional and warm. "Chief Johnson, this is Director Patricia Hammond from the State Fire Marshal's Office. Do you have a few minutes to talk?"

Steve's stomach tightened. These monthly calls were getting old, his standard polite refusals apparently insufficient. He glanced at Sue, who was studying the framed commendations on his wall.

"Yes," Steve said.

"I want to be direct, Chief Johnson. We're prepared to offer you the Deputy State Fire Marshal position in Charleston. The salary is one hundred and forty-five thousand annually, with a full benefits package, relocation assistance, and a clear path to State Fire Marshal within five years. This is a significant step up from your current position."

Steve's mouth went dry. They had upped the salary, obviously trying to sway him. He made eighty-two thousand in Laurel Ridge. The difference could mean college fully funded for Lindsey, more retirement security, and more financial breathing room.

"That's a very impressive offer." Steve said.

"You're exactly what we need in Charleston," Director Hammond pressed. "Your leadership during the Maple Ridge wildfire response last spring demonstrated exceptional crisis management. Your community engagement model in Laurel Ridge is precisely the approach we want to implement statewide. You'd be heading up training initiatives, policy development, and coordinating with local departments across West Virginia."

Everything she described represented goals Steve had once obsessed over. Recognition. Advancement. The opportunity to shape fire safety policy for the entire state. This was the career pinnacle he'd sacrificed his marriage pursuing.

"Can I have a couple of days before I give you my decision? I have many things to think through and consider."

"Of course," Director Hammond said. "We need an answer by Friday, December seventeenth. I'll email you the full offer package this afternoon. We really hope you'll consider this seriously, Chief Johnson. You'd be an asset to the state office."

"Thank you, I'll be in touch by Friday," Steve said, his eyes on Sue's suddenly rigid posture.

He hung up. "That was about a State Fire Marshal position in Charleston."

"Go on." Sue's voice was flat.

"They've been trying to recruit me for months—"

"Months?" Sue set her sandwich down with precise movements. "You've been talking to them for months?"

"Not talking, exactly. They've been calling. I've been saying no," he said as he leaned forward. "But this offer is significantly more than before. The salary alone would mean—"

Sue stood abruptly. "State Fire Marshal. That's a big opportunity."

Steve blinked at the careful neutrality in her tone. This was wrong. Her body language, her voice—everything screamed retreat.

"It is," he said cautiously. "They're offering a deputy position, one hundred forty-five thousand a year, full benefits—"

"You kept saying no?" Sue's voice had gone tight. "For months, they've been calling, and you kept saying no?"

"Well, yes, because I wasn't interested. But now that we're—"

"Now that we're what, Steve?" Sue's hazel eyes had gone hard. "Back together? So suddenly the job is worth considering?"

Steve stood, alarm bells clanging in his head. "No, wait—Sue, I want to discuss it together as a couple—"

"Discuss what exactly? Whether I'm willing to move to Charleston? Whether Lindsey should change schools? Whether your career is more important than my life and my business here or Lindsey losing the only home she's ever known and all her friends?"

"Sue, no—that's not what I meant—" Steve moved around the desk, but Sue stepped back.

"For years in our marriage, you made career decisions without me." Her voice shook. "You chose ambition and your own selfishness over family. And I thought—" She pressed her lips together, a tear escaping down her cheek. "I really thought you'd changed."

"I have changed!" Steve's voice rose, desperation clawing at his chest. "That's why I want to include you in the decision—"

"There shouldn't BE a decision, Steve!" Sue's voice broke. "The fact that you need time to think about it tells me everything I need to know."

Steve reached for her, but she jerked away from his touch. The rejection hit like a physical blow.

"Sue, please listen—"

"No." She grabbed her purse from where she'd set it beside the chair, her hands trembling. "You listen. If you want that job in Charleston, take it. I mean that. But if you go, we're done."

"That's not fair—"

"Fair?" Sue's laugh was bitter. "You know what's not fair? Spending six years rebuilding my life, learning to be happy alone, finding peace with our past—and then opening my heart to you again only to watch you do the exact same thing that destroyed us the first time."

"I'm not doing the same thing!" Steve's frustration warred with fear. "I'm trying to include you—"

"By asking for time to THINK about whether you want to choose your career over us?" Sue wiped at her tears with angry movements. "That's not including me, Steve. That's hedging your bets."

"That's not—Sue, if you'd just let me explain—"

"I deserve someone who doesn't have to think about choosing me." Sue's voice steadied, going quiet in a way that terrified him more than her anger had. "Someone who doesn't need a couple of days to weigh whether career advancement is worth more than the woman he claims to love."

Steve's throat closed. "I do love you."

"I love you too." Fresh tears spilled down Sue's cheeks. "But I will not be second place to your career again. I won't do it to myself, and I won't do it to Lindsey."

"You're not second place—"

"Then why do you need time to think about it?" Sue's voice cracked. "Why isn't your answer an immediate no?"

Steve opened his mouth, the explanation sitting on his tongue—that he wanted to discuss it WITH her, that asking for time was about respecting her enough to include her in major decisions, and that he was trying to be the partner he'd failed to be before.

But looking at her face, at the pain and fear and protective anger written across every feature, he realized she couldn't hear him right now. She was back in their marriage, watching him choose work over family again and again until she'd had nothing left but divorce papers and survival instinct.

"Sue—"

"Call them back, Steve." Sue's voice was firm now, clear despite the tears. "Give them your answer. But understand that your answer to Charleston is also your answer to me."

She turned toward the door.

"Wait—" Steve moved to follow, but she held up her hand.

"Don't." The single word stopped him cold.

She walked out.

Chapter 33

Sue's hands shook as she pried open the gallon of sage green paint, the screwdriver slipping twice before she managed to pop the lid free. The smell of fresh paint filled her nostrils—sharp, chemical, and grounding. She grabbed a clean paint roller from the supply box and snapped it in place with more force than necessary.

The restaurant buzzed with activity around her. Graham's crew worked in the kitchen installing the new ovens, their voices carrying through the open doorway. Two of her servers were painting the wall behind where the counter would be. Carla was working on her laptop.

Sue ignored all of it.

She poured paint into the tray with steady movements, her jaw clenched tight enough to ache. The sage green pooled in the plastic container, smooth and even.

She grabbed the paint tray and a ladder, carrying both to the far corner of the dining room where a freshly primed wall waited. Away from the others. Away from the concerned glances, she could feel tracking her movements.

She set up the folding ladder with sharp, efficient motions. Positioned the paint tray on the small shelf. Grabbed the paint roller, climbed the ladder, dipped her roller into the sage green, and pressed it against the wall.

The first stroke released something inside her chest—a tight coil of fury that had been building since she'd walked out of Steve's office. She rolled the paint in long, aggressive strokes, covering the primer with brutal efficiency.

"Can I have a couple of days before I give you my decision?"

The words replayed in her head with perfect, torturous clarity. Steve's voice on the phone, professional and calm, asking for TIME to think about whether a job in Charleston was worth more than the life they were rebuilding.

Sue's roller hit the wall again, harder this time.

She'd sat in her SUV for several minutes after stalking out of the fire station, hands gripping the steering wheel while tears blurred her vision. She'd cried until her chest hurt and her throat was raw.

Then the tears had shifted into something else. Something hot and sharp-edged.

Anger.

At herself for being stupid enough to trust again. For opening her carefully guarded heart to the man who'd already proven he'd choose career over family. For believing that six years and some humble words and a few weeks of working side by side meant anything had fundamentally changed.

At Steve for making her hope. For looking at her like she hung the moon while apparently keeping his options open in Charleston. For trying to include her in a decision that shouldn't require discussion in the first place.

At the universe for letting this happen again. For dangling happiness in front of her and then snatching it away the moment she'd reached for it.

She had wiped her face, checked her reflection in the rearview mirror, and done her best to fix her makeup with shaking hands. Then she'd driven to the restaurant because what else was there to do? Fall apart? Give up? Let the reopening she'd worked so hard for slip because her ex-husband was apparently still the same ambitious, career-obsessed, and selfish man?

No.

She'd survived once. She'd survive it again.

"Sue?"

Carla's voice came from behind her, careful and concerned.

Sue kept painting. "What?"

"Honey, what's going on?"

"Nothing."

"Sue—"

"I don't want to talk about it." Sue's roller moved faster, the paint spreading across the wall in neat, even lines. "I just want to work."

Carla's footsteps retreated.

Sue climbed down the ladder, moved it three feet to the right, and climbed back up. Dip, roll, cover. Dip, roll, cover. The repetitive motion gave her something to focus on besides the ache in her chest and the horrible certainty that she'd been right to walk away.

Graham appeared at the edge of her vision, his expression concerned. "Sue, you okay?"

"Fine." She didn't look at him. "Ovens going in smoothly?"

"Yeah, but—"

"Good. Let me know if you hit any snags."

Her brother hesitated, clearly wanting to push, then thought better of it. His footsteps retreated toward the kitchen.

Her phone sat on a nearby table, screen dark and silent. No calls. No texts. Nothing from Steve.

Which meant he was still thinking it over. Still weighing Charleston's one hundred forty-five thousand dollar salary and prestigious position against staying in Laurel Ridge with her and Lindsey.

Sue's stomach twisted. She climbed down, repositioned the ladder again, and attacked another section of wall.

The physical labor felt good. Her shoulders burned. Her arms ached from holding the roller at awkward angles. Sweat gathered at her temples. She welcomed all of it—anything to distract from the thoughts circling her mind like vultures.

What if she'd been too harsh? What if Steve really had just wanted to discuss it like partners?

No. Sue shut down that line of thinking immediately. She'd learned this lesson already. Steve didn't get the benefit of the doubt when it came to career decisions. He'd used up that grace years ago when he'd chosen overtime and certifications and advancement over his wife and daughter.

If he wanted her—truly wanted her—his answer to Charleston should have been immediate.

"I'm not interested. My life is here."

That's what he should have said. Not, "Can I have a couple of days before I give you my decision?"

She finished the first wall and moved to the second, her movements mechanical. The sage green was beautiful—exactly the warm, inviting shade she'd imagined.

This was her restaurant. The business she'd built with determination. The community gathering place she'd poured her heart into.

It was almost ready. New ovens, fresh paint, updated equipment. Saturday's reopening would be perfect—the private party for Laurel Ridge Community Church members and all the people who'd supported her through the fire and the rebuilding and the journey back to this moment.

But standing here with her paint roller dripping sage green onto the drop cloth, Sue felt hollow.

None of it meant anything without Steve.

The realization hit her with devastating clarity. This restaurant, this success, this carefully constructed life of independence and self-sufficiency—it was empty. A beautiful shell with nothing inside.

She'd been lying to herself for six years, pretending she was fine alone. Pretending independence meant happiness. Pretending she didn't need anyone.

But she needed Steve. She loved him. She wanted him here, helping her paint these walls and plan the reopening and build a future that included both of them.

And he was in his office at the fire station, presumably thinking over whether Charleston was worth leaving her.

Sue blinked hard against fresh tears. She would not cry again. She'd cried enough.

She climbed down from the ladder and surveyed her work. The sage green looked beautiful.

Sue picked up her phone, the screen lighting up at her touch. 2:02 PM. No missed calls. No texts.

She set the phone down and climbed back up the ladder. She had work to do. A business to run. A daughter to raise.

A daughter.

Sue's hands stilled on the paint roller, sage green dripping.

Lindsey.

Their daughter, who'd been so joyfully and innocently delighted to see her parents falling in love again.

What was she going to tell her?

Your father was offered a job in Charleston. He's thinking about whether we're worth staying for.

No. She couldn't say that. Couldn't make Steve the villain in their daughter's eyes even if he deserved it.

We realized we rushed things. We're better as friends.

Lindsey wouldn't believe that.

She dipped her roller in the paint again and pressed it against the wall, the sage green spreading in long strokes.

Maybe she'd tell Lindsey the truth. That sometimes love wasn't enough. That adults had to make hard choices about careers and futures. That her father loved her completely, even if he'd chosen Charleston over staying in Laurel Ridge.

The roller moved across the wall, mechanical and steady, while Sue's mind spun through impossible explanations and heartbreaking conversations she wasn't ready to have.

The restaurant's front door stood propped open, cold December air drifting in along with the sound of traffic on Cedar Avenue. Christmas music played from someone's radio in the kitchen. Laughter echoed from Graham's crew in the kitchen.

Sue continued painting the wall, alone with her thoughts and her breaking heart and the terrible certainty that she'd have to tell her daughter that happy endings didn't always happen.

Even when you prayed for them.

Even when you hoped with everything you had.

Chapter 34

Steve stood frozen in his office doorway, staring at the empty hallway where Sue had disappeared minutes ago. The sound of her footsteps had faded, replaced by the ordinary noise of the fire station—someone laughing in the bay, the radio crackling with routine traffic, and the hum of Monday afternoon operations continuing as if the world hadn't just tilted sideways.

He turned back into his office. Sue's half-eaten sandwich sat abandoned on the desk. Her water bottle, still on his desk. The chair she'd occupied when everything had been easy laughter and comfortable partnership.

"Then why do you need time to think about it? Why isn't your answer an immediate no?"

Her words echoed in his head, each syllable a sharp blade. Steve sank into his desk chair and pressed the heels of his hands against his forehead.

He'd been trying to include her. Trying to show growth by not making unilateral decisions about their life together. In his mind, asking for time meant respecting her enough to discuss major choices as partners.

But all Sue heard was hesitation.

All she saw was the old Steve—the man who'd chosen his career over family.

The horrible irony of it made his chest ache. In trying to be better, he'd come across as exactly the man who'd destroyed their marriage. The man who needed time to think about whether his wife and daughter were worth more than professional recognition.

Steve ran his hands through his hair, the motion doing nothing to ease the pressure building behind his temples.

"I deserve someone who doesn't have to think about choosing me."

She was right.

She was absolutely right.

The realization settled over him with crushing clarity. It didn't matter what he'd intended. What mattered was what Sue needed to hear. She needed an immediate, an unequivocal NO to Charleston. She needed to see that there WAS no decision to make.

He reached for the phone.

His hands were steady as he dialed. The line rang once. Twice.

"Director Hammond speaking."

"Director Hammond, this is Fire Chief Johnson." Steve's voice came out firm, clear. "I've made my decision. The answer is no. Thank you for the opportunity, but my life is here in Laurel Ridge. I'm not interested in relocating."

A pause on the other end. "Chief Johnson, I understand this is a big decision. Perhaps if you took the full-time frame we offered—"

"I don't need more time." Steve cut her off gently but firmly. "I appreciate everything you've offered, but I'm staying here. My family is here. My community is here. This is where I belong."

"I see." Director Hammond's professional warmth had cooled slightly. "Well, if you change your mind—"

"I won't. But thank you again for the offer."

Steve ended the call before she could respond.

The decision was made. Charleston—declined. The prestigious position, the substantial salary increase, the career pinnacle he'd once obsessed over—all of it, gone with a thirty-second phone call.

And he felt nothing but relief.

But Sue wouldn't believe a phone call was enough. She'd walked out of his office in tears, convinced he was repeating the same patterns that had broken them before. Words wouldn't fix this. Explanations wouldn't heal the wound he'd accidentally reopened.

She needed to see his choice. Feel it. Trust it.

And he knew exactly how to show her.

Steve stood, grabbed his coat from the hook behind his door, and shut off his office lights. His mind raced ahead, planning and calculating what he needed to do.

He walked down the hallway toward the bay, his footsteps purposeful. The station buzzed with its usual afternoon energy—Luke and two other firefighters were washing Engine Two, water streaming across the concrete floor. Ray was organizing medical supplies near the ambulance bay. Mark was working on equipment maintenance in the corner.

"—told him that carburetor needs replacing—" Mark's voice drifted toward Steve, but the words didn't register.

Steve walked through the bay, past the gleaming fire engines and the smell of cleaning solution and the sound of casual conversations happening around him. His entire focus had narrowed to a single point: what he needed to retrieve, where he needed to go, and what he needed to say.

"Chief?" Mark called out.

Steve kept walking.

He pushed through the door to the parking lot, cold December air hitting his face. His truck sat three spaces down, snow still clinging to the hood from last night's light snowfall. He climbed in, started the engine, and pulled out of the lot without looking back.

Laurel Ridge passed by his windows—familiar streets and businesses he'd known for sixteen years. Martha's Diner, with its cheerful window displays. The Book Nook, with its seasonal book recommendations posted on the door. Earl's Hardware, where Sue's father had finally started warming to him again after years of justified coldness.

He turned onto Chestnut Street and pulled into the parking lot of his apartment building—a two-story brick structure that housed eight units total, nothing fancy but clean and well-maintained.

He took the stairs to the second floor two at a time, his keys already in his hand. The hallway was quiet, most residents at work during the afternoon hours. Steve unlocked his door and stepped into his apartment.

The space was neat, sparsely furnished—a couch, a coffee table, a small dining set he rarely used. His bedroom held a bed, a dresser, and a nightstand. Everything functional, nothing excessive. He'd learned to live with less during the years after the divorce, and the simplicity suited him.

Steve went straight to his bedroom closet, pushing aside hanging shirts and work uniforms until he reached the back corner. A small safe sat on the closet floor, black metal with a keypad lock. His fingers moved automatically through the familiar code: 1-2-0-4. Lindsey's birthday.

The safe clicked open.

Inside were important documents—his birth certificate, social security card, and the deed to a piece of land his grandfather had left him. And beneath those papers was a small velvet box.

Steve lifted it out.

His hands remembered the weight of it. The texture of the navy-blue velvet, slightly worn at the corners.

He remembered standing in a jewelry store in Beckley fourteen years ago, nervous and excited and absolutely certain he'd found the woman he wanted to spend his life with.

He opened the box.

Sue's original engagement ring rested on the white satin interior. A simple gold band with a single diamond solitaire—not large, not flashy, but clear and beautiful in its honest simplicity. The wedding band that matched it sat beside the engagement ring, both returned to him six years ago when Sue had filed for divorce.

"I can't stand looking at it anymore."

Her voice had been hollow when she'd said it, standing in his apartment doorway with Lindsey at her parents' house and legal papers making their separation official. She'd held out the rings without ceremony, her hand steady despite the tears on her cheeks.

Steve had taken them, and they'd sat in his safe ever since. A reminder of what he'd lost. What he'd destroyed through his own selfish ambition and blind obsession with career advancement.

He'd thought about the rings often over the past few weeks as he and Sue had grown closer. He'd been planning to have the engagement ring reset. Take the center diamond and add more stones around it. Make it bigger, more impressive. Create something that looked expensive enough to match the second chance she was giving him.

But looking at the ring now, Steve realized that would be old Steve thinking.

The man who'd believed bigger and flashier meant better. The man who'd tried to prove his worth through achievements and recognition instead of through steady, faithful presence.

This ring was perfect exactly as it was.

Simple. Honest. Real.

Just like the love he was offering her now—not the flashy promise of a man who thought he could buy forgiveness, but the humble commitment of someone who'd learned what truly mattered.

Steve closed the box and slipped it into his coat pocket.

He left his apartment and took the stairs back down to the parking lot.

Steve's hands were steady on the wheel as he drove back through Laurel Ridge, his breathing calm despite the urgency pulsing through his veins.

Sue's Pizza appeared ahead on his right. Graham's truck was parked out front. He saw Sue's vehicle in the small parking lot on the side of the building.

He pulled in behind Graham's truck and cut the engine.

Chapter 35

Through the large front windows, Steve could see Sue standing on a ladder painting.

He closed his eyes, one hand gripping the steering wheel while the other touched the velvet box in his coat pocket.

God, please. Let her hear me this time. Let her see what I'm choosing.

He took a deep breath, released it slowly, and climbed out of the truck.

The cold air bit at his face as he walked. Christmas music drifted from inside the restaurant along with the sound of voices.

He pushed open the propped-open door and walked in.

Several heads turned immediately. Carla looked up from where she sat with her laptop at a table, her expression shifting from neutral to concerned the moment she saw his face. Graham stood in the center of the dining room on a stepladder, taking measurements of the ceiling, his tape measure extended. Two of Sue's servers paused mid-brush-stroke on the wall behind the counter.

Sue didn't turn.

She continued painting, her roller moving in steady strokes across the wall, completely absorbed in her work. Or pretending to be.

Steve stood just inside the doorway, his heart hammering.

"Sue."

Her entire body went rigid. The paint roller stilled against the wall.

"Unless you've called Charleston and told them no, don't even come closer." Her voice was controlled and measured, but Steve could hear the tremor underneath.

Silence fell over the restaurant. The Christmas music from the kitchen radio seemed suddenly too loud. Everyone had stopped working, all eyes shifting between Steve and Sue's back.

"I called them," he said. "Right after you left. Told them my answer is no."

Sue's shoulders tensed, but she didn't turn around.

"Sue, can you please come down from that ladder?"

"No." Her voice had gone thick with emotion.

He walked closer, his boots echoing on the floor until he stopped near her. He looked up at her rigid back.

"Please."

"Why should I believe you?" Sue's voice cracked. "You said you wanted a couple of days before giving your decision."

"I know." Steve's throat tightened. "And I was wrong for saying that. I was trying to include you in the decision, but there was no decision to make. I knew you wouldn't want to follow me to Charleston, and I shouldn't have second-guessed and thought that maybe you would have an opinion."

Sue still didn't turn, but her knuckles had gone white where she gripped the paint roller.

"It's always been you, Sue. It's always going to be you. I'll walk away from the fire department completely today if you tell me to."

Sue finally turned on the ladder.

Her eyes were red-rimmed and swollen from crying. Sage-green paint streaked her cheek and dotted her hair. Tears had left tracks on her face. She was the most beautiful thing he'd ever seen.

"Come down. Please."

Sue descended slowly, one rung at a time. She reached the second-to-last step and stopped, her eyes locked on his face, searching for something—truth, maybe, or the courage to believe him.

Steve dropped to one knee.

Her breath caught audibly. She grabbed the ladder for support, the paint roller falling from her hand and clattering to the floor, rolling across the drop cloth and leaving a sage green trail in its wake.

Everyone in the restaurant froze. The only sounds were the Christmas music and Sue's shaky breathing.

Steve pulled the velvet box from his coat pocket. His hands trembled slightly as he opened it, revealing the simple gold band and single diamond solitaire that had sat in his safe for six years.

"Sue Marie Smith. I broke your heart in ways I can never fully repair. I chose career over family. Ambition over love. Success over the woman who made my life worth living."

"I lost everything that mattered. And I deserved to lose it." Steve's vision blurred with his own tears. "But somehow—by grace I don't understand and definitely don't deserve—God gave me a second chance. You gave me a second chance."

He drew a shaky breath.

"I don't want Charleston. I don't want the deputy state fire marshal position. I don't want prestige or recognition or anything except you. I want Sunday dinners and Christmas mornings and growing old together right here in Laurel Ridge."

Sue was crying now, both hands pressed against her mouth.

"Will you marry me? Again?" Steve's voice broke on the words. "Let me spend the rest of my life proving that you're my first choice. Every single day. Without hesitation. Without question."

Sue tried to speak but couldn't. More tears streamed down her face, falling onto her work shirt.

She climbed down the last two rungs and stood directly in front of him.

"You kept my ring." Her voice was barely a whisper, breaking on every syllable.

Steve stood, taking her trembling hand in his. "Of course I kept it. I could never let it go. Just like I could never really let you go."

He lifted the ring from the velvet box. Sue's hand shook as he slid it onto her finger. The diamond caught the light, throwing tiny rainbows around.

Sue stared at it. "I always loved this ring."

"So no resetting it?" Steve managed a watery smile. "I was going to ask if you'd like to choose a different—"

"No." Sue's head snapped up, her eyes fierce despite the tears. "This ring is perfect. Just like it is."

Steve's heart expanded in his chest. "Does that mean yes?"

"Yes." Sue's voice strengthened, clear and certain. "It's always been yes with you, Steve."

He pulled her into his arms and kissed her.

The restaurant erupted in cheers. Carla was crying openly, one hand pressed to her chest. Graham grinned from his stepladder, his tape measure forgotten. Sue's servers were clapping and crying simultaneously. Someone in the kitchen let out a whoop that echoed through the building.

Sue pulled back slightly, laughing through her tears. "I have paint in my hair."

"I don't care." Steve cupped her face, his thumbs brushing away tears and paint streaks.

"And probably on my face."

"Still don't care."

Sue's laugh was watery but genuine. "I got paint on your coat."

"Best thing that ever happened to this coat."

Graham climbed down from his ladder and walked over, clapping Steve on the shoulder. "Welcome back to the family, brother."

Carla appeared at Sue's side, pulling her into a fierce hug. "About time you two got it together."

"We have a wedding to plan!" one of the servers called out.

"Christmas wedding?" someone else suggested.

Sue turned back to Steve, her hand pressed against his chest. "This Saturday... opening day," she said softly, for only him to hear. "If that's not too soon."

"This Saturday is perfect," he said as he covered her hand with his. "Though tomorrow would be even better."

He kissed her again, longer this time, while everyone celebrated around them.

Chapter 36

The sanctuary doors opened, and Sue took her father's arm as the first notes of the processional filled Laurel Ridge Community Church. Through the candlelit space decorated with evergreen garland and white flowers, past pews filled with everyone who'd watched their story unfold, she could see Steve waiting at the front of the aisle.

Earl squeezed her hand. "Ready?"

Sue's eyes found Steve's across the sanctuary. He stood beside the altar in his uniform—a navy double-breasted jacket with gold-trimmed epaulettes and polished buttons catching the candlelight, his department badge gleaming on his left chest, his nameplate reading S. Johnson on his right. Gold-embroidered "Laurel Ridge Fire Department" patches decorated the sleeves, gold stripes denoting his rank as chief. Everything about him was polished, pressed, and perfect.

But it was his face that made Sue's breath catch. The way he looked at her—like she was his whole world.

"Ready," Sue said.

They began their walk down the aisle.

Sue wore the same white dress she'd worn fourteen years ago—simple, elegant, with lace sleeves and a flowing skirt.

Lindsey stood at the front as maid of honor, wearing a deep green dress that made her dark hair shine. Her face was radiant. Beside Steve, Mark stood as best man in his own dress uniform, grinning broadly.

The church was packed. Sue's mother sat in the front row next to Gail, both women dabbing at their eyes. Tom and Dan sat beside Gail. Graham and Matt were also seated near Anna. Carla had claimed a spot with Martha, both of them crying. Ray sat with Luke and the rest of the fire department crew, all in their dress uniforms.

Pastor Andrew waited at the altar, his face warm with joy as he watched them approach.

Sue and Earl reached the front. Her father turned to her, his weathered face soft with emotion.

"I'm proud of you," Earl said quietly. Then he looked at Steve. "Both of you."

Steve's voice was thick. "Thank you, sir."

Earl placed Sue's hand in Steve's, then stepped back to sit beside Anna.

Sue and Steve stood facing each other, hands clasped, while Pastor Andrew's voice filled the sanctuary.

"Dearly beloved, we are gathered here today in the sight of God and these witnesses to join together Steven Michael Johnson and Susan Marie Smith in holy matrimony." Andrew's eyes crinkled with warmth. "Again."

Gentle laughter rippled through the congregation.

"Some might say a second wedding is unusual," Andrew continued. "But I say it's a testament to grace. To forgiveness. To the God who specializes in making all things new."

"Steve and Sue's story isn't just about romance rekindled. It's about two people who learned—through pain and loss and years of growth—what truly matters. They learned that love requires humility. That marriage demands sacrifice. That family is worth more than any professional achievement or personal ambition."

Andrew looked between them. "And they learned that God's timing, while often mysterious, is always perfect."

"Steve, Sue—you've walked through fire together. You've experienced the destruction of what you once built together. But like Sue's restaurant, you've been rebuilt. Stronger. Wiser. More beautiful than before."

Pastor Andrew opened his Bible. "First Corinthians thirteen, verses four through eight: 'Love is patient, love is kind. It does not envy, it does not boast, it is not proud. It does not dishonor others, it is not self-seeking, it is not easily angered, it keeps no record of wrongs. Love does not delight in evil but rejoices with the truth. It always protects, always trusts, always hopes, always perseveres. Love never fails.'"

He closed the Bible and looked at them both. "Steve, do you have vows you'd like to share?"

Steve nodded, his eyes never leaving Sue's face. "Sue, fourteen years ago I promised to love you for better or worse, in sickness and health, until death parted us. I broke those promises. I put my career before you, my ambition before our family, and my pride before our marriage."

His voice roughened with emotion. "I can't change the past. I can't undo the pain I caused or erase the years we lost. But I can promise you this: for the rest of my life, you will be my first choice. Every morning when I wake up, every decision I make, and every moment I'm given on this earth—you will come first."

"I promise to be present. To listen when you speak. To value your dreams as much as my own. To support you in everything you do. To love you not just in the easy moments but in the hard ones."

"I promise to choose you, Sue. Every single day. Without hesitation. Without question. For as long as God gives me breath."

Pastor Andrew turned to Sue. "Sue?"

Sue drew a shaky breath. "Steve, when I walked down this aisle the first time, I was twenty years old and completely certain our love could survive anything. When our marriage fell apart, I thought I'd lost that certainty forever."

She squeezed his hands. "But standing here now, I realize I was right the first time. Our love can survive anything. It survived years of hurt. It survived divorce and distance and all the walls I built to protect my heart. It survived because it was never just our love—it was God's love working through us, even when we couldn't see it."

"I promise to trust you. Not blindly—we've both learned that lesson—but with the wisdom that comes from knowing you've changed. I promise to communicate instead of withdrawing. To ask for help instead of insisting on independence. To build our future together instead of trying to control everything alone."

Sue's voice strengthened. "I promise to love you with an open heart. To celebrate your successes without fear. To support your calling while maintaining my own. To be your partner in every sense of the word."

"I choose you, Steve. Today and every day after. With gratitude for second chances and faith in God's perfect timing."

"The rings?" Andrew asked.

Mark stepped forward, producing two gold wedding bands from his pocket—the same rings they'd exchanged fourteen years ago.

Steve took Sue's ring, his hand steady as he slid it onto her finger. "With this ring, I thee wed."

Sue took Steve's ring, her fingers trembling slightly as she placed it on his hand. "With this ring, I thee wed."

Pastor Andrew raised his hands. "By the power vested in me by God and the state of West Virginia, I now pronounce you husband and wife." He grinned. "Again. Steve, you may kiss your bride."

Steve pulled Sue into his arms and kissed her—a real kiss, deep and full of promise. Then, in a move that made the congregation gasp and laugh simultaneously, he dipped her low, supporting her weight as the kiss continued.

The church bells began to ring, their joyful peal echoing across Laurel Ridge's valley.

When Steve finally pulled back and helped Sue upright, both of them were laughing and crying at once. The sanctuary erupted in applause and cheers.

They turned to face their community as Pastor Andrew announced, "I present to you Mr. and Mrs. Steven Johnson!"

More cheers. Lindsey threw her arms around both of them, creating a three-person hug in front of the altar while cameras flashed and people whooped their approval.

They processed back down the aisle together—Steve and Sue with linked arms, Lindsey bouncing alongside them, all three smiling. At the doors, Lindsey ran ahead to check outside.

"Wow!"

They stepped out into the December afternoon. Snow had started falling during the ceremony, light flakes drifting down from the blue sky. And there, parked in front of the church, sat Engine One—the main fire truck, decorated with white ribbons and greenery, polished until it gleamed.

Mark and Luke walked around Steven and Sue outside the church and stood beside the fire engine, matching grins on their faces.

"Your chariot awaits," Mark announced with a mock bow.

Luke opened the passenger door. "Mrs. Johnson?"

Sue laughed. "You're kidding... I can't believe you did this."

"Oh, I'm dead serious," Steve said, guiding her toward the truck. "We're riding to the reception in style."

Mark and Luke helped Sue up into the passenger seat, her white dress billowing around her. Steve walked around the truck and lifted Lindsey up on the driver's side, then climbed in himself. Lindsey settled between her parents, her face alight with joy.

Mark and Luke climbed into the back compartment. The engine roared to life.

Steve pulled away from the church with the siren giving a short celebratory whoop. They paraded up and down the streets throughout Laurel Ridge; people stopped on the sidewalks to wave and cheer. Shop owners came out of their businesses. Cars honked. Children pointed and jumped with excitement.

Sue looked at Steve across Lindsey's head. He was already looking at her, his expression so full of love it made her chest tight.

"I love you."

"I love you too."

Lindsey grabbed both their hands. "This was the best day ever!"

After a few trips through town, Steve turned onto Cedar Avenue, and Sue's Pizza came into view.

The restaurant was transformed. Every window glowed with warm light. White lights outlined the building. A banner across the front read "GRAND REOPENING" on one side and "CONGRATU-LATIONS STEVE & SUE" on the other. The parking lot was packed with cars.

Steve stopped in front of the restaurant. Graham stood waiting on the sidewalk with a huge grin, ready to help Sue down while Steve helped Lindsey and Luke and Mark hurried inside.

"Love you, sis," Graham said, hugging his sister.

The restaurant was beautiful. The sage-green walls glowed in the soft lighting. Tables and chairs filled the dining room, every surface covered with white tablecloths and centerpieces of evergreen and white flowers. The Christmas tree in the corner sparkled with lights. Garland draped across the new counter, where Carla stood beaming.

But it was the people who made it perfect. Every pew from the church seemed to have emptied into Sue's Pizza. Both families gathered near the front—Earl and Anna, Tom and Gail, Dan, Matt, and Graham. Carla and the entire restaurant staff wore matching aprons. Martha dabbed at her eyes with a handkerchief. Ray raised a glass in salute. Pastor Andrew and Lily found seats at a table near the window.

The buffet tables along the back wall groaned with food—pizzas, yes, but also pasta dishes, salads, breadsticks, wings, calzones, Stromboli, and every appetizer Sue had added to her new menu. Pitchers of water, sweet tea, lemonade, and coffee sat ready. And on a special table near the Christmas tree, a simple three-tier cake from the Taste of Heaven Bakery waited, decorated with white frosting and fresh flowers.

"Speech! Speech!" someone called out.

Steve and Sue looked at each other, then Steve stepped forward slightly, his arm around Sue's waist.

"Thank you all for being here," Steve's voice carried across the crowded restaurant. "For celebrating with us. For supporting Sue through the fire and the restoration. For welcoming me back into a family I didn't deserve to rejoin."

Sue leaned into him. "We're grateful. For all of you. This restaurant—this community—it's not just walls and ovens and fresh paint. It's people. It's relationships. It's love made visible."

"Cheers! Let's eat!" Carla called out. "Before the food gets cold!"

Laughter erupted as people moved toward the buffet tables. Sue's staff sprang into action, serving food and refilling drinks and making sure everyone had what they needed.

Steve guided Sue to the head table, where Lindsey had already claimed her seat between them. After the line went down some, they filled their plates—Sue with her favorite pizza combination, Steve with the new pasta primavera she'd added to the menu, Lindsey with enough breadsticks to feed three people.

The celebration flowed around them. Conversations were filled with laughter. Children ran between the tables. The smell of fresh pizza and garlic and Christmas pine-scented candles created something magical.

After everyone had eaten, Mark stood and clinked his glass with his fork. "Time for toasts!"

He raised his glass. "I've worked with Steve Johnson for many years. I've watched him lead our department with integrity and courage. But I've also watched him become something even better—a man who knows what truly matters." Mark's voice grew emotional. "Steve, you're not just my chief. You're my friend. And Sue, you're the woman who made him whole again. May your marriage be blessed with all the joy you both deserve."

"Hear, hear!" echoed around the room.

Dan stood next. "As Steve's younger brother, I got to watch him fall in love with Sue the first time. And for reasons that only God understands, I also sadly watched their marriage fall apart. And now—" His voice caught. "Now I get to watch them build something even more beautiful. To second chances and God's perfect timing."

More cheers and clinks.

Then Earl stood, and the restaurant went quiet.

Emotion softened his weathered face as he looked at Steve and his daughter. "I'll be honest. When Sue told me she was giving Steve another chance, I was worried. Protective. I remembered the pain I'd watched my daughter endure, and I didn't want her to go through that again."

Steve reached for Sue's hand under the table.

"But God showed me how wrong I had been in my judgment of Steve and showed me that my worries were a waste." Earl's voice strengthened. "Steve, you are the man I always hoped you'd be. You deserve my Sue-bug's love. I thank you for your forgiveness of my judgmental ways, and I pray for nothing but happiness for the both of you."

Earl raised his glass, his eyes bright with tears. "Steve, welcome back to our family, son. And Sue—" His voice broke. "I'm so proud of you. For your strength, for your forgiveness, and for your courage to hope again."

Sue was crying openly. Steve's arm tightened around her shoulders.

"To Steve and Sue!" Earl finished.

The restaurant erupted in agreement.

Before anyone else could stand, Lindsey jumped up from her seat, a folded piece of paper in hand. "I want to say something!"

Pastor Andrew smiled. "The floor is yours, Lindsey."

Lindsey looked between her parents, her young face radiating pure joy. "Grandma Anna and Grandpa Earl helped me with this because... well... you know I can ramble on sometimes."

Steve and Sue smiled as Lindsey opened up the piece of paper she held in her hands. "Dear Mom and Dad. I've been praying for this since I was old enough to pray. Every night. Every morning. Every time I saw Mom looking sad or Dad looking lonely."

Her voice wavered. "Sometimes I thought He wasn't listening. But Mom and Dad both taught me that God's timing is perfect even when we don't understand it."

Lindsey wiped at her tears. "Mom and Dad, you were right... God's timing is perfect."

Steve and Sue both stood and walked toward Lindsey.

"Thank you for giving me my family back."

Sue pulled Lindsey into a fierce hug while Steve wrapped his arms around both of them.

There wasn't a dry eye in the restaurant.

***

The evening continued with more laughter and conversation. Sue danced with her father while Steve danced with his mother. Then Steve and Sue took to the floor together for their first dance as a reunited couple, swaying to a slow song while everyone watched with satisfied smiles.

Later, Sue found herself standing near the Christmas tree with Carla, watching Steve talk animatedly with Ray and Mark.

"You did it," Carla said softly. "You got your happy ending."

Sue smiled. "Steve and I both did. God did this. We just had to learn to trust Him."

"And trust each other again."

"That too."

As the evening wore on, the celebration showed no signs of slowing even as the December darkness settled outside. But finally, as the clock neared nine, Pastor Andrew found Steve and Sue.

"I think it's about time for the happy couple to make their exit," Andrew said with a smile.

Lindsey appeared at Sue's elbow, and she hugged her. "Thank you for being the best maid of honor."

"And the best daughter," Steve added, ruffling her hair.

"And the best prayer warrior," Lindsey said with a grin. "Don't forget that part."

The crowd began to gather as word spread that Steve and Sue were leaving. They made their way to the door, stopping to hug and thank everyone along the way. Earl embraced Steve for a long moment, whispering something that made Steve nod with emotion. Anna kissed Sue's cheek and pressed something into her hand—a small, wrapped package with instructions not to open it until later.

At the door, Pastor Andrew raised his hands for quiet. "Before Steve and Sue leave, I'd like to offer one final blessing over their marriage."

Everyone bowed their heads.

"Heavenly Father, we thank You for this day. For the redemption it represents. For the grace You've poured out on Steve and Sue's relationship. We thank You for never giving up on Your children, even when we give up on ourselves."

Andrew's voice was warm and full. "Bless this marriage, Lord. Strengthen it through trials. Grow it through joy. Use it as a testimony of Your faithfulness and Your power to make all things new."

He paused. "May Steve and Sue's love reflect Your love—patient, kind, and never failing. May their home be filled with laughter and peace. May their family continue to grow in grace and truth. And may they never forget that their story is ultimately about You—Your timing, Your redemption, Your perfect plan."

"Amen" echoed through the restaurant.

Steve and Sue stood at the threshold, arms around each other, looking back at the community that had carried them through their darkest seasons and now celebrated their brightest moment.

Steve turned to Sue, his hand cupping her face. "You ready, Mrs. Johnson?"

Sue smiled up at him, her heart so full it almost hurt. "I've been ready since the day I met you years ago."

"I'm ready too." Steve's voice was low, meant only for her. "For all of it. The ordinary days and the extraordinary ones. The hard conversations and the easy laughter. Growing old together right here where we belong."

He kissed her then, sweet and sure, while their community cheered one last time.

When he pulled back, Steve's eyes were bright with joy and promise. "I love you, Sue Johnson. Today and every day after."

"I love you too," Sue whispered.

They walked out into the December night together, snow falling softly around them, the warm light from Sue's Pizza spilling onto the sidewalk behind them. Inside, the celebration continued—their family, their friends, and their community rejoicing in the love story that had found its way back to the beginning.

And Sue knew with absolute certainty that this wasn't an ending at all.

It was a beginning.

The best one yet.

Leave A Review

I f you enjoyed this book, please consider leaving an honest review on Amazon

Visit Our Website:

www.tarabaisden.com

Visit Our Amazon Author Page HERE

Find Us On Social Media:

Facebook

Facebook Author Page

Instagram

Also by Tara Baisden

<u>**Laurel Ridge Series**</u>

#1. Season of Hope

#2. Finding Grace

#3. His Perfect Plan

#4. Love Redeemed

#5 Snowbound Blessings

#6 Sheltered Hearts

#7 Restoring Faith

#8 Love Rekindled

#9 Where She Belongs

#10 Shelter in His Arms

#11 Where Love Stands

#12 The Pieces We Mend

#13 Where Love Grows

#14 Where Hearts Heal

#15 Harvest of the Heart

#16 Heart of the Season

#17 Season of Forgiveness

#18 Threads of Grace

<u>Riverbend Valley Series</u>

#1 A Cowboy's Second Chance

#2 Wanderlust & Wild Horses

#3 Heartstrings on the Horizon

#4 Runaway in Riverbend Valley

#5 Mended Hearts

#6 Healing Hearts

#7 Home to Lost Creek

<u>Mistletoe Falls Series</u>

#1 Whisk Me Under the Mistletoe

#2 Once Upon a Christmas

#3 The Mistletoe Express

#4 Candy Canes & Sweet Dreams

#5 Wrapped Up in Christmas

#6 Jingle All the Way Home

About The Author

Tara Baisden is a Contemporary Christian Inspirational Romance author who proudly calls the beautiful state of West Virginia her home. Nestled on a sprawling mountainous property, she is surrounded by the peace and serenity of nature. Her days are happily spent in the quiet of country life, writing heartwarming stories of love, faith, and second chances. Tara also enjoys quilting, working in her garden, tending to her beloved pets, and soaking in the beauty of her surroundings.

With deep roots in West Virginia, family is everything to Tara. One of her favorite pastimes is gathering on the front porch with loved ones, sharing stories, laughter, and enjoying the simple, meaningful moments that life offers. When she's not crafting her novels, Tara can often be found exploring the rich history of her home state, visiting local historical sites, and, of course, stopping by every bookstore she passes! Her passion for reading and discovery always fuels her next adventure.

Tara is the author of the Laurel Ridges series of novels, as well as the Riverbend Valley series of novels, of which have been beloved by fans of inspirational romance. Her novels reflect her love for faith, family, and the timeless beauty of the world we live in.

Known for her sweet and clean romances, she creates characters that feel like family and settings that make readers want to visit again and again.

You can find out more about Tara and her latest releases at www.tarabaisden.com or follow her on social media for updates and behind-the-scenes glimpses of her writing process. Stay connected—you won't want to miss the heartfelt stories of love and family she has in store!

About Laurel Ridge

Welcome to the fictional town of Laurel Ridge, West Virginia!

Nestled deep in the heart of the Appalachian Mountains, Laurel Ridge is a place where time slows down, allowing visitors and residents alike to enjoy life's simple pleasures. With its quaint, brick-paved streets, historic storefronts, and the ever-present backdrop of rolling hills and dense forests, Laurel Ridge is a hidden gem that attracts tourists looking for both serenity and adventure.

A Rich History

The town was founded in the early 1800s by pioneering settlers who were drawn to the fertile land and abundant natural resources of the region. Laurel Ridge began as a small logging community, relying on the towering forests that covered the surrounding mountains. The New River, one of the oldest rivers in the world, provided an essential transportation route for lumber, as well as a lifeline for the early settlers.

As the years passed, the town evolved from a logging outpost into a thriving hub for craftspeople and artisans. By the late 19th century, it had developed a reputation for its hand-crafted furniture, textiles, and pottery, all made by skilled locals. The town's proximity to the New River also made it a destination for adventurous souls seeking to kayak, fish, or hike along the riverbanks.

A Place of Renewal

Though the logging industry faded by the early 20th century, Laurel Ridge adapted to the changing times. Its natural beauty and deep connection to West Virginia's mountain heritage drew travelers from near and far, transforming it into a beloved tourist destination. Local shops, run by generations of the same families, line the town square, offering handmade goods, locally sourced foods, and, most of all, warm hospitality.

The town's signature event, the Harvest Festival, began in the 1930s, celebrating the craftsmanship, music, and traditions passed down through the generations. Each year, visitors flock to enjoy live Appalachian music, taste locally grown produce, and witness demonstrations of old-world techniques like blacksmithing and weaving.

A Town of Faith and Community

At the heart of the town stands Laurel Ridge Community Church, a small, white clapboard building with a steeple that reaches toward the sky. Built in 1876, the church has been a pillar of faith and strength for the community for over a century. Its bell, crafted by the town's original blacksmith, has been ringing on Sunday mornings ever since, calling townsfolk to worship and reminding everyone of the enduring values of faith, hope, and love.

The church's history is intertwined with the town's, serving as a refuge in difficult times and a gathering place in moments of joy. Over the years, the church has grown to include an outreach center that supports local families and tourists in need, providing everything from free meals to spiritual counseling. The church's welcoming atmosphere reflects the town's deep sense of unity and service.

A Growing Tourist Haven

Today, Laurel Ridge has grown to a population of around five thousand people, yet it has managed to retain its small-town charm. Its thriving tourist industry draws visitors year-round. Tourists can stroll through mom-and-pop shops, and dine at the beloved Martha's Diner, famous for its homemade pies and retro charm. The town square, with its white gazebo surrounded by flowering bushes, is often the site of outdoor concerts and farmers' markets, creating a sense of nostalgia and small-town pride.

For nature lovers, the New River offers breathtaking views and the thrill of adventure, whether it's fishing in its crystal blue waters or hiking along the rugged trails that weave through the wilderness. Tourists and locals alike cherish the scenic beauty, often finding peace in the simple pleasures of watching the river flow or taking in the panoramic vistas of the Appalachian Mountains.

Laurel Ridge, with its rich history, strong community spirit, and natural beauty, is more than just a tourist destination—it's a place where past and present blend seamlessly, offering everyone who visits a chance to experience the best of West Virginia's mountain heritage. You'll find that Laurel Ridge is a town that captures the heart.

Welcome to Laurel Ridge. I hope you fall in love with this charming small town and its residents.